My He...

on
Mackinac
ISLAND

My Heart Belongs

on Mackinac ISLAND

Maude's
Mooring

CARRIE FANCETT PAGELS

BARBOUR BOOKS
An Imprint of Barbour Publishing, Inc.

ISBN 978-1-68322-088-6

Adobe Digital Edition (.epub) 978-1-68322-089-3
Kindle and MobiPocket Edition (.prc) 978-1-68322-087-9

Series Design: Kirk DouPonce DogEared Design
Model Photography: Lee Avison/ Trevillion Images

Published by Barbour Books, an imprint of Barbour Publishing, Inc., P.O.
Box 719, Uhrichsville, Ohio 44683, www.barbourbooks.com

*Our mission is to publish and distribute inspirational products offering
exceptional value and biblical encouragement to the masses.*

 Member of the
Evangelical Christian
Publishers Association

Printed in the United States of America.

Dedication

In memory of William Henry Fancett (1918–2003).
Thanks for taking me to the island, Dad!

Acknowledgments

Every book is for God Almighty—only He could make my stories happen. And God bless my family for their support: Jeff, Cassandra, and Clark, you've made so many trips to Mackinac over the years to indulge Mom's love of the island. Thank you, Rosemary Wellington, for making Mackinac Island come alive for me with your personal tour all those years ago, in a way I hadn't experienced while living and working there. And kudos to Bob Tagatz, the Grand Hotel's historian, for his passion for bringing this historic treasure's past to life and for answering all my questions while we were staying at the hotel and researching for this book. Thank you, also, to Margaret Doud, owner of the Windermere Hotel, where we also stayed and researched for Maude's fictional inn.

My pastor, Rev. Larry Jones, wrote a wonderful sermon based on a "Prince and the Pauper" theme that ended up being delivered by Rev. Seth Caddell when Larry encountered travel difficulties. That sermon segued with my spiritual theme and inspired me to expand it for both my hero and heroine. I love those God-inspired sermons! Thanks, Larry and Seth!

Thank you to my Beta readers Regina Fujitani and Diana L. Flowers, and my advance readers Andrea Stephens and Julia Wilson, and to my Pagels Pals members, who keep me lifted up in prayer. So many folks have worked with me on this manuscript over the years, including Julee Schwarzburg, who consulted on the proposal; Susan Brower, who helped with the edits for the Maggie Awards (this manuscript was a finalist in Unpublished Manuscripts, Inspirational Novels); and Julie Gwinn, who did substantive edits for the full manuscript. Thank you, Becky Fish, my wonderful editor from Barbour, for your help, and Becky Germany for believing in Maude's story. Thank you all for putting your mark on this story!

Chapter One

Mackinac Island, Michigan
Monday, June 3, 1895

Maude Welling's twelve-year-old brother, Jack, raced across the waxed wood floor of the soda shop, straight toward her, then skidded to a halt.

"Greyson's back!" His loud pronouncement caused several people seated at nearby tables, to cease their conversation and look up.

Perched atop an oak stool at the counter, Maude choked in surprise on her cherry phosphate and struggled to maintain her balance. Finally, he was home—and she would see him face-to-face. She pushed the frosted glass away and grabbed the napkin from her lap and wiped her mouth, dread and excitement comingling in her gut. She looked down to inspect her white cotton pin-tucked bodice.

Finding a tiny spot above her waist, she frantically dabbed at the crimson dots. "I need some seltzer water, quick."

Al spritzed some seltzer on a clean white cloth and passed it to her.

"Thanks." Luckily the red stain began to blot up. "There. That's better."

Hands shaking, Maude slid her uncle's reconciled account records across the marble counter to him. Soon Father would allow her to resume handling the Winds of Mackinac record keeping, once she was married to her childhood sweetheart. "Your books are all in order now, Uncle Al."

He winked at her. "You need to get to the dock."

Beside her, Jack shifted from foot to foot, his jaw muscles twitching.

She realized that he hadn't said another word since coming into the shop.

Something was wrong. Maude's sweetheart had returned to Mackinac Island. Everyone should be smiling, happy for her. Even Maude's own hands perspired, as they did when she was afraid, not when she was excited.

Jack drew closer and tugged at her mutton-leg sleeve. "Sis, he's got someone with him—real pretty redhead."

Maude stiffened from the top of her pinned-up hair, down to her tail-bone. No word from Greyson in over a month. She glanced at her bare left hand. Snapping her mossy-colored short capelet up from the coatrack, she draped it across her arm.

"What would you know, Jack? He was probably just being polite to someone."

Jack scowled. "Yeah, right. Thought he was gonna marry you—not some old carrot top." Her brother ran out into the street, the bell ringing as the glass-paned door slammed shut.

Maude exited the soda shop, lifted her skirts, and crossed the busy street to the wharf, dodging carriages and piles of manure the horses had left and the street sweepers had yet to clean up. Her phosphate fizzed inside her gut. She pressed a hand over her mouth, feeling the cherry-red liquid churning. Removing her hand, she pressed her lips together and strode toward the docks. When a chill, stiff breeze greeted her, she wrapped her capelet over her shoulders and tried to button it as she walked, but the large buttons wouldn't cooperate. She pulled the garment close, overlapping the front and hugging herself tight.

Maude gasped for breath as she wove among the passengers at the dock. She spied Jack as he ducked behind one of the narrow whitewashed wood buildings that trailed onto the waterfront.

Arrivals chattered happily as they clustered around their luggage in the center wood platform on the boardwalk that surrounded the dock. Liveried men, all in various colors denoting their particular inn, toted the boxes off and hoisted them into the baggage drays bound for the hotels.

Maude moistened her lips as she spotted her old beau, so handsome in a suit she'd never seen before. Greyson stood beside a huge black-leather trunk, which was banded by contrasting brown straps. Adjacent to him stood a slim woman with red hair—just as Jack had said. Sucking in a breath, Maude waited for the tightness in her chest to ease. *Relax. Breathe slowly. Inhale in, then exhale out.*

As the porter pushed the luggage toward one of the island's cabs, Greyson turned and looked directly at Maude. Then flinched. He said something to his companion and pulled the young woman in Maude's direction. Maude froze; her feet glued to the boardwalk like the green-flocked wallpaper newly hung in their parlor.

Jack popped out from behind the dockmaster's building. He squinted at the red-haired woman as he often did insects he was about to secure inside a mason jar. The woman snapped her fan against Greyson's arm, and he ceased dragging her.

Now the young lady floated along the wide wooden planks of the walkway, her gauzy confection of a dress billowing in the light lilac-scented breeze. Lace, embroidery, and glistening tiny beads seemed to cover the entire fitted bodice. A House of Worth gown—one advertised in the latest edition of *Harper's Bazaar*. Maude glanced down at her simple blouse and skirt—a country bumpkin's clothing compared to this woman's elaborate attire. Maude had ceased wearing mourning and had been so happy to wear something with color again. But now, she wanted to run home and don her black frocks to hide.

Everything within her urged Maude to flee, even as the duo edged closer to her.

"Maude?" Greyson raised his tall hat, golden hair glistening beneath the midday sun.

When they were children, she and Greyson had enacted a play about the French Revolution. Why did she suddenly feel as though he was about to take her hand and haul her off to the executioner?

A tremor twitched the young woman's full lips as she linked her arm through Greyson's.

Standing several feet back from the couple, Jack pointed at the stranger then turned to address Maude. "See, I told ya so!"

Heat seared Maude's cheeks as her brother raced away toward the park across the street. She turned and watched him go, wishing she could chase after him.

When she turned around, Greyson's companion narrowed her eyes and scanned Maude from her scuffed boots to her white blouse tucked into her wide-banded skirt, lingering on her waistline, which was, thankfully, very slim. "Greyson, aren't you going to make introductions?"

When he responded, wind from the lake rushed past Maude's ears, obscuring what he said, except for "...Anna."

Once again, the young woman withdrew her arm from Greyson's grasp. As the young woman minced toward Maude, swirls of titian hair dipped beneath her wide-brimmed hat.

Extending a lace-gloved hand, a glittering bulge visible on her left ring finger, the woman offered a tight smile and a challenging stare. "I'm Anna Luce—Greyson's wife."

Heartbeats hammering in Maude's chest escalated, reminiscent of the months of incessant noise from the construction of the Grand Hotel eight years earlier—when Mother had wondered if their inn would survive with such competition.

"I...I see...." But she didn't, as her vision faded slightly.

Surely even Mrs. Luce, Greyson's mother, didn't know, for she would have told Maude. What would the poor woman think when she discovered her son was now married to someone other than Maude?

Greyson extended a hand, but she recoiled.

Maude forced a breath and exhaled as slowly as she could, waiting to calm her nerves. Betrayal knifed her gut, and she clasped her hand to her stomach.

"Excuse me...."

She strode from the dock, her heel catching on an uneven board. She yanked her heel free. Two angry tears spilled, and she wiped them away with the back of her hand.

"Maude!" Greyson's voice trailed her.

"Let her go, darling," his wife urged.

And against the backdrop of island breezes, birdsong, and carriage wheels, Maude heard Greyson walking out of her life, with Anna.

Ben Steffan pulled at his starched linen collar, anxious to leave the White Star Line steamship behind. Painful memories of a different voyage rushed over him. Yet this time, he stood aboveboard, not in steerage. Ahead, Mackinac Island, an emerald jewel, lay nestled within Lake Michigan's azure velvet. Even from miles out he spotted the clifftop outline of the Grand Hotel, his destination. *Pristine beauty.* No wonder the wealthy flocked here each summer. Perhaps even Roosevelt, who had urged Mackinac's National Park status, might be spotted. But Ben wasn't here for a political or social column, despite being the society columnist for the *Detroit Post.*

Soon they moored. Two other gentlemen, who'd appeared as nervous as Ben was trying to not be, moved alongside two young ladies and offered assistance disembarking the ship. Was their aim on the island to find a wealthy wife? Ben would have to draw upon all his observational skills to spot the targets for his article. Despite his qualms about this charade, if he hit pay dirt with this story, Banyon may finally make him assistant editor. And he could finally afford to support a wife, should he ever have time to court someone.

The scent of engine smoke dissipated as Ben merged into the crowd heading off the dock. A winsome brunette bumped into him, wafting the scent of musky flowers. As Ben met the woman's gaze of open appreciation, his cheeks warmed. Apparently well-dressed "Friedrich König" was worthy of appreciation. His boss had outfitted him at a gentleman's store in Detroit, and Ben's transformation was quite complete.

No. How well he knew that one's character—one's heart and soul—wasn't altered simply by donning fine attire. If only the young women who read his exposé might realize the same.

Around him, the crowd separated into jagged queues that edged toward a line of carriages stretched seven deep. Gold embroidered letters "*GH*" glistened in the sunlight on one surrey's red topper.

He strode forward, not wanting to miss his conveyance. Almost there, a bronze-haired beauty with wet rosy cheeks, whirled toward him and ran smack into his chest. When he grabbed her shoulders to steady her, he looked over her shoulder and caught the glimpse of familiar faces behind her. *Greyson Luce and Anna.* What were they doing here? The couple moved away toward a small one-horse carriage.

Shoulders stiffening, Ben took one step back from the woman in his arms.

"I'm very sorry, miss. *Ich habe dich nicht gesehen.*" Obviously, something had distressed her, and from the looks Anna and Greyson cast her way, they had something to do with it.

The young lady before him stood erect as a queen, her tiny cape fluttering in the breeze, hands now fisted. Corkscrew curls trailed her long neck, which was streaked with angry red. Despite her angst, here was a woman of fortitude. Or had she thought he'd insulted her in German? He lapsed into his native tongue when stressed.

"Of course you couldn't see me. I plowed right into you."

"You speak German?"

"A little." She sniffed, and Ben offered her his handkerchief. She accepted the linen square. She kept her head lowered, shame etched on what little he could see of her features.

Dressed in plain but well-made clothes, she appeared to be an islander. Something about her called to his heart. He didn't trust in emotions—he was a journalist, and facts were what mattered. But right now, he longed to understand how she felt. Must be the island air and the boat trip unsettling him.

"Miss, is there anything I can do to help you?"

A deep blast from the ship's horn startled him. His shoulders jerked against the constraints of the tailored jacket, but she appeared unaffected by the intrusion.

For a split second she raised her pretty amber eyes, tears spilling down her flushed cheeks. Just as quickly she lowered and shook her head.

Focus, Ben. Pay attention to your job. He needed to get to his carriage.

"Excuse me, miss, but I must get to my lodgings." Ben drew his straw boater low over his eyes.

"Yes, please don't let me keep you." With that, she lifted her skirts and moved swiftly away from him.

He'd not even introduced himself. He was Friedrich König now, wealthy industrialist, and headed for the Grand Hotel. He recollected his conversation with his editor, and could almost smell the man's pipe smoke and the scent of paper fresh from the press. His editor, Banyon, hadn't mentioned Anna and Greyson would be on Mackinac, yet he knew of Ben's "friendship" with Anna.

A slow sizzle, like tinder catching in the fireplace, began to burn. Was Banyon setting him up? He rubbed his chin then headed toward the line of carriages, now thinning, as one after another of the drivers directed the horses to pull their conveyances away from the curb.

Ben moved on to the loading area.

A strongly built black man dressed in full livery, his wide gait steady, approached. "Grand Hotel, sir?"

"*Ja.*"

"Name, sir? I'll get your baggage." He pulled out a pad of paper and a short pencil.

"Friedrich König." If he kept saying it, maybe he'd even believe it himself.

The stranger's compassion unnerved Maude, as had that glimpse of admiration she'd caught in his eyes—even though her face had to have been red with humiliation. It was as though God had allowed her that tiny moment of kindness to assuage the pain Greyson's betrayal had delivered.

Even early lilacs couldn't entice her attention as she strode on the curving wood walkway toward the Winds of Mackinac. Woodsmoke from chimneys nearby tickled her nose. She didn't bother to wipe her cheeks, for more tears would follow. Angry, rage-filled tears. When Father found out about Greyson's marriage, he'd sell the inn, and then. . .

Seagulls swooped overhead and squawked. She longed to screech along with them—to throw back her head and rail at the injustice of having Greyson marry another. *Oh God, why me?*

You refused him.

She sniffed. She'd not really refused him—she'd asked for clarification. And then his letters dropped off. He'd never sent word that he was courting another woman, much less about to marry her. *Two-timing scoundrel.*

Maude continued walking alongside Lake Michigan. Sunlight dappled the azure water as sailboats' canvases unfurled. She belonged here with a sense of connectedness that was in her blood. She and Greyson were Mackinac Islanders: year-round residents, not some tourist or seasonal visitor. Not a stranger—like Anna.

Not a stranger like the man who'd held her at the wharf. The best marriages were those formed by long-term relationships and mutual respect and friendship, Father had insisted.

How had Greyson managed to woo and win a wife in such a short time?

Greyson's accusation from their last private encounter, at Christmas, echoed in her mind. "You never loved me. Not as a woman loves a man she wants for a husband." He'd certainly pressed that point enough for her to know it was true—she'd always pulled back from his rather frantic kisses and embraces.

Sadie Duvall's warnings—were they true? "He's after one thing, Maudie—and it isn't what you think." And what did that mean?

After she arrived home, Maude went to their private parlor, seated herself at the Baldwin piano, and poured herself into a favorite Tchaikovsky piece, her fingers pounding the instrument as though she could overpower the discordant melody in her heart. But to no avail. She ceased the melancholy piece. Tentatively, she began to play the strains of her own composition, this song full of crescendos more hopeful—of finding one's own true love. She pulled her tingling fingers from the piano, as though the inanimate object discerned her ambivalence. Why did her thoughts continue to drift off to the stranger rather than to her childhood sweetheart?

She rose and arranged her skirts before moving toward the fireplace. Soft footfalls announced their new maid—her friend Sadie's sister. Although it sometimes seemed awkward to have her friend's sister in their employ, Maude was happy the girl received steady pay and was safe, fed, and warm every night.

Bea Duvall set down a box of cleaning supplies and rags near the hearth. "She fired her, Miss Maude."

"What?" She'd not yet grown accustomed to Bea's cryptic messages. "Who fired whom?"

"Sadie's been fired. She's looking for a job."

Maude reached an unsteady hand out to the back of the nearby divan. "Mrs. Luce can't..."

"You go tell her that, then." Bea huffed and commenced polishing the revolving mahogany bookcase near the wall. "Greyson's wife, the new Mrs. Luce, fired her. Too bad you weren't her."

The Grand Hotel's porch stretched several football fields long. Ben forced himself to not gawk. He affected a blasé air as he approached the building. Gleaming alabaster white, it nestled high on the hill overlooking woods and verdant fields. Pavilions punctuated the lush grounds here and there like Bavarian Easter eggs nestled in rye baskets. A folly built at one end of the lower park was meant to entice sweethearts, no doubt. Would he find himself entangled there with someone who believed he was the wealthy Friedrich König?

Once inside, the multitude of crystal chandeliers rivaled anything he'd viewed as a newspaperman covering the swankest events in Detroit. Yet the decor was more "affluent rustic camp" for a fair amount of the building, particularly the halls leading to the bedchambers. Unpainted paneling covered the entryway, which was as wide as his entire apartment building in Detroit. Overhead, the coffered wooden ceiling with its impressive intersecting beams and sunken panels suggested a large lodge in the north woods. Yet moving into the social areas, the decor became more formal.

Highly polished hardwoods and marble reflected in the gilded baroque mirrors in the spacious lobby.

Ben followed the man toting his baggage to a semicircular walnut counter, behind which a silver-haired clerk wiped his glasses. Adjacent stood a large, rectangular, wheeled cart, similar to those used at the newspaper to transport papers to carriages for delivery, but this one was covered with luggage.

"König," the porter told the clerk. "Friedrich König."

Donning his eyeglasses, the man blinked at Ben before bowing quickly. "Welcome, Mr. König. You have one of the diplomat rooms—one of our best."

"Very good."

"I'm Mr. Morris, and we've been directed to assign a manservant to you." The clerk handed a heavy brass key to a tall dark-skinned servant wearing the hotel's distinctive red jacket. "Blevins will be caring for your needs, since you didn't have your valet accompany you."

"No." Because he had no valet.

When the men frowned, Ben corrected himself. "I mean, ja, I'd appreciate the assistance."

The porter grinned over his shoulder. "This way, sir."

Following the red-jacketed man down the hallway, Ben again appreciated the difference a fine pair of shoes made. He'd had neither foot nor leg discomfort, which he often did running all over the city in his old broughams. And his jacket's cut facilitated his movements, as well.

A young woman attired in a low-cut gown sashayed by them, fixing her gaze on Ben.

"Good afternoon." His voice came out low, almost a growl. He didn't find such immodest attire appealing. But Friedrich König might, and he needed to act the part. He smiled at her in what he hoped was a charming fashion.

She raised one golden eyebrow. "Good day." Her accent was pure New York. She slinked past.

Two doors down, the employee paused. After turning the key in the door, the servant pushed through, bringing the cart ahead of Ben. As he entered the room, a faint musty odor battled with the breeze, wafting in through the open, expansive mullioned windows. The hotel had only recently been reopened for the season. Extravagant wallpaper in hues of ivory covered every wall. A large bed covered in sumptuous silks featured prominently in the room.

"I'll put your clothes up for you, sir." Blevins chuckled. "I do have other duties, but I'll be assigned to you as your manservant."

He recalled his uncle's manservant, Hans, an overworked but loyal man who used to slip Ben *pfefferminze* candies. "Go ahead and unpack then."

"Yes, sir." He opened the heavy brass latches on the black leather trunk stamped in gold with "CROSLEY'S LUGGAGE," the London shop being the finest purveyor of such goods and on loan to Ben from his boss.

The big man began hanging Ben's clothes in the armoire.

Crossing to the window, Ben gazed out at the brilliant blue water and whistled in appreciation. Then realized such behavior could be considered crass. He fisted and unfisted his hands.

"Your first visit here, sir?"

"Ja. Indeed." Ben assumed a casual slouch, attempting to give the air of a wealthy gentleman accustomed to such digs. But his uncle would have stood erect, soldier stiff, awaiting orders. Ben straightened.

"If I can be of any assistance to you, please let me know." He lifted Ben's undergarments between two meaty hands and transferred them to the open bureau drawer.

Ben needed a friend in his corner, inside the hotel. And he didn't want to ask for assistance from too many people. This man seemed to be an honest fellow.

But a little cash incentive couldn't hurt.

"Ask for Ray downstairs at the counter." He grinned. "Mr. Morris is the only one calls me Blevins."

"Thank you, Ray." He pulled out some crisp bills, but the man shook his head.

"No tipping at the hotel, sir." The man's brilliant white teeth contrasted with his dark skin.

He'd forgotten the hotel's policy. He shrugged and grinned, and then Ray's features relaxed.

Ben frowned at the dark, liquid-filled cut-glass decanters that covered a low table. "You can remove those from the room."

Another faux pas—most wealthy young men would be celebrating the premium brandies, sherry, and whiskey contained in the crystal containers.

"Always good to wait on a fellow temperance man."

"Yes, a temperance man. That's right." But Friedrich König would surely imbibe. "At least when I'm keeping my own company. For business, I must keep up appearances or I'll be considered staid."

Ray's dark eyebrows pulled together and then relaxed. "There's a dance tomorrow night in the ballroom, sir. Sure to be plenty of young ladies there—including some who live nearby. Some you might know, you being from the city and all."

Fear prickled up the back of Ben's neck. He could identify most of the elite from Detroit because of his work. Hopefully they'd not recognize him if he crossed their paths. He strafed his hand over his naked jaw. *No more thick beard.* And his unruly hair had been cut in the latest fashion. He'd even begun oiling it and using pomade to keep his thick hair well dressed.

Might he get a chance to see the young lovely he'd spied earlier at the docks? Would the young woman reside in one of the fancy "cottages" that dotted the cliff side like miniature castles? He cringed. Without love and Christian charity, even life in a castle could bring *das Elend*, complete misery.

Chapter Two

*O*nly a day had passed since Maude's encounter with the kind stranger at the wharf, but it seemed several had trailed by. She'd tossed and turned all night long as dreams became nightmares, but turned out to be the truth when she awakened. Greyson was married. They'd not be wed this summer. Nor would they run the inn together.

She was thoroughly humiliated, but in her heart of hearts she was more angry than lovesick. For months now, God had seemed to be telling her that Greyson was not the man for her. With Greyson's marriage, deception's cloth had been lifted from her eyes—not sheer bridal veil mist but a heavy swath of wool thrown free.

Sitting at her dressing table, brushing out the knots in her hair, her errant thoughts diverted back to the man at the dock. Tall and well dressed, the newcomer to the island had never been on Mackinac before—she'd have remembered. His behavior and strong features suggested a man of purpose.

Rarely had she daydreamed about Greyson. Maybe he was right—she hadn't loved him, not like when two were to be married. Last night she'd prayed for Greyson and Anna and asked God to help her to forgive them. She chewed the inside of her lip. Next, she'd need to pray to forgive herself. She should have obeyed the prompting of God to write to Greyson at school and share her concerns. Regardless of what he had done, she, too, had a responsibility she'd overlooked.

Three light knocks on the door announced Bea. "Good morning, Miss Maude."

"Good morning." She continued pulling the brush through her waist-length hair.

"Wish my hair was so pretty."

"Thank you." Maude glanced into the mirror, wishing that, rather than her medium brown hair, she viewed the ebony tresses that were the Cadotte women's legacy—as was this inn. "Your eyes are beautifully expressive."

The girl's cheek turned crimson. "Always give me away, miss. Don't be wishing that."

Maude laughed. "Have you heard anything from Sadie?" She set down her boar-bristle brush.

"Yes, I went home and treated my little sisters to ice cream while Sadie looked for work, again. Nice having my own money to spend, Miss Maude." Bea rocked back and forth in her sturdy black shoes.

She couldn't help smiling at the girl's pride in doing something kind. "I spoke with Father last night about Sadie." She'd not worked up the nerve yet to tell him about Greyson, but she'd have to face him this morning and get it over with. "He'll address the matter this afternoon with both Mrs. Luces." Not that Maude expected Greyson's new wife, Anna, to reinstate Sadie, but Father should at least say something since they'd been paying for Sadie's help.

"There's no need." Bea opened the chifforobe and retrieved a hanger for Maude's wrapper.

"Why is that?" Maude stood so Bea could help her get ready.

Bea took Maude's dressing gown from her and hung it. "Sadie's found a spot."

"Wonderful!" Maybe it would be easier than caring for poor Mrs. Luce.

The girl examined the garments hanging in the center of the wardrobe, chewing on her lower lip.

"I'd like the skirt that Jane just pressed."

With Bea's assistance, Maude soon stepped into her skirt. "Who is Sadie working for?"

"The tavern."

Maude stiffened. "What?"

"Needed something right away, and Foster had an opening."

Mr. Foster? The proverbial cat could have gotten her tongue, for Maude couldn't find another word to say. The man was the worst employer on the island. A bald-faced liar, with the shiny pate to match.

Bea pulled a matching blouse from the armoire. "Don't you have the church's social meeting this afternoon?"

Groaning, she held out her arms. "I forgot." She waited as Bea slipped the sleeve on and then walked behind her to button the back.

"Won't all those ladies ask about Greyson?"

Maude sucked in her breath as together they tucked her blouse into her skirt band. "I think you're right."

"You *might* be too upset to go to those old biddies' meeting." Bea handed Maude her stockings, and she sat on the vanity chair and pulled them on.

"It's true. I didn't sleep well." Maude fished her everyday shoes out from beneath the vanity. "They aren't biddies—they've all been very sweet to me, especially since Mother died."

"Begging your pardon, but none of those ladies lifted a finger to help us when Pa went missing." Moisture glinted in Bea's green eyes.

Maude exhaled a puff of air. "I'm sorry."

"Not your fault." Bea bent and helped wrap the laces over the large black hooks on the shoes and then expertly tie off the bow.

"I best get down to breakfast."

"I've got to run to the kitchen and see if Jane needs help serving."

Maude followed Bea downstairs. They parted in the hallway, where Jack was just entering the family's private dining room. Maude strode in behind him and ran smack into the back of her chair at the oval table. "Oh!"

"You're getting even clumsier, Muddie!" Jack grinned as he moved behind her and pulled her Windsor chair out.

She frowned at him. "Don't call me that."

He laughed. "Aren't you gonna thank me for holding your chair for you?"

"Thank you, Jack." Praise might not be perceived as such when said through gritted teeth, so she tried again but with a sweeter tone, "You're becoming quite the gentleman." Unlike Greyson, who'd not even bothered to warn her he was pursuing Anna.

Father, seated by the bay window, sun streaming in over his shoulder, looked up from his copy of the *Free Press*.

Oh, no. Too late. She cringed, recognizing his piercing glance. An accusation was forthcoming.

Father's glasses slid down the narrow bridge of his nose. "I hear Greyson is home."

Should have realized that by now every islander had likely heard the story.

Jack, now seated opposite her, chomped on a peach, juice trickling down the cleft in his chin. "Yeah, he's got himself a real purty redheaded wife!"

Removing his reading glasses with one hand, Father snapped his paper closed with the other. "Who'll run this hotel then?"

"I will." Maude deftly speared a piece of sliced peach from the blue willow china bowl set before her. Hadn't she proven she could keep accounting books straight?

Stony eyes glared unblinking at her. She wouldn't look away. Unflinching, she stared back at her father. When he averted his gaze, she didn't feel she'd won anything. Disappointment clouded Father's eyes. A sheen of moisture filmed them, and his complexion remained ashen. Worry gripped her heart as a cramp began in her stomach. He needed to go to the mainland to see a specialist—but he wouldn't go.

"Maude, we've had this conversation many times. I've made my position clear."

One of the maids tapped on the door. "Hot breakfast ready, sir."

"Bring it in." Father's grumpy tone contradicted his command.

The young woman glided past Maude and set a tray before her father. The savory scent of bacon, eggs, biscuits, and fried potatoes tempted her appetite.

"Are ye eating this mornin', miss?" The servant's Irish brogue announced her recent arrival in America and her origins.

"Yes, Jane, if you have any left after the guests are served." They'd had a family arrive earlier than expected. Maude had failed to send to the mainland for extra groceries. She'd been too busy hiding in her room and fretting over Greyson. She pressed her hands to her cheeks—what had happened to her? She'd always been so unflappable. But it wasn't every day a girl got jilted.

Her father frowned. "No need to wait, Maude."

To wait—for love again? She blinked at her father. Then dropped her hands as he pointed to the tempting food Jane set before her.

Stomach rumbling, Maude succumbed and filled her breakfast plate. Cook had outdone herself with the eggs. And the bacon was perfect. Hadn't they been out of it, though?

"I ran down to Uncle John's store last night." Jack grinned and grabbed an extra biscuit for himself. "Got some extra stuff for that new family we got."

Father shook his paper out and cleared his throat. "Thought you children should know I may sell the inn."

Bacon stuck in Maude's throat, almost choking her. She cleared her throat as icy tentacles of fear seemed to trickle down it.

"You can't!" At Maude's raised voice, Jane's ruddy cheeks reddened further, and she tugged on her frilly apron before slipping out the door. "This hotel belonged to Mother's family for decades."

She fisted her hands until her nails bit into her palms. How dare he? What could he be thinking? She loved this gorgeous island—couldn't imagine living anywhere else. Furthermore, Mother had prepared her since childhood to take over the running of the inn—she said per Grandmother's will that Maude would be inheriting eventually. Uncle Robert, her mother's younger brother, had yet to meet with Father about the stipulations in the will. But he'd hinted that she should prepare herself. Could it be that Father would sell off the inn and all their properties purposefully, to ensure she wouldn't be running it? She pushed her plate away, suddenly queasy. "Father, I don't see how. . ."

If possible, Father's skin glowed even paler than minutes earlier. "Quite enough, young lady!"

Young? At almost twenty-one and now with Greyson married, she'd soon be considered—an old maid. She had to do something. "Sorry, Father."

He scrutinized her face before his features relaxed again.

"Here. Read the local paper—I'm finishing up the *Free Press*."

Jack passed her the thin local newspaper, the *Islander*. Maude flipped to the back, tremors in her hands shaking the thin pages. Print inside a square box advertised: "*Wanted for immediate employment—Grand Hotel seeks local workers. Contact Mrs. Ada Fox, Housekeeping Manager.*"

She knew about running a hotel. If Father wouldn't allow her to assume management of the inn, Maude would look elsewhere. Today. She'd prove herself capable.

Bea entered the room, her clothing clean but the hem dragging and a small patch peeking through in the pleats in her skirt. The girl reached over Father to pour juice from a silver pitcher into his goblet.

"Thank you, Bea."

"Yes, sir." Their new maid bobbed, but the bow in her hair flopped forward and she shoved it back awkwardly with her hand.

Jack covered his mouth, but Maude could see that he was stifling a laugh. She cleared her throat and shot a scolding look in his direction. Bea's face crumpled, and she poured a splash of juice, just a jot, into Jack's glass before coming around the table.

When their father went back to his newspaper, Bea wrinkled her nose at Jack.

"Hey!" the boy protested.

Father's head shot up. "Young man, you shall conduct yourself with decorum at this table."

How many times had Father fussed at Uncle Robert to do the same when he had lived with them? Where was Captain Robert Swaine now? And why wasn't he answering her letters?

Ben allowed the manservant assigned to adjust his cravat.

"How you like dinner last night, sir?"

Mostly Ben had enjoyed learning more about those seated at his table. "I met some interesting people." Like Marcus Edmunds, who purported to be a wealthy Detroiter, but whom Ben had never met on the social scene, which he covered for the paper.

"Good." Ray Blevins assisted Ben into his superfine wool jacket. "Find the billiard room earlier?"

"Sure did." Ben stretched out his arms, amazed that his sleeves, for the first time in many years, were tailored expertly and hit perfectly at his wrist. "Played with Casey Randolph." Whom he suspected of being a man in pursuit of wealthy conquests.

"You gonna give Mr. Randolph a run for his money if that Miss Ingram sees you tonight."

"She was all eyes for him at the billiard tables."

"Mr. Ingram a lumber baron." Ray adjusted the jacket sleeves until they lay perfectly at Ben's wrist. "He sure he gonna find his girl a good match up here."

"That so?" Would Ingram discern that Casey Randolph was all polish and no substance?

"Yes, sir." The servant nodded. "Enjoy the dance."

"I won't be dancing."

Ray slipped almost silently from the room.

Ben tucked a pencil nub and a minuscule square notepad in his pocket, in case he needed to jot a note.

Inside the ballroom, crystal chandeliers illuminated the inlaid mahogany-and-oak dance floor, around which were clustered tables covered in pristine linen tablecloths. He scanned the room. No bronze-haired vision—the woman from the dock. Many families sat together. Single people lingered by the dance floor. A mixed group surrounded an ice sculpture of a swan—similar to one recently pictured on the cover of the *New York Times* social section.

If only this exposé could garner the attention that New York papers had given to tales of Britishers seeking American heiresses for their fortunes. Maybe then Ben's life would finally fall into place. Finally—a promotion, a raise, and journalistic respect.

Marcus joined Ben and pointed toward the arched entryway. "Can you believe someone as rich as Anna Forham would marry an island sap?"

Anna floated into the room, on her husband's arm. Her crème anglaise skin glowed beneath the hotel's new electric lights.

Ben moved back farther into the shadows. He'd not stay. If he watched Greyson and Anna waltzing, then he risked being discovered.

"Greyson Luce was engaged to be married to the daughter of an island inn owner."

Slacking his hip, to affect a nonchalance he didn't possess, Ben inquired, "Which one?"

"Prettiest one on that curve as you approach the Grand. Light lemon color."

"I meant the young lady, not the inn."

"Oh." Marcus shrugged. "I don't know."

Greyson Luce was engaged to an island girl. Instead he married Anna. Could that have been the fiancée crying at the wharf? Granted that girl looked angry, rather than devastated over the loss of the love of her life. Still. . .

As the band began to play, Marcus glanced in Miss Ingram's direction. "Excuse me, I see Myra is here." He headed off toward his target.

If Ben got a scoop on Anna, daughter of their newspaper owner's rival, both Ben's editor and he could benefit. But pursuing such a story would be mean-spirited. Surely Banyon hadn't sent Ben up with muck-raking in mind.

After only a night on the island, how might he feel after several weeks? Editor Banyon's suggestion to pose as a wealthy businessman seemed so persuasive at the time, but now Ben felt more like a spy than a journalist.

Ben turned on his heel and returned to his room. When he entered, he stepped onto a piece of paper. Ben bent and retrieved the telegram. Already Banyon was issuing directives from afar. Ben groaned as he read the terse words, "*Expose Luce.*"

Crossing to the bed, he flopped down on his back, shoes and all. Did his editor simply wish to humiliate the owner of their rival publisher? And so soon after Zofija Forham's death. Other than Greyson Luce having ended his relationship with the loveliest creature Ben had laid eyes on, there were no leads on Luce. While Banyon expressed his belief that Luce had pursued Anna for her money, he'd never tasked Ben to investigate. Until now. Had Banyon set him up with a diversionary story as a pretext to muckrake against the Forhams?

Chapter Three

*A*rguing with himself hadn't gotten Ben far the night before. Today he'd take action—and deal with his conscience later. This research might afford him the chance to encounter the cinnamon-haired beauty again. He'd argue the point with Banyon when he crossed that threshold.

Standing at the top of the steps at the Grand, Ben took in the sweep of azure lake water dotted with whitecaps as he prepared to leave the property, which covered many acres.

He descended the steep hill adjacent the Grand Hotel. After another ten minutes of walking, he paused and scanned the occupants of two carriages that rolled down the main road, then continued on, the breeze inconsistently following him. Marcus said Greyson's former fiancée lived in a yellow inn at the sharp curve with a grassy knoll across from it.

Sweat broke out on Ben's forehead and he removed his hat and tucked it under his arm. He walked on past beautiful homes. Soon he'd be in the outer rim of the business district where several hotels and inns clustered near the water.

Would he once more see those flashing eyes, or had the young woman recovered from the shock—if indeed the beauty from the docks was Luce's former fiancée?

Dodging a pile of horse droppings, he crossed the street and stepped onto the boardwalk near the well-maintained early Victorian inn. Guests clustered on the porch surrounding the yellow clapboard building. A servant girl rolled a tea cart past them.

Near the street, a white-haired groundskeeper clipped at boxwoods. He looked up. "Beautiful morning, eh?"

Ben paused. "Ja, but I tell you what—it would be lovelier yet, if I can locate a young woman I met at the dock when I arrived." He hoped his smile might assure the gardener that he wasn't an evildoer.

The worker ceased cutting and wiped a shirtsleeved arm against his forehead. "Young lovelies coming to the island all the time nowadays."

Ben ran his tongue over his lower lip. "I think she might be a resident."

The gardener's thin lips rolled together. "We've not too many young beauties on the island. Sadie Duvall is one. Blond hair, robin's-egg-blue eyes."

"No, brunette."

The older man blew out a puff of air. "Ah, that beauty might be Mr. Welling's daughter." He jerked a thumb toward the well-kept inn behind him.

Ben's heart rose into his chest as he read a sign hanging from a shingle— WINDS OF MACKINAC. Was this where Greyson's abandoned fiancée lived?

"Does she have golden-brown hair and stand about so high?" He raised his hand up to just above his own shoulder, which was taller than the groundskeeper. The young lady stood tall, but she might have been wearing high-heeled boots beneath her skirts.

Both men watched as a young woman stepped around from the back of the inn, a filmy scarf secured her wide straw hat beneath her chin. Her gray skirt and jacket, trimmed in ribbon, perfectly displayed her femininity with her blouse tucked into the tiny waist of the skirt. A jacket, almost military in cut, was anything but soldierlike in appearance.

He'd not realized he'd been holding his breath until the other man jabbed a finger at him. "I'm guessin' that's who you were lookin' for, eh?"

The gardener chuckled and went back to his chores. But then he looked up, his eyes narrowed. "We look after our own here on the island, sir. Just be sure you understand that, eh?"

Warning acknowledged, Ben tipped his hat at the man. Now what? He had to have this story, but he had no desire to cause this young woman even more distress than she'd suffered at the hands of Greyson Luce.

Stepping back, he bumped into a budding azalea and almost fell.

❤

Maude raised her parasol to shield her eyes from the strong sun reflected by the lake. Who was Mr. Chesnut speaking with by the street? She'd heard the groundskeeper when she'd come around from the back of the house and through the side garden, where she'd paused to inhale the scent of the lilacs. He was talking with a man who had a low voice, and she hoped it wasn't one of his drinking buddies. Their gardener had finally sobered up long enough to come back and perform his job adequately again.

Rounding the brick walkway and raising her umbrella to protect her skin from the sun, she spied a tall man whose wide shoulders perfectly filled out his expensive suit. Slicked back dark hair circled above his collar and beneath his bowler hat. Maude pressed a hand to her chest. The man from the docks.

A gust of breeze brought a heady mix of all the perfumes of the flowers Gus cultivated for them. Heavenly. She inhaled deeply as she joined the two men.

Gus looked up. "You know this fella?"

Cringing, she lowered her parasol and leaned on it for support. "I'm afraid I quite literally ran into him at the docks."

The stranger's eyes met hers as a gentle smile tugged at his lips. "I'm glad to see you looking better today."

Had she looked so awful, then? She pressed a hand to her cheek.

A rosy tint tinged his high cheekbones. "*Ach*, I did not mean that as it sounded. I mean—you looked very upset, Miss. . ."

"Maude Welling. And thank you, I was having a. . .difficult day."

Gus snorted then scuffled off toward the side garden. She thought she heard him mutter something about Greyson, but she wasn't sure.

"I'm Friedrich König." The newcomer touched his fingers to his hat brim.

"Nice to meet you, Mr. König."

"And very nice to meet you, Miss Welling." His lips twitched as though he hesitated to say something.

"I'm off to my uncle's shop. Is there anything I can help you with?"

"No, but I'd be happy to escort you." His voice dropped into a lower register.

What would people say if they saw her strolling with a man so soon after Greyson's marriage and their broken engagement?

She met his direct gaze. "I'm afraid I must decline. But I do thank you for your kind concern, Mr. König." It was entirely improper for a stranger to call upon her. But the thought made her want to beam. This island visitor was someone she'd like to know better.

When disappointment flickered over his fine features, a twinge of regret pierced Maude's reserve. She chewed on her lower lip lest she blurt out that she'd love to stroll with him.

"Miss Welling, I regret if I have caused you any discomfort by stopping to share my regards."

A niggle of apprehension worked through her. Mr. König spoke with a touch of German that thickened and then trailed into a strong Midwestern speech pattern—as though he was making an effort to appear more European than American. More fashionable, at the Grand, to be from the Continent. If he was affectatious, perhaps a dose of Pastor McWithey's sermons might help cure him.

"Mr. König, if you are looking for a church to attend while you're on the island. . ."

"Ja, I am." His affirmation caused her heart to skip a beat.

"Mission Church is where my family attends." Surely tongues wouldn't wag over a stranger being invited to services. Or had she just offered more fodder to the island gossips?

He tipped his hat. "Until then." With a rueful smile, he departed.

Maude watched as he strode down the boardwalk—in the exact direction she was headed.

As she walked, Maude silently berated herself for not allowing the dashing stranger to walk with her. That would have shown Greyson, wouldn't it—if she had?

After arriving at the soda shop, Maude climbed up high on the stool and peered over the counter at the proprietor. "I wish you'd hire Sadie."

Maude blew out a puff of air. She couldn't bear her friend working at Foster's awful tavern.

"Nope." Uncle Al dried the last soda glass and set it on one of the long shelves on the wall behind the counter.

"Why not?" Maude accepted the lime sarsaparilla that her uncle set before her as she accepted his daily log sheet.

"She'd be in the way."

"Sadie could make things easier for you." Thirsty, Maude slurped her drink, embarrassed at the loud noise she made doing so.

One of the Islander Hotel's groomsmen, seated nearby, laughed and jerked a thumb in her direction.

Maude glared at him. He wasn't from the island. The hotel must have brought him in for the summer. Handsome in the extreme, with his chestnut hair and a thick handlebar moustache, but not so distinguished-looking as Mr. König. Maude stared the smirking young man down until he turned his attention back to his own drink. The other fellow seated beside him guffawed.

Uncle Al shook his head. "That's why—for one thing. Sadie's too pretty for her own good."

"I can't tolerate these insufferable men who come to the island for the season to work and then think we island girls are easy pickings." Maude drew in one last loud slurp for effect, noting, with satisfaction, that the good-looking fellow ignored her this time. His buddy, however, leaned forward and winked at her.

She frowned. These gawking men made her feel as furious as she had when the soldiers, formerly at the fort, trailed her and Sadie around. But the man from the Grand somehow brought other sensations to her. She shrugged her shoulders, the chilly sarsaparilla sending shivers through her. Or was it from thinking about Mr. König?

Her uncle resumed his chore.

"Do you really think Mr. Foster's is a good place for her? You know what people say about him."

"Maude. . ." Uncle Al sighed, exhaling loudly. "Right now, you need to concern yourself with your own affairs."

"What do you mean?" She leaned back on the stool.

Al rubbed his forehead. "Maude, there's rumors. . ."

She raised her hand to stop him. "Please, no rumors, just facts." Mother had firmly instilled in her to avoid listening to gossip.

He reached beneath the counter and pulled out what appeared to be a calling card. He passed it to Maude. "Get the details from this man. I don't know the specifics, but he will."

She glanced at the bold black type font. STEVEN HOLLINGSHEAD, ESQUIRE, ATTORNEY AT LAW, ST. IGNACE, MICHIGAN.

For her uncle to push this on her, he must have his reasons. Maude tucked the card into her reticule, her hands trembling as she snapped the latch closed.

Already off kilter, her world seemed to have dipped even further askew.

Ben pretended to read the notices in the island post office, as he listened to several islanders converse with the postmaster.

A young clerk held an envelope aloft. "Sir, this letter is marked 'private,' but the recipient lives at an inn. What do I do with it?"

Ben's ears perked up.

"Who's it addressed to?" The silver-haired man continued to pull envelopes from a box and sort them into piles on a nearby table.

"Miss Maude Welling."

From the corner of his eye, Ben saw the postmaster look up. "Well, she's often at the soda shop, which her great-uncle owns."

"Should I run it over there then, sir?"

Ben resisted the urge to offer to deliver it to her.

"Looks like it's from an attorney, sir."

"Oh, just put it in the inn's box." The postmaster cleared his throat. "Can I help you with anything, young man?"

Ben turned to face the counter. "Yes, please, two stamps."

After receiving the stamps and his change, Ben made his departure out into the fresh island air. He crossed the street and headed toward the stores near Cadotte's establishment.

Soon he was leaning against the whitewashed wall of the tobacconist's, beneath the shadow of an overhang. Ben watched as Maude made her way from the soda shop across the street to the wharf. He jingled the coins in his pocket. Time for a Coca-Cola and a chat with the shop owner.

Time for Ben to get to know Mr. Cadotte better. And then, his beautiful great-niece. As he entered the soda shop, the silver-haired man behind the counter turned to face him. He wore a heavy white apron tied at the neck, over a black-and-white-striped shirt, the far-too-long sleeves pushed up by his armbands. A black bow tie was affixed perfectly straight beneath his narrow collar. And his blue eyes, as Ben approached, remained steady.

Sliding onto a high, counter-height chair, Ben met the man's wary gaze. He offered what he hoped was a charming grin, but this Al, of Al's Soda Shop, wasn't returning the smile. Ben averted his gaze to the board behind the slender man.

"I'd like a Coca-Cola, please."

With an almost imperceptible nod, the man pivoted and grabbed a glass from a shelving unit covered with soda and sundae glasses then filled the glass. Ben glanced around at those gathered there. If he judged correctly based on the well-worn clothing, most were island workers. If he were in Detroit, he'd be dressed in a similar fashion and not be gathering the stares he collected now.

Al placed the drink before him, and Ben passed him the coins for payment. The man swiftly rang up the sale on his brass cash register, popped open the drawer, deposited the money, and slammed it shut. Ben flinched. From the man's compressed lips, he wondered if he could get anything out of him. But he'd faced far worse.

Ben sipped his sweet cola. "Nice shop you have, sir."

The man scratched his pale cheek. "It's not for sale."

Chuckling, Ben met the man's eyes. "I'm not buying. But I am enjoying."

One corner of Al's narrow lips twitched. "Good. Anything else you want?"

The door banged open, and a young ebony-haired boy ran up beside Ben. "Hey, mister."

Al scowled. "Just because my great-nephew can get away with that behavior doesn't mean you can, you whippersnapper. Now go out and come back in like a gentleman."

The offender hung his head, retreated, and then returned, the door gently jingling the bell as he reentered and approached the counter. "Mr. Al, why don't you pretend I'm your great-nephew?"

"Because you ain't. I've only got the one, and that's Jack."

When the child had difficulty getting up onto the seat beside him, Ben stood and hoisted him up. The look Al shot him was a mix of gratitude and apprehension as he grabbed an ice-cream scoop, seemingly anticipating the boy's request.

"I wish I was Jack. I'd have free phosphates any time I wanted. And all the ice cream, too."

Al snorted. "Is that what you think?"

"Uh-huh." The child placed two coins onto the counter. Not enough for a scoop of ice cream.

Ben slipped his hand into his coat pocket and pressed the proper amount between his fingers. Then he removed his hand and placed it behind the child's ear.

The boy leaned away but Ben extended his palm, revealing the money. "Why do you hide your money in your ear? Is this an island thing?"

The boy blinked up at Ben. "Hey that's magic—like Miss Maude does, too."

"Maude Welling?"

"You know her?"

"Ja. She's very pretty."

"She's my Sunday school teacher. She's my friend Jack's sister."

Grinning, Ben sipped his soda, observing Al as he dipped out a large scoop of chocolate ice cream for the boy. "I bet she's nice to all the children."

Al slid the glass bowl in front of the boy. "How do you know Maude?"

"I met her when I arrived. At the docks."

The man's silver eyebrows bunched together. "She doesn't normally wander around over there."

"Yes, she does, Mr. Al. I saw her talking with Mr. Greyson."

The shop proprietor narrowed his eyes at the child, who began shoveling ice cream into his mouth. He shifted his gaze to Ben. "No offense, mister, but we keep our family matters to ourselves on this island."

Ben fought the urge to keep his journalist's poker face in place and affected an air of concern. "I understand."

"Nuh-ah." The boy raised his head from his treat, chocolate dripping down his chin. "You're always bragging about Jack and how he's gonna end up in the Olympics."

"That's different. Jack's athletic feats have been covered in the newspapers even as far as Detroit."

A chill of apprehension slipped through at the reminder that Ben lived in the small world of journalism. He shouldn't give up so easily, but by the set of her great-uncle's jaw, it was clear he'd get nowhere with him. He'd try a different tactic elsewhere.

The boy cocked his head at Ben. "Mr. Al is right. You're nice, but no one's gonna talk with you about Miss Maude. You're too old to come to my Sunday school class and see her."

Al gave a brief laugh. "One bit of advice I can offer you, young man. Don't even think she'd consider courting with you."

He wasn't worthy. That he knew. And the reminder was enough to send him out the door.

"She's got to get over two-timer Greyson first." The boy dropped his spoon and covered his hand with his mouth.

Throughout the overcast afternoon, Maude delivered mason jars of soup to shut-ins from church and inquired about positions for Sadie. But islanders were more interested in gossip about Greyson than in helping her friend. She couldn't do anything about Greyson or seeing the attorney right now, but she could try to make Father see reason.

Once home, she handed Bea her hat and parasol. "Is my father here?"

The girl pointed to the office adjacent to the reception area, the door open.

Maude stepped inside, the stale odor of cherry tobacco and dust revealing that yet again Father hadn't allowed the maids to completely clean what he considered his domain. He'd not allowed Maude to assist him with the books, even though he knew she balanced Uncle Al's ledgers down to the penny. *No, instead Greyson was supposed to marry her, and only then could he deign to allow her to perform office duties.* Father was an ostrich—his head firmly stuck in the sand.

"Father, I thought we might talk."

He gestured to a high-backed Eastlake chair across from the desk.

She sat, arranging her muslin skirt around her. "You can't be serious about selling the inn." This was her grandmother's legacy to her. Mother inferred the inn wouldn't go to Father when she died. But with Uncle Robert nowhere in sight since her mother's death, nothing had moved forward to settle the estate. And Maude hadn't seen the will. That could be why her grandmother's brother gave her the business card.

Father pulled on the corners of his moustache. "Need to look at other options."

"Such as?"

"The Welling farm, which my parents bequeathed me."

The last time Maude had visited the Welling farm was during hay season, and she'd suffered her worst breathing attack yet.

She gritted her teeth then forced her jaw to relax. "But it's the season now, and we're fully booked out!"

"Jack needs to go to Lower Michigan. He's the best runner in the state of Michigan. He wants to start training for the Olympics soon."

Had he forgotten that Maude couldn't live on a farm? She clenched her hands. "He can't be in the next Olympics."

"No, but four years from then—perhaps."

Maude unfisted her hands and examined the angry red lines dug into her palms by her nails. "Do you really think he's that good?"

"Quite simply, yes—he's an outstanding athlete."

"But Jack is only twelve years old." She plucked a tiny peppermint from the milk-glass bowl on his desk and popped the sweet treat into her mouth. "He's a child."

"Do you think I push him?"

"No, but. . ." He'd certainly pushed the marriage with Greyson.

"Would do us good to get off this island—away from the bad memories." Father closed his eyes momentarily.

"I love this place. I belong here." *I thought I stood to inherit this inn.*

Her father laid another ledger atop the teetering pile on his desk. "You have no real life here, Maude—you should be out with other young people your age—dancing, being courted by young men, raising your own family."

"I want to run this hotel."

"You—are—not—married." His face flushed crimson.

"This is a new era, Father." From the open window, the sound of carriage wheels and horses' hooves echoed on the street outside. "Mother helped run this inn—and look at the other Cadotte women."

He scowled. "Cadotte women, indeed! We could be put out of this home at any time."

"What?" Her chest began to squeeze. "How?"

"I'll leave that for your uncle to explain."

"Robert? He's here?"

"No, but I expect him soon."

"But. . ."

"Enough! I'll say no more." He slammed his palm on his desk.

Chapter Four

Would he cross paths with Miss Welling today? As Ben walked down the hill Thursday morning, in search of a bicycle sturdier than those at the Grand, he kept checking the pedestrians, hoping he'd see her. A garishly painted wood-frame bike stand stood near the Wellings' inn. Stacks of lake-bottom rocks formed a half wall and surrounded the shack, located near the beach.

As he arrived, a pasty-faced adolescent male peered at Ben over the top of the *Free Press*. Not Ben's periodical.

The youth set the newspaper down. "Morning. What can I do for you?"

"Thinking about riding over to check on Greyson and Anna Luce. I know them from Detroit."

Light-colored eyes darted back and forth. "Don't have any bikes for rent today."

"The sign says 'available.'" Ben pointed overhead.

"It's wrong. I should have flipped it." The boy turned the sign.

"What about those three over there?"

"Sorry, mister."

The sound of bicycle spokes whipping air met Ben's ears just as he turned to spy a youngster speeding directly toward them, his eyes wide with fright. Ben's heartbeat ratcheted upward. With a pile of rocks ahead, the boy had no place to stop. His leg muscles bunching in anticipation, Ben began to move as the tawny-haired boy stood up on his pedals. Ben ran forward, darting around the wall. As his bike crashed into the stony stack with a sickening crunch, the youth leaped into the air.

Ben dove, like he used to do playing football, and caught the boy in his arms before falling to the ground, arms wrapped around him. Heavier than Ben had guessed, and probably older than the ten years he'd estimated. The boy's weight smacked Ben to the ground, sending a jolting pain through his ribs as they connected with the rocks at the wall's bottom. Mein Gott, *oh, Lord, this hurts!* He rolled over twice, flexing his limbs so he'd not crush the boy. His back throbbed from where he'd landed. Something ripped—his coat. But he'd gotten the youth to safety. He released his grip, and the child scrambled to his feet.

"You all right, mister?"

Searing pain originated in his ribs then flowed to the back of his head. "Ja, I think so."

The boy rubbed his head. "Thought I was a goner."

The bicycle vendor joined them. "What ya think you were doin', Jack, eh? You think you've got some kind of special powers you can fly?"

Cringing at the worker's harshly spoken words, Ben stood and patted the boy's back. Pain spiked through him, and he gasped.

"*Nur ein Unfall*—an accident is all." His mother's frequent soothing words had come to his lips as easily as setting linotype for an advertisement. Would Banyon forgive him the cost of a new jacket? Ben pulled the torn clothing off, unbuttoned his cuffs and rolled the sleeves up. Felt more like himself again despite his aching back.

"Aw, I'm always having accidents." Jack swiped at the blood trickling from scrapes on his bare arms.

The other youth snorted. "Because you're always rushing somewhere, Jack."

"Do you run?"

"Best on the island!" The boy offered a gap-toothed grin.

The bicycle-shop employee guffawed. "Fastest in Michigan—he beat some snot-nosed punk from the Grand last summer—no disrespect meant, sir, if you're staying there. That kid was the top runner in the whole state." The youth's words tumbled out like a falling tray of typeset.

"Jack!" A woman's breathless voice accompanied the swish of skirts as Maude Welling surged toward them.

Ben's back ribs pulsated.

The boy sprang up and hugged her. "Sis, you shoulda seen it—this stranger. . . Hey! What's your name anyway?"

"Mr. König." On her lips, the false name rang true.

"Anyway, Muddie—he leaped in the air and caught me before I would have crashed into the rocks over there, hit my head, broken my neck, and died!"

Muddie? It must be his endearment for Maude. Ben's nose twitched as he stifled a grin, and a groan.

Lips trembling, Maude squeezed her brother tighter. "Don't say such things." Her lovely voice caressed Ben's ears.

Careful to not breathe too deeply, Ben inhaled slowly. "Your brother has greatly overstated my help."

The bicycle-stand clerk feigned jumping and catching a ball. "You should have seen it, Miss Maude. Just like catching a football!"

"Sir, thank you for saving my brother."

Sir? In my dreams, she calls me "darling."

Jack tugged at Maude's elbow, but she ignored him. Standing this close to the handsome Mr. König, she could see the tiny laugh lines in his strong face. Muscles bunched beneath his pushed-up shirtsleeves, and his broad shoulders stretched the cambric fabric of his shirt.

Maude averted her gaze, suddenly uncomfortable.

The man winced and bent over.

"I think Mr. König got hurt, sis."

Mr. König held up a hand and straightened. "It's nothing." He swiveled away from them and grabbed his ripped jacket, streaked with dirt and grass.

Jack dug the toe of his boot into the grass. "I'm sorry you got hurt helping me, mister."

"It's all right." The man's breathy voice alarmed her. Was he so injured he couldn't draw in a whole lungful of air?

"I'll be fine once I get back to the Grand and lie down."

Maude suddenly felt like she'd taken a blow, too. This man was staying at the Grand Hotel. Where she sought employment.

"Listen, if the pain worsens, please go visit Dr. François Cadotte. Tell him what happened. And that I told you we'd take care of the bill." What was she saying? This stranger likely could buy her uncle's office if he wanted. She chewed her lower lip.

"Miss Welling, I am..."—his sensual lips twitched—"I wish to say I am—"

A shrill whistle pierced her ears. Jack pulled his fingers from his mouth and waved frantically at an approaching carriage. "Stan! Can you take this fella up to the Grand Hotel?"

Stan pulled the carriage to the side of the street. Maude waved a finger at Friedrich König, as she might Jack. "You need to see the doctor. I'd feel terrible if something happened to you." Almost as wretched as she felt right now, knowing that if she was granted the job at the Grand, she may run into this man again. This very handsome man.

Friedrich König mounted the steps into the back of the empty coach.

"Perhaps we shall meet again, Miss Welling?"

As long as it wasn't at the Grand.

Chapter Five

*B*en awoke Friday to his back ribs spasming as though he were Adam and Maude his Eve—and she'd been pulled free from him. What a woman. Intelligent. Competent. Perhaps not the words many men used to describe their ideal woman, but they were correct for him. Moreover, she was even more beautiful that he'd remembered. Her dainty hands were satin soft. How he wished those silken hands were holding his.

A triple knock at the door announced his breakfast tray.

"It's open. Come in!" he hollered, as if he were back at the newspaper. Ben slapped his hand against his forehead and tried to rise from the high bed to open the door. But the swelling around his ribs wouldn't allow the movement.

"Mr. König? You all right, sir?" Ray pushed the cart into the room, multiple covered trays stacked atop. The scent of bacon and eggs wafted toward him.

As he sat up, pain shot through him. "I don't know." Sweat broke out on his brow.

The servant pushed the cart near the secretary table and then crossed the carpet to the bed. "You need help?"

He'd broken ribs before in fights on the streets of Chicago. "It's not broken, I think, but. . ." He unbuttoned his pajama shirt.

Ray rubbed his broad chin. "Want me to take a look?"

"I thought if I stayed in bed and slept overnight, it might improve, but *nein.*"

Ray cocked his head. "You in a fight?"

Ben laughed, but when his ribs complained, he pressed his hand to his side and stopped. "I caught a flying boy."

"You don't say—a flying boy? Can't say I've seen any 'round here myself."

"Poor kid flew off his bike, and I caught him. Only thing was the rocks behind me didn't make for a soft landing."

"Ouch."

"Exactly."

"Maybe you best see the doc."

"Do you think you could get me some Dr. McLean's Volcanic Oil Liniment?" Papa swore by the noxious-smelling stuff when he'd worked too hard at the factory.

"Yes, sir. And maybe you need some rib tape?"

Ben met the man's eyes. "How'd you know?"

"Used to box." The man grinned and held up his meaty fists.

"Me, too." And he was none too proud of it.

"Ya don't say. I was a heavyweight. How's about you?"

Ben wiped his brow. "Nein, just fight to keep the thugs away. In Chicago."

"Thought you was from Detroit?" Ray cocked his head to the side.

"Was brought up in Chicago and moved to Detroit later." At least that was the truth. He blew out a long sigh. Ben was already tired of the charade. Might as well bring Ray in on the secret—he seemed trustworthy enough. "I'm a newspaper reporter, not a rich industrialist. And not an aristocratic German." His uncle had made sure of the latter.

"Won't tell a soul, sir." The man raised his bushy eyebrows then placed one finger over his lips.

"I'm trying to get a scoop on men who come here to chase wealthy women—lying, conniving, cheating—whatever they need to do to get the young women to fall in love with them. Once they are married and the parents find out who the scamp really is, there is little recourse because of the divorce laws."

"Hmm, I think we got some sweet ol' gals bein' chased by men like that right here at the Grand. I told Miss Fox about one just today." Ray began to brush Ben's dinner jacket off.

Had he said anything about Ben to her? "I see." He cleared his throat.

The man beamed. "Don't you worry—I know you be a good man, and I didn't say nothin' about you to Miss Ada."

"Thank you." He recognized the woman from Detroit. And somehow connected her to Greyson Luce. But how?

En route to the Grand, with sore muscles from canoeing with Jack the previous evening, Maude headed up the hill to the imposing structure built atop the lower bluff. *Drat!* Why did the handsome stranger Mr. König have to show up at the bicycle shop yesterday, right when Maude had decided her only chance at employment was at the very hotel where he was staying? But she wasn't about to get sidetracked by someone staying for the summer—likely less—no matter how good-looking he was. No matter that he had injured himself saving her brother. If she kept trying, she could convince herself she had no interest in the man. No. She couldn't talk herself out of her fledgling feelings for him. But how would she avoid him if he saw her there? At least in a short time, Friedrich König would return to wherever he was from.

Straightening her best skirt, she scanned the groups of people attired in workman's clothing, at the back of the hotel. The employees clustered near early blooming hydrangea bushes, some of the men smoking. She edged toward what must be the servants' entrance. She'd left her bicycle behind in her cousin's stable, not wishing any of the servants to take notice of her spiffy new machine.

She flexed her feet. The walk up the hill, in her stiff new boots, was sure to bring blisters. She entered the building. Never had she seen a hall so long. Few islanders worked inside the ostentatious building. Which was to her benefit, because there'd be little chance of running into them here if she obtained a position. The cavernous Grand Hotel still smelled of fresh-cut pine, eight years after it had been built. As she trod the spotless wood floor, passing maids pushing rolling carts, she detected hints of paint, lemon oil, and beeswax, as well.

A woman with skin the color of coffee set her dust rag aside. "Help you find your way, miss?"

"Mrs. Fox's office?"

"The housekeeping manager?" The servant cocked her head.

Should have worn something simpler. "Yes."

"Follow me." The solidly built woman led Maude down the long hall.

Flowers dotted almost every surface in the corridor, bright shades of red, yellow, and lilac. As lovely as they were, each step hammered caution through her. Although the Grand had brought additional business to the island, most natives of Mackinac didn't want anything to do with the showy place. Certainly, her family hadn't, other than supplying goods.

Framed pictures of exotic locations lined the walls in the middle of the long hall. Brass placards affixed to the bottom of the gilded, oversized wood frames named castles, pyramids, Central Park, and river locations. Likely destinations that the wealthy travelers to the hotel had also visited and would find familiar. So unlike the paintings at her inn.

The maid waved an arm toward an alcove. "This is Mrs. Fox's seating room."

"Thank you."

Maude walked beneath the scalloped arch. Within, black-leather padded seats lined the walls. *What am I doing here?* No one would hire her. But she couldn't have Father sell the inn and take them to the mainland.

Pulling her skirts close, she sat in the chair closest to the arch in case she changed her mind and left. She needed this job to prove herself. Maude tugged at her gloves, removed them, and tucked them inside her reticule.

The minutes ticked by, and Mrs. Fox's office door, stained in tones of darker mahogany and lighter cherry, remained closed. An unvarnished placard, mounted in the center of the upper door panel, proclaimed "ADA FOX, HOUSEKEEPING MANAGER," and hung askew. It needed adjusting.

Maude rose and stepped cautiously over the rich red-and-green Persian rug then hesitated at the door, her hands shaking. Behind this door sat the woman who could make her dreams come true. Or deny them. *The sign must be straightened.* Maude adjusted the placard until it sat perfectly even. Quick footsteps from within the office echoed before she could step away. The heavy door opened inward.

Maude straightened as she stood face-to-face with a compact woman dressed in fine but serviceable clothes. Such as she should have worn for this visit.

The matron stared at her with dark eyes. "Can I help you?"

"I'm here about a job."

"I see." The lady raised one eyebrow. "Do you make it a habit of creeping up and standing behind doors?"

Oh, no, this was going badly. Perspiration beaded Maude's upper lip. "No, ma'am, it's just that your sign was off kilter." She was off kilter, too.

"Off kilter?" A smile tugged at the woman's thin lips. "Oh, you mean that board they stuck up there?"

"Yes, ma'am."

The woman sighed. "The proper frame should arrive soon. Then all will be set aright."

"Yes." If only Maude's own situation could be fixed so easily. Greyson's wed to Anna Forham. Prickles of indignation sped down her arms.

"Come in." The lady whirled into the office, revealing multiple layers of petticoats beneath her skirt, and stepped behind a sturdy, dark-stained table used as a desk.

Maude followed and sat where directed. She held out her application, and the woman took it.

Dear Lord, what am I doing here? She inhaled and smelled only her fear—creeping through her pores as she awaited her interview. The salt-and-pepper-haired woman before her held up Maude's application and scanned it before setting it back on her desk—unadorned save for a gilded photo frame.

"Have you any experience with housekeeping, Miss. . ."

Maude didn't intimidate easily, but the matron's stern appearance flustered her. *Lord, I need this job if I'm going to prove to Father that I can run the hotel.* She met Mrs. Fox's direct gaze. "Welling. Maude Welling."

Brown eyes behind silver frames widened, and for a moment something flickered over the woman's features and then vanished. Had she recognized her name? "Miss Welling, I've come from Detroit where I ran a very tight ship. I expect the same here."

"Yes, ma'am." Maude looked down at her lap. "I have years of experience here on the island."

"Where?"

"At the Winds of Mackinac."

The housekeeping manager's lips compressed. "The Winds of Mackinac, you say?" Mrs. Fox's tone held steel.

"Yes." *Bad move, wrong thing to have said.*

Did Mrs. Fox know Maude was the daughter of the proprietor?

"I'm expecting the owner shan't want you coming over to us. Did you manage to secure a letter of reference?"

"Not from my employer"—Maude explained, barely managing to avoid saying *father*—"but my teachers and other businessmen on the island have offered me letters." Maude placed them atop the table.

After several minutes examining the references, the woman nodded. "Most impressive." She offered a tight smile. "You realize you can't come dressed. . ." Mrs. Fox waved a hand toward Maude.

Her cheeks heated, as the woman's eyes flicked from Maude's elaborate hat to her double-breasted cropped jacket, her best herringbone skirt, and down to her shining new short boots.

"You'll need to pick up your uniform. It will be deducted from your wages, as will your housing, which will be at—"

"No, thank you, ma'am—I won't require lodging. I have. . .relatives on the island."

The woman's features froze, but her index finger tapped on her spotless desktop.

"Thank you for this opportunity." Maude pressed her fingers to her mouth. She was gushing.

The woman's mouth twitched into a smile. "Your enthusiasm is appreciated. We run a tight ship here, and while I can be demanding, you'll find I reward those whose work is exemplary. And you, my dear, will be on my list to watch!"

"I hope I don't disappoint you." *Or my father.*

Mrs. Fox's features hardened. "Keep to yourself. Be a good girl. Work hard—and you'll do fine. Don't mix with the guests, nor for one moment be alone with a man in any of the rooms. I'll explain more of our rules when you work on Monday."

"Yes, ma'am. What time should I arrive?"

"By four should be fine."

Maude swallowed. She'd not risen before seven o'clock in her life. "Yes, ma'am."

Sumptuous fabric almost tethered Ben to the high bed. How had he returned to his grandparents' Bavarian estate? No—it was his uncle's now. He struggled to move, but pain surged through him. He was on Mackinac Island. Abed at the Grand Hotel even though it was midday. At this rate, he'd never get his story done.

The door opened. Light from the hallway spilled in across the emerald floral carpet.

"Just me, Mr. König." Ray crossed the room, opened the brocade curtains, and lifted the shades. "Thought I'd let you sleep a little longer before you changed, sir."

"What's the time?"

"Nearing lunch, sir, so I figgered you best be rising. And I brought you a telegram from the front desk, right there." He handed it to Ben.

"*GL a fraud,*" his editor had telegraphed. "*Pursue story.*"

He moved his legs to the side of the bed, intense pain shrieking through his back. *Oh, Gott, bitte hilf mir. Oh, Lord, please help me.*

"Sir?" Blevins rushed to his side. "You look like you gonna pass out."

"Ja, we should go to the doctor." His image, in the mirror across the room, swam. Ben closed his eyes. Instead of slipping into his own comfortable and well-worn tan dungarees, shirt, and tweed jacket, he'd be forced to don the attire of a well-to-do industrialist.

"I can send him right up, sir."

"Nein. The island doctor."

"We got one right here for our own people."

Two birds with one stone—he'd have the island doctor check him and make discreet inquiries about Greyson. "Ray, help me get dressed, and then let's get to the town doctor."

After her interview terminated, Mrs. Fox insisted that Maude acquaint herself with the hotel layout. The hotel made the Winds of Mackinac inn minuscule, yet the inn possessed three full stories and occupied several acres of land, including a park adjacent to the waterfront. The Grand Hotel truly deserved its name. But she needed to get home instead of perusing.

She paused around the corner from the assistance desk, which occupied an alcove between the two wings.

"I require a carriage to go see the town doctor." Mr. König's voice carried into the hallway.

Oh, no, he was worse. But Maude dare not approach him here.

"We have our own physician on staff—"

"I wish to see Dr. Cadotte." Mr. König's commanding tone brooked no argument.

Oh my. Was he distressed that he'd helped save Jack? What if Father found out—would he say she needed to keep better track of her brother?

She'd get to the doctor's office as soon as she could. Maude would need to pay for Friedrich König's medical bill so that Father wouldn't hear of it. If he did, he'd worry even more about Jack, and that might cause him to have another spell. Her own heart clutched at the thought.

"The carriage can be ordered, but it will be about twenty minutes."

"Fine." Mr. König's words sounded as though he'd ground them between his teeth.

As stealthily as she could, Maude slipped around the corner. Then ran all the way down the hall, dodging maids as she ran for the exit and toward her cousin's shop to change and get her bike. She had twenty minutes or so to get to the doctor's office, explain all to her uncle, and pray that Mr. König would be well. What if something was seriously wrong with him? Outside the hotel, she continued to run, not pausing until she reached Stan's stables.

Her cousin waved to her. "Maude—your filly comes in on the afternoon ferry."

"Oh, no." She'd forgotten both her quarter horse and Jack's Thoroughbred were being returned from the Upper Peninsula where they'd wintered.

Stan slid the stable door farther open, allowing in more sunlight. "I'll rent her out if you can't give her exercise."

Without Robert there to ride with and Jack always bicycling now, it would be best.

"Yes, please!" she called out as she jumped onto the bike then hitched up her skirts and pinned them. She should defy Father and get some bloomers. "And pray for Friedrich König—he's the man who saved Jack. He's hurt. I'm going to François's office to let him know he's coming."

"Sure will."

Maude rode as quickly as she could. Her uncle's office was less than a mile away. She flinched as she rode alongside a dray piled high with hay bales. She was always afraid one was going to fall off the top and crush her; they were stacked so high and not even secured with rope.

Soon she arrived at the physician's office. Surely he could fix up poor Mr. König. What a pity it would be if the kind man sustained injuries requiring an early return home to Detroit.

Why did her plans for the summer all have Mr. König as a shadowy figure in them? Canoeing, picnics, bike rides, carriage rides, and perhaps even a theater production. How would she do any of those things if she were to work at the Grand six days a week? Much less ride her mare. Without Greyson, Sadie, and Uncle Robert to frolic with, would she even have a social calendar to fill anyway?

❤

Gott sei dank. Ray had obtained permission to accompany Ben to the town doctor's office. God be thanked, because Ben almost dropped to his knees from the pain. He panted slowly as the hotel employee half carried him into the white clapboard-sided building.

Once inside, Ben sat at a colonial-looking oak bench—austere with no padding. Ray removed his hat and approached the young woman at the counter, whose shocked expression presumably sprang from seeing a black man in this office.

"Can I help you?"

"Yes'm." Ray twisted his hat in his hands. "Mr. König here got hurt yesterday and a Miss Welling tell him he can come see Doc Cadotte."

The woman rose and peered around the servant at him. Ben started to scowl at her and then regretted his action.

"Is he staying at the Grand? I saw the carriage."

"Yes'm."

"Well, he shouldn't be here, then, eh? He should be treated up there." Her staccato pronunciation of her words hammered home that she was aggrieved. Yet the office otherwise seemed empty.

A flimsy door opened, and Miss Welling exited, a nervous smile affixed to her pretty face. "Thank you, Doctor."

"Glad to help, Maude." The man leaned over and attempted to kiss her forehead. She pulled away and glanced at Ben.

What was she doing here, and was the doctor, with graying hair, Miss Welling's new sweetheart? It wasn't unheard of for a woman to marry a man many years her senior if he was well situated. Judging from the spartan office, however, this man wasn't wealthy—although Ben knew some of the very well-to-do chose to hide their assets. Dr. Cadotte wouldn't be the first. Indeed, the wealthiest woman in America, Adelaide Bishop, was rumored to live like a skinflint.

Maude took several steps toward him. "Mr. König—are you much worse?"

"Ja, afraid so."

Eyes like rich caramel scanned his face and torso before Maude sat down on the bench with him. Her hands outstretched, for a moment he thought she might take his hands in hers, but then she clutched them together in her lap.

The receptionist joined them. "You know Mr. König, Maudie?"

The young woman's cheeks flushed. "I do. He saved Jack from crashing into the bicycle-shop barrier. Mr. König fell onto the rocks."

"Oh." The receptionist slowly walked to the still-open door where the physician remained, looking over a notepad.

The woman whispered in his ear, and the doctor nodded. "Mr. König, come back with me."

Ray bent over from his waist, with dignity. "You want help, sir?"

Ben guarded his right side, keeping his arm close to his body. "Ja."

Maude rose and stepped back, her smile tremulous. "Mr. König, I must get home and help with some functions at the inn tonight. But I'll check with François, that is Dr. Cadotte, tomorrow to see how you are."

The lovely islander moved nearer him, wafting the scent of lilacs. "And I've paid your bill."

When she left, the door closing behind her, a chill of absence surged through Ben. How could he already mourn the loss of her company when he barely knew her?

An hour later, after being poked and prodded, Ben realized why Maude's words about the bill troubled him so much. How had she known he would require the doctor—for certain? What was she doing there in the first place? Why hadn't she seemed surprised to see him? Odd—but as a reporter he seemed to question even the most innocent of actions. He exhaled, sending a sharp pain through his back.

The doctor probed Ben's back ribs. "Mr. König, might I inquire as to your relationship with Maude?"

Ben swallowed, wishing to ask if the physician commonly tried to kiss young women patients. "I've only recently met her—and her brother."

Cadotte laughed. "You'll run into Jack all over the island—he's never still."

When the man's prodding fingers ceased torturing his ribs, he placed a wet and malodorous, camphorated cloth over them and began to wind cloth around Ben's torso.

"Too tight?"

"Nein."

"You'll need to leave this poultice on several days. Then I want to see you back." The man continued his bandaging and then tied off the cloth.

"You don't kiss all your patients, do you, *Herr* Doctor?" Ben coughed into his hand.

The doctor laughed. "You'll see people all over this island hugging and kissing Maude. She's the island's sweetheart."

With good reason—even a newcomer like he could see she was beautiful, kind, and gracious.

"Sit tight here for a moment."

I was able to save this boy. Thank You, Father, for putting me in the right place at the right time. And, Lord, if You could show me what Your plan is for me, I am willing to listen. And if You have a place in my life for this lovely lady, Maude, then thank You. But provide a way, for You know I have no provision for her.

With this injury, would his research and story be sunk? The plaster on his back tightened as he drew in a deep breath.

Before long, the doctor eased the door open to the room and touched the bandage. "Drying up nicely." He handed Ben his shirt.

"You must be a special man, Mr. König, for Maude to speak so highly of you."

"Special? Nein—I'm as ordinary as they come." Hadn't the thugs on the streets of Chicago tried to ram that into his head? He was a nobody—the son of immigrant factory workers and himself a newsie, selling papers on the street. He'd sworn to himself that one day his byline would be in a big paper. And God had granted his wish. As he fastened his cuff links, something niggled at him. Had he ever really asked the Lord to help him? He and God hadn't been on good terms back then. A flush heated his neck.

"You all right, Mr. König?" The doctor placed a firm hand on Ben's shoulder.

"Ja."

"Well, regardless of what you think of yourself, Jack's family is grateful. And we on Mackinac Island open our arms to those whose kindness and bravery protects our own."

Ben found himself speechless. Had he just gained entrée and the "right" to speak with islanders and get answers about Greyson Luce? He pictured his engraved nameplate—BEN STEFFAN, ASSISTANT EDITOR.

The doctor removed his hand and took two paces toward the door before turning around. "Unfortunately, one of our own—that wastrel of a beau Maude had, didn't realize what would happen when he up and married another woman."

Greyson and Anna? A knot formed in his gut—a double-tied lover's knot. A knot that had come unloosed.

"This beau—he was from the island, also?"

"Yeah. A fellow named Greyson Luce." The man scratched at his cheek. "Used to be a good island fellow. But now..."

Confirmation from a reliable source. While the physician chattered away, Ben took mental notes, his fingers itching to write the information down. All was fitting together. Maude crying at the docks, with Luce and Anna behind her. Marcus's comment that Luce's former fiancée owned the inn on the curve. As a journalist, he needed that verification.

"I have met this Greyson Luce in Detroit, I believe, with Miss Forham."

A muscle in the man's cheek twitched. "Was he sporting her about all year long?"

Ben nodded his assent. "He squired her around to a number of social events."

Dr. Cadotte shook his head. "I guess Greyson had us all fooled—even his own mother."

Did he? What about Anna?

Mrs. Forham's plea, before her death, echoed in his conscience—*"Look out for my girl."* The sweet lady, a native of Prussia and a cast-off daughter of a duke, like his mother, had recognized Ben's resemblance to his grandfather and uncle but had kept his secret to the end, as far as he knew. But every time he covered a social event she'd attended, Zofija Forham approached him, placed a gloved hand on his arm, and prevailed upon him to keep an eye on effervescent Anna, who could disappear into a crowd in the wink of an eye. Had the lady meant she had suspicions and wanted Ben to keep her daughter out of the Detroit newspapers? Had she used his sympathies as another person rejected by his aristocratic German family to spare the Forhams embarrassment?

Maybe so.

Banyon was under no such compulsion, though.

"I'm sorry for Miss Welling's maltreatment."

A muscle in the doctor's jaw twitched. "Greyson was a cad of the first caliber. We'll not be tolerating anyone breaking Maude's heart, eh?"

The look he gave Ben, with his gray eyes narrowed, would have frozen him on the spot. Except for one thing. "Doctor, she doesn't look to be too heartbroken to me."

Rubbing his chin, the physician's eyebrows knit together. "You know, I think you're right."

So either Miss Welling was more cold-natured than she appeared, or she'd never given her heart to Luce. He prayed for the latter.

Chapter Six

Saturday afternoon was Maude's personal shopping day. Since she would begin work on Monday, she'd make good use of her time.

Maude set out for town, the breeze carrying lilac and wildflower scents. Sapphire water, bordered by turquoise, leaped as opal waves scattered the blue beauty. A lovely matched pair of gray mares pulled a surrey toward town—Pastor McWithey waved as he and his sweet-faced wife passed by.

Up ahead, pedestrians crossed the street from the docks to the various stores in the heart of town. Soon she arrived at Uncle James's shop. Bolts of pretty pink-and-white cotton fabric displayed in the window caught her eye. Maude ducked into the mercantile and inhaled the scent of lemon soap and bayberry candles. Kerosene lamps for sale dangled from hooks hanging in the overhead beams.

From farther back, a familiar voice carried to her ears. Greyson Luce's.

"Oh, Mrs. Cadotte, you're just as lovely a lady as ever. And this is my bride, Anna."

Greyson and his flattery. Funny how quickly the pain had turned to irritation. Not just with Greyson, but with herself. In this very shop, she'd last purchased material to sew a special dress to accommodate his mother's infirmity.

Anna's hand grazed the handle of a nearby pram and settled there. She and Greyson stood in front of the infant-needs section of the store. Surely it was coincidental. They'd only been married a short time.

Maude hurried from the emporium, crossing the street toward the docks. She reached the dock side of the street as one of Stan's drays drove by, piled high with luggage. She waved to the driver, and he nodded back at her.

Seagulls dipped and snatched up pieces of bread from someone's breakfast abandoned at the docks. When she paused at the landing, she spied a steamship moored. Cadotte line.

Her uncle's boat. Uncle Robert had to be here somewhere.

A flash of red caught her eye. Attired in a red flannel shirt, her uncle was so trim and his cheeks glowed with such health that she almost didn't recognize him. But he wore his blue-tinted lenses—a dead giveaway. She blinked and then stared, trying to convince herself it truly was Uncle Robert. He looked as he had about ten years earlier and much closer to his age of thirty.

He watched her in amusement from a nearby bench.

Moving toward him, she sidestepped walkers milling about. "You're here."

"Yes, I am, Maudie." He cupped her elbow, the feel comforting, stabilizing.

A tear slipped down her cheek.

He pulled her into his arms. Gone was his thick beard. Robert's chin felt warm and smooth against her forehead. "Kept hoping I'd see you in St. Ignace."

"I didn't get over at all this year." She recalled at ten years old, standing here with her mother's younger brother, him offering to sail her to St. Ignace to watch the lumberjacks' contests. "I don't care about those silly things," she'd insisted—but she had. Oh, how she'd wanted to go and see those big men roll the logs beneath their feet, throw axes, and chop down trees, the mighty pines landing with an earth-shaking thump. But when she'd gone to the mainland during haying season, she'd had to be rushed back home. Her cheeks heated remembering her humiliation at ruining the trip for everyone.

Robert sucked in another breath and released her, holding her at arm's length. "Maudie, I'd hoped I'd run into you."

"About time you came back!" She couldn't believe he'd really stayed at St. Ignace so long—almost a year.

Boat horns sounded. She jumped. Then they both laughed.

"How long can you stay away from your boat?"

His hazel eyes met hers. He shrugged then averted his gaze. "My new boats won't be ready until next season."

"I'm so sorry." She'd heard about the fire on one, and the other sank in

Lake Superior during a gale.

"Me, too." Pain flickered over his handsome features. "Gave up my captain's seat so Captain Blake wouldn't leave me for another line."

"That was generous of you."

"Good business decision." He shook her hands lightly. "Besides, I have some things to take care of here on the island."

What was wrong with him? He was acting as skittish as the chestnut horse she'd just seen.

Dropping her hands, he drew in a long breath. "I won't be staying at the inn."

"I see." But she didn't. "Of course, we'll miss having you."

He barked out a laugh. "I doubt your father will feel that way, but I'm hoping I can get him to see reason."

Maude frowned. "About what?"

Robert cocked his head. "Let me get things resolved with him first, and then I'll share with you. All right?"

"I guess I have no choice."

"Don't worry, he's got his head in the sand right now, but I'll pull it out now that I'm here to assist." He winked.

She needed to tell him, in case he hadn't been told. "Have you heard about Greyson?"

He squeezed her hand. "You were too good for him. Time to look elsewhere."

At the Grand? Would being there give her a chance to learn more about Mr. König?

"Dr. Cadotte prescribed this medication for three times a day." The town druggist handed Ben a blue bottle.

"*Danke.* Thank you." Ribs aching badly, he pulled out his wallet.

"No need. Miss Welling came by yesterday."

"But I insist."

Cigar smoke drifted toward them as a brown-suited customer approached the register.

"Aren't you the fella who saved Jack's neck?" the druggist asked. "I'm Jack's uncle, Henri Cadotte—the doc's brother."

Which meant the good doctor was also Maude's uncle. "Ah, well, I'm not so sure I saved his neck, but maybe some other bones."

The druggist smiled at Ben. "We're grateful for what you did for our little athlete. Mark my words—Jack Welling will be an Olympic champion one day." He squared his shoulders. "Everyone is proud of that boy."

"And everyone loves his sister." The druggist pointed out the window where Maude Welling stood—embracing a strapping gent.

"Such a shame about Robert losing several of the ships this winter, isn't it?"

"Captain Swaine has lost a lot this past year," the other customer agreed.

"Humph, he's gained a few things, too."

Outside, dressed in what looked like a lumberjack's flannel shirt, the man clutched Maude's elbows and stared down at her with undisguised love then wrapped his arms around her. She clung to him as though the man had given her life-sustaining breath.

Ben had no right to be jealous. Yet he was. Completely irrational.

Henri patted Ben's back, and he flinched. "Come on, I'll walk you over to Maria's Café. She's my sister, and I'm sure she'd like to treat you to a nice meal for rescuing our nephew."

And would she treat Ben to a portion of island gossip? "Ja. Thank you."

By the time they stepped out into the street, Maude and Captain Swaine had disappeared. The two men waited for the steady stream of carriages and bicycles to stop long enough for them to cross.

"Maria!" Henri called out to a handsome woman with wren-brown hair. She smiled at them from behind the counter.

"Sis, this is the fella who helped Jack."

Maria glanced around at the customers. "Just make sure his father doesn't hear that. Peter worries too much about that boy as it is!"

A waitress, who looked to be a younger version of Maria, carried steaming platters of corned beef and cabbage past.

"Would you like the special?" Maria smiled at Ben. "On the house."

He'd eaten so much watery cabbage and beef growing up that Ben could no longer stomach it.

"Try the baked grayling. It's fresh." Henri pecked a kiss on Maria's cheek.

"And overfished." Maria arched an eyebrow. "But we'll enjoy it while we still have it."

A young girl, perhaps thirteen or so, finished pouring coffee for four elderly men seated at a table in the center of the square-shaped café and joined them. "You eating, Uncle Henri?"

"No, have to run. But help get this man a grayling platter."

Maria led Ben to a table as Henri departed.

The young girl directed him to a table. Light freckles dotted her pert nose. "Get ya some coffee, sir?"

"Ja, danke."

A pucker formed between her blond eyebrows.

"I'd like some coffee. Yes, thank you."

"Only one who ever excelled in German at school just finished up college."

He hazarded a guess. "Greyson Luce?"

"Yup." She bent forward. "He can't be too smart, though—he dumped the sweetest and nicest girl on the whole island."

Ben nodded. "I've only recently met Miss Welling and her brother, but I'd agree."

Her eyes grew large. "So you're the man who saved Jack, eh?"

"Some say so."

"They're my cousins." The girl bobbed her head and then left them. Ben needed to ask about Greyson, about Swaine, about the Wellings.

So absorbed was he with the questions he wanted to ask them, he didn't realize the proprietor was standing at his elbow.

"Well, Mr. König, I think the girls have got everything under control. Do you mind if I sit with you for a moment?"

"No, please do."

She pulled out a chair and sat across from him. "It's a shame that Maude has gone through so much. Between her mother and other things. . ."

She pursed her lips together tightly.

Ben stretched his neck. "If you mean Mr. Luce's behavior, I'm already aware he broke his vow to her."

Maria's dark eyes scanned his face. "Well, in fairness to Greyson, I'd say they weren't suited. And if rumors are true about his wife, then. . ." She clamped her lips together as though she'd said too much.

Ben gauged whether to push for more information. "We have to trust in God."

"Well, thank God you saved my nephew."

Her daughter returned with a cup of coffee. "Cream pitcher is right there, sir, and the sugar."

"Danke." Glancing up at her, he met a pair of twinkling eyes. Her enthusiasm reminded him of his sister's bubbly personality. A pang in his heart caused him to avert his gaze back toward her mother.

The girl moved to another table.

Maria sighed. "I don't know what Maude would have done if she had lost Jack, especially with her father sick now."

Her father ill. "At least she has Captain Swaine to help her."

Maria glanced around the café before leaning across the table. "Robert was always such a fine young man. But if I were you, I wouldn't mention his name—or Greyson Luce's—to too many people around the island."

What had the captain done?

Maude's cousin returned with a plate of fish and potatoes. "Here ya go, sir."

Maria stood. "I best get back to work. Nice chatting with you."

"Thank you." He set his napkin on his lap, inhaled the scent of onions and herbs that seasoned the fish, and took one bite. *Delicious.*

Behind him, the café door was opened and then closed.

"Maude!" the proprietress called out. "Jack's rescuer is right there."

Ben removed the napkin from his lap and stood as Maude moved toward him. "Miss Welling." The twinge in his side was nothing compared to the discomfort he had knowing she was associating with a man whom islanders were concerned about.

"I'm just popping in for some coffee."

He assisted her into the chair that Maria had just vacated and then sat. "The coffee is very good. Strong." Unlike the sludge he drank back at the newspaper.

"Are you feeling better?" Her pretty features bunched in concern.

He patted his pocket. "Dr. Cadotte's prescription should help."

"You must be worse, then." Her scolding tone was mild but effective.

"Nein. The doctor said aches were part of the healing process."

Maria returned and poured a cup of coffee for Maude. "Some pie to go with that?"

"No, thanks, Aunt Maria."

The restaurant owner pointed to Ben's food. "Eat up before it gets cold, eh?"

"Please do, Mr. König." Maude nodded at him.

"Ja." He chuckled and then sampled the perfectly flaky fish.

The young waitress returned and whispered into Maude's ear until the island beauty pulled away and glared up at the girl. "You'd best not be spreading any rumors."

Turning toward Ben, Maude raised her eyes upward as the girl departed. "My cousin, Caroline, thinks you are very handsome, Mr. König."

He raised his napkin to his mouth and set it back down. "Is that all she said?"

Maude blushed. "No."

"What does she say of Captain Swaine?"

Her face crinkled in confusion. Ben's cheeks heated. "Your uncle pointed him out to me, when the two of you were. . .in the street."

"Caroline would say he was old." Maude laughed and poured cream from a tiny pitcher into her coffee and then added three cubes of sugar. "Robert's health regimen has greatly improved his appearance, though."

Ben raised his eyebrows in question and sipped his black coffee.

"I'd say he's quite handsome." A cloud suddenly passed over her face.

"I've heard nothing but good things about him."

"Oh?" Her voice held a note of caution. "You don't strike me as the chatty type, Mr. König."

"Sometimes." He grinned at her and pierced a potato chunk. He needed to be careful not to blow his cover.

Her eyes narrowed slightly. "Islanders don't normally converse with visitors."

"Ja. But they're so pleased I saved Jack. I think they're so excited about their island sprinter that they're gushing with words for me."

"Ah, the island gossip chain has already transmitted the news, then." She sipped her coffee.

"Ja. I've heard so many things at the Grand, too."

"Such as?" Her chin jerked up a little higher.

Ben shrugged, hoping to get this safely back on topic and extricate himself from the suspicion he was casting on himself. "Captain Swaine would be a good husband and provider."

Perhaps the dark-haired man was the real reason Maude didn't appear to be grieving her broken engagement. Other than her tears at the wharf.

"That's no secret."

Ben shouldn't be wasting his time mooning over the island girl. Needed to further explore the potential stories from the Grand. Preferably for articles that Banyon would accept rather than something about his rival's daughter. His boss had never seemed the vindictive sort, although he'd often complained bitterly of Forham's tactics in journalism.

Maude cocked her head to the side, ringlets bouncing against her ivory neck and trailing down her bodice. "Are you all right, Mr. König? Are you in a lot of pain?"

"Not too bad." Tomorrow would be the Sabbath. The best place to get information might be at church, if after-service conversations were anything like those in Detroit and Chicago. "Does your invitation to attend church still stand?"

She flushed and raised her coffee to her lovely lips. Setting the cup into its saucer, she met his eyes. "I was making you aware of our place of worship. Anyone is free to attend."

Disappointment was chased away as a physical reaction of anger shot through him. A recollection commanded his thoughts. Years earlier King Otto had begun a persecution of the Catholics in Bavaria. Father hadn't been able to practice his faith—definitely not after he married Mother. The children had been baptized in the Protestant faith.

"Ja, that's a good thing that any who wish may attend."

Tonight, he'd have to get cracking on all his potential articles. Even the one that included Maude's name. Still, looking at her pretty face, he'd have to push himself hard to get typing.

Chapter Seven

*S*urely it was pain that kept Ben awake and not guilt at what he'd begun typing. Now he was late getting to church. From its peeling paint, sagging shutters, and crumbling shingles, the place could use repairs.

Two stragglers loitered at the door—one of the boys turning to gawk at him.

"Whatcha doin' here?" Jack Welling drew out the last word as though it was the very last place on God's green earth that he'd expect to see Ben.

He shrugged. "They serve good coffee here in the fellowship hall, ja?" Hopefully the Mission Church's coffee klatch served up enough gossip to be chased for actual truth.

"Yup." Jack jerked a thumb to point to the basement of the building. "Dad says they just don't allow us whippersnappers."

"Aw, I like coffee." The other boy dashed inside, leaving Jack behind.

"We were gonna sit in back together." Jack's shoulders rose and fell.

"Sit with me, then." Ben planned to observe. And listen well.

"Nah, I better take you up to sit with Muddie and Dad."

Ben stiffened. "Nein." He had no desire to sit next to Maude's new beau, if Captain Swaine also attended.

But the boy darted ahead of him up the stairs and into the church. Exhaling loudly, Ben followed Jack and took a few long strides to catch up to enter the narthex. Inside, the two doors to the sanctuary were open, and the seats that lined either side were about half filled. He could have easily slid into an open pew without detection. The entire interior was painted white, even the pew backs, which gave the building an austere feeling.

In a loud stage whisper, the boy called, "Come on! It's up front."

Instead of hiding in the back as he'd planned, Ben would be on display. He stifled a groan when parishioners turned to look as they strode forward.

Jack stopped at the end of a pew where only the two Wellings sat. Mr. Welling leaned slightly forward to give his son a stern look. Jack ignored the silent admonition and sprinted to the back of the church. Welling's sigh could be heard all the way at the end of the pew.

Bronze coiffed hair gleamed with light from the stained-glass windows as Maude gestured for him to move closer. Ben slowly maneuvered down the pew to join them.

"Mr. König, how good to see you here." She offered a radiant smile.

His heartbeat raced as he sat beside her. She wanted him here, after all. Might Maude even care for him? Warmth flowed through him. Interrupted immediately by the wheezy sound of an untuned organ.

"Oh dear." Maude's knuckles grew white as the organist, a pleasant-looking young woman, attempted to coax some semblance of good sound from the ancient instrument.

Ben scanned the room. A piano hid in an alcove to the right.

"They need to replace our organ, but we haven't the funds yet." Maude's sweet lips pinched together.

When the minister raised a palm toward the organist, the screeching sound ceased. Red-faced, the poor woman stood. *Wie pienlich*—how embarrassing. With eyes downcast, she trod back to her seat. But Ben felt dozens of eyes pinned on him rather than on the organist. Did the parishioners know he was tasked to expose one of their members? He'd not seen Luce on his way in. Was he wrong in assuming he attended the same church as Maude did?

After the doxology and prayers, the minister stood to preach.

"Today I will speak about *The Prince and the Pauper* and how that relates to our Christian walk." Adjusting his clerical collar, he scanned his audience.

Ben cringed. How did the man know that Ben, like the pauper in the story, was acting the part of a prince—but only momentarily?

"Be still, and know that I am God."

Shivers washed through Ben's body.

"Are you well?" Maude placed her small cotton-gloved hand on his much larger one. Her fingers looked perfect lying atop his.

"Two shall become as one."

She pulled her hand away, settling both in her lap.

The preacher continued, "God has made us all princes."

Ben shifted in his seat.

"As well as princesses." Reverend McWithey smiled beneficently at Maude and several young women up front.

"He makes us all heirs to His kingdom."

Ben felt like a section of linotype being examined for defect or error.

"And God makes heiresses of His kingdom, too."

Mr. Welling coughed.

"Some of you think you are paupers. You've never accepted that you have already been given keys to the kingdom—so you don't live a kingdom-honoring life. Some of you knew you were sons and daughters of the Lord but chose to live an ungodly life. Others are only about to hear the good news of salvation and eternal life in Christ."

As the man went on, Ben's convictions grew. So much of how he viewed himself was based on seeing himself as in an impoverished state and lamenting that he wasn't living in a manor house. Much of this feeling was based on his parents' reaction to their reduced state after his uncle, who'd inherited the family estate in Germany, refused to honor his grandparents' wishes that Ben's family live in their own part of the manor house and be free to come and go as they wished. That had suited his traveling musician parents. But his uncle became ashamed of Ben's family, calling his parents gypsies and itinerants.

Ben had only vague recollections of the day they'd come home to the estate to be told they were no longer welcome. All their possessions had been packed, and they were told to find housing elsewhere. Only they hadn't. Instead, his mother, crushed by her elder brother's hostile actions, sought a life for them in America, losing Ben's sister on the way.

He blinked back the tears that threatened his eyes. When the sermon ended, Ben wished only to leave and be alone with his demons. With his memories of the pauper he'd become. And his ribs had begun to hurt again. He had no trouble making his excuses to the Wellings before he returned to the hotel. So much for overhearing coffee klatch gossip.

❤

Poor Mr. König. It had been very nice to see him again, but between her concern for the kind man and Reverend McWithey's sermon about lies and the trouble they caused, Maude's head ached. Extra coffee at the church hall hadn't eased the pain, either. She vowed that before she slept on this Lord's Day, she must address a few things. She stood in the hallway of the inn on the first floor, preparing to take action.

Beginning tomorrow, her days belonged to the Grand Hotel. She'd have to wake before daybreak, travel to the hotel, and check in precisely at 4:00 a.m. She opened the front door to exit onto the wraparound porch. She smelled Father's cherry pipe smoke and followed the scent.

Brilliant pink mixed in the evening sky, above golden striated clouds and tipped down onto the azure blue water of the straits, its low waves rolling in on the nearby beach. Cool early night breezes ruffled her puffed sleeves, and Maude grasped her arms at the elbows as she approached the man who denied her the fulfillment of her plans to run the inn.

"Maude?" Father's lips flattened. "Did you need something?"

"I'll be up early tomorrow morning, Father, so don't wait breakfast on me." She kissed his forehead, smelling his Ayer's Hair Vigor tonic.

"Fine. Sleep well."

Would she? Knowing she was employing a deception? "Good night."

Maude retreated inside then down the hall to the inn's rear exit, in search of Bea. Lifting her skirts, she trod down the back stairs of the inn and out to the detached laundry room. A whoosh of moist, starch-scented air greeted her.

"Hello, miss." A rosy-cheeked Jane lifted sheets from one tub and into another while Jeanette turned the crank on the rotary clothes washer nearby. Half past eight at night and Jane had served breakfast to them at eight that morning. *What a long day.* Jane wiped her wrist against her forehead, where curls clung to her brow.

"I'm looking for Bea."

Maude's gut twisted. She was about to involve her friend's sister in her scheme. Bea emptied the chamber pots and tidied up before breakfast so she'd be able to help Maude rise in the morning.

"She's in bed, miss."

"Thank you." Maude returned to the inn and went to the girl's room, on the servants' hall. Light beneath the door revealed she was yet awake. Maude tapped on the door, and Bea opened it.

"I need a favor."

"What?"

"Can you please wake me when you start your morning rounds?"

Bea's eyes widened. "Why?"

"Don't ask." Maude smiled faintly and motioned as though holding a key to her lips and locking them. "Mum's the word, Bea."

The girl imitated Maude's movements and added a motion of throwing away the key.

Had Maude just enlisted the help of the one person most likely to share her activities with anyone who would listen?

Chapter Eight

Something jabbed Maude—Huron warriors attacking and nudging her with their spears, their faces painted black and red. They hissed at her in their unintelligible dialect. They'd take her from Fort Michilimackinac as they had her grandmother many times removed.

Maude sat up in bed, gasping.

A dark form loomed at her bedside. "Get up." Bea's command echoed in her ears.

"Oh, Bea. . ." Maude took two long, slow breaths. "What time is it?"

"It's the devil's own hour, Pa always said—three in the morning."

Maude groaned. "Thank you."

The girl rustled around the room, lighting the gaslights.

Maude threw back her covers then slid from the high bed.

Bea clucked. "Best get moving if you have someplace to go."

The girl was downright irritating.

Maude bent beneath her bed to retrieve her maid's uniform. "Can you help me?"

"Not my job."

"Yes, but. . ." Ire rose. "If you wish to keep your position, help me, and mind your tongue." Remorse washed over her as soon as she'd uttered the words.

Bea moved closer and unbuttoned the gown's back closing. Why was her nightdress not buttoned in the front? She'd turn it around tonight. No need in relying upon Bea.

The girl bent and lifted the gown so swiftly that it caught Maude by surprise and she fell back against the bed.

"Sorry." The girl's accompanying sniff stabbed Maude's heart.

"I'm sorry for snapping at you." Maude squeezed the girl's thin shoulders.

"It's all right."

She'd leave her camisole on and change her undergarments that night. "I'll need a bathwater this afternoon, Bea. Can you tell the workmen? I'll be using the tub in the laundry house."

"Yes, ma'am."

"Don't call me that—it makes me feel a hundred years old." Getting up this early had her feeling double her age, already.

Hours later, bone weary at the Grand Hotel, Maude lost count of the number of ceramic chamber pots she'd emptied before the sun had risen. The senior housekeeping staff followed behind her, their stoic faces masking whatever opinions they had of her lack of skills.

As she closed her last room behind her, another door nearby flew open.

One of the senior maids, Amanda, who'd look more at home in a tavern, with her brassy hair and overly made-up face, emerged.

A tall dark-haired man in blue pajamas threw his arm out toward the long hall. *Friedrich König.* "Out! And don't come back. I will be speaking to Mrs. Fox of your behavior."

She'd been warned of men who tried to take advantage of the maids and was told to run from the room if that happened. Had this man attempted an offensive behavior? Was he a rogue and trying to throw suspicion off onto the maid?

Maude ducked her head and pulled her cap low. Heart hammering in her chest, she turned her attention back to her task. The offended servant headed straight for Mrs. Fox's office.

What if I'm assigned his room? A million pins jabbed her thick hair into a severe bun, and her black-and-white maid's uniform masked her figure, hanging limply from her shoulders. Surely he'd not recognize her.

Maude continued on her rounds, sweeping, polishing, and wiping until she feared her shoulder socket would come loose.

The lower staff's immediate supervisor, Mrs. Stillman, passed by. She lifted the brass watch that dangled from her bodice and announced, "You're late for break. Follow me."

Breakfast scents carried from the servants' dining room—five hours after her first shift, at 9:30 a.m. At home about now, she'd be preparing to go down and eat with her family. Was Jane this exhausted when she served breakfast?

After entering the long narrow room, Mrs. Stillman waved Maude toward the table's far end. "You eat last. You're newest."

Maude's stomach squeezed in protest. "Yes, ma'am."

Waiting for the food to be passed to her end of the table, Maude tapped the arm of the dark-skinned woman adjacent. "What time does shift end?"

Brown-black eyes shone dark against the whites of her eyes as they widened. "Don't you know, girl?"

"No."

The heavyset woman tossed back a glass of milk. "Off the clock at half past two."

"Two thirty?" Maude resisted a groan.

"Um-hum." The older woman's full lips drew up into a shy smile. "I'm Dessa. I have the top floor."

If Maude had the top floor, then she'd have less chance of bumping into Mr. König. "I'm Maude. I'm assigned rooms on the main floor."

"You startin' down heah?" The woman's thick Southern accent carried the last word out in two syllables.

"Yes."

The maid sniffed. "And you brand new?"

Maude stiffened at the woman's accusatory tone. The other servant averted her gaze.

When the food finally made it to them, Dessa turned Maude's way again. Little remained in the bowls of biscuits, grits, eggs, sausage, and potatoes.

"Ain't enough grits to take three bites." Dessa divided the amount in two and passed the bowl to Maude.

"You can have my grits."

"You sure?"

"Yes, ma'am." In her fatigue, she'd lapsed into what she'd always called older women. And why shouldn't she call this coworker 'ma'am'?

"Ma'am?" The woman chuckled. She pushed the last of the creamy hominy grits onto her plate.

"Dessa?" Maude cleared her throat. "Do you think Mrs. Fox put me on the first floor so they could watch me closely?"

Chewing on a buttered biscuit, the servant closed her eyes, her face beatific as if savoring every morsel. "Mebbe so."

"Do you think they don't really want any local girls working here?"

"This be the first year they hired any of ya'll."

"I was afraid of that." She emptied her portions onto her plate—filled only about a third full. She bowed her head and offered up a quick prayer.

When Maude opened her eyes, Dessa smiled. "You a good reminder to me of what I forgot to do—thank the good Lord that I got a roof over my head, food in my belly, and that I ain't a sla—" Her head shot up.

The room came to a hush as Mrs. Fox, attired in a black day dress, entered the room. "Continue on. Don't let me disturb you."

As the manager made her way down the long table, she periodically stopped and squeezed a shoulder or bent to whisper something in one of the maid's ears. A frisson of concern shot through Maude. Not only did she have to work later than she thought, which would intrude on her time with Jack, but she'd be exhausted when she returned. Plus, she'd be changing her clothes at the stable during peak time rather than closer to the lunch hour.

Mrs. Fox stopped at the end. "Maude, I need to speak with you privately."

Ben stood as soon as Mrs. Fox and another woman entered the parlor outside the head housekeeper's office. *Herr König must demand that his maid be replaced.* He couldn't allow that blowsy servant into his room again or tolerate her suggestive behavior. The woman should be fired. Mrs. Fox, as usual, presented a perfectly starched appearance, her shoulders square in her puffed-sleeve jacket. Alongside her, a maid with her cap pulled low over dark hair in a severe bun stared down at her shoes. Her ill-fitting garment appeared clean but not pressed. *Odd.*

"Mrs. Fox?"

"Yes, Mr. König?"

"I wish to speak with you about the incident with one of your maids."

She raised a hand. "We can discuss that once I've sent my newest maid on her way."

The young woman stepped behind Mrs. Fox and ducked her head farther, as though fearful of him.

He cleared his throat. "Ma'am, I want you to know that I would never make overtures toward one of the maids." Overture, a musical term for decidedly unseemly behavior. "Nor shall I succumb to anyone's brazen behavior."

"Quite understood."

The maid continued to cower behind the older woman.

"I require a replacement."

"Of course, sir."

The servant practically crouched behind Mrs. Fox's shoulder. "I don't want anyone to fear me on your staff."

"I have the matter well in hand. In fact, I'm about to discuss your situation with this young lady." Mrs. Fox's shoulders shifted beneath her tightly constraining jacket. "She's quite—demure—as you can see."

Demure? She was downright cowed.

Ben had to avoid any situation that might bring him further scrutiny, and he must keep up the appearance of a wealthy, aristocratic German man accustomed to having his way.

He held up his hands. "Mrs. Fox, I cannot have someone coming and going who is afraid of her shadow—I'd find that intolerable."

❤

Afraid of her shadow? He was intolerable, not she. Maude sucked in a breath full of outrage and peeked over Mrs. Fox's shoulder. How dare he? And he'd been so kind to Jack. He'd even come to church.

Mr. König had yelled at one of the maids and chased her from his room. Had the maid refused to bend to his wishes in some illicit regard? Maybe he was protesting too much over his own innocence.

Her stomach squeezed its meager contents into the size of one of Jack's baseballs in her gut. So this was the genuine article—the real Mr. König. He examined his gold-cased watch. He couldn't be bothered by the servants. Friedrich König had the power to have her dismissed if he didn't care for her. Or if Mrs. Fox agreed with his assessment of her and found Maude unsuitable. Prickles of fear raced down her back.

Bowing her head in subservience, Maude stepped to the housekeeper's side and bobbed a curtsy. "Begging your pardon, sir, but I'm more than willing to do as Mrs. Fox directs me for the care of your room."

Mr. König cast her a sidelong glance then directed his gaze toward Mrs. Fox.

The matron stood erect, unmoving. "Can you accept this new maid's assignment? For the morning shift only, mind you."

What would Maude be doing in the afternoon?

"This is a hotel, after all, Herr König, not a private estate." Mrs. Fox raised an eyebrow at him.

Surprisingly, the handsome young man blushed.

All the servants tittered about the wealthy, aristocratic bachelor. They said not only was he a rich factory owner, but he also had titled family in Europe. He'd certainly not acted the part when he was with her in the community. Maude hadn't realized at first that the maids were referring to Friedrich König, whom she had thought of as her new friend. The rude man. A deceitful man who was only kind to others when it suited him. Then why had he helped Jack?

"She should suit." His haughty tone chilled her.

"Glad you agree. Is that all?"

He hesitated a moment then gave a brief nod before departing the parlor.

Mrs. Fox sighed. "What an eccentric young man. I can't figure him out."

There was more to Mr. König than met the eye. "Perhaps that isn't necessary."

Mrs. Fox chuckled. She entered her office and waved to a chair then took her own.

The little knots in Maude's back began to unwind.

"I must tell you why I called you in." The woman's countenance became more serious.

Maude frowned.

"I failed to apprise you that yours is only for a part-time position."

"Part-time?" She wasn't sure whether to crow in relief like the roosters that morning or protest. After all, her father might not be very impressed with a half-time position.

"Yes, eight hours, not the usual ten, and you'll work only five days, not six."

She nodded in agreement.

"Now, let's go over what you'll need to do when you come in tomorrow—for Mr. König's room especially."

"Do you think he might have"—Maude searched for an appropriate word—"bothered Amanda?" The servant asserted to every maid in the supply room, where they gathered, that he had.

Mrs. Fox's intent gaze fixed Maude to the spot.

"God's Word tells us to believe the best of everyone."

"Yes, ma'am."

Mrs. Fox clasped her hands together. "He also tells us to be wise as serpents and gentle as lambs. And you, my dear, are a lamb—but even the lamb must understand the snakes among us."

But she didn't specify whether she meant Amanda or Mr. König. Maude wasn't about to ask—she'd have to find out for herself.

Chapter Nine

At least she'd not tipped over any chamber pots. Maude's second day of work proved more difficult than the first, with Mrs. Stillman dogging her steps.

Heading out and across the street, she made a beeline for Danner Stables, owned by her cousin Stan. "Best on the island," proclaimed the sign hanging by the stable office.

Maude stepped into the barn, the hay causing her to sneeze. If she remained here too long, her chest would begin to tighten.

"Stan?" She wished they had time to chat—she needed someone to talk to.

A slender young man rose from sitting on a hay bale in the shadows.

"Better get back there and change, Maudie, whilst we've got no customers." Stan jerked a thumb toward the tack room.

So her cousin, like everyone else, had no time for her, either. "Thanks, Stan." Moisture pricked at her eyes as she strode through the hay-strewn floor. She sneezed and stepped into the tack room. Pulling the flimsy wood door shut, she fastened the rope loop around a large rusty nail, securing the door.

As she undressed, thin streams of light shone between the wood slats framing the room. If only Bea were there to assist, it would go more quickly. She pulled her blouse over her head and held her breath at the odor. Her over-blouse would require washing as well as her skirt. She patted her undergarments—they too would need laundering. She shuddered, recalling how one of the guests at the Grand, a society girl from Lansing, had Maude unfasten not only her boots but her corset, too. Did Bea react the same way to her? From now on she'd ask the servant to assist only when she truly couldn't fend for herself. Or she wouldn't buy clothing that required others' assistance.

A sharp rap on the door startled her. "Better hightail it, Maudie. Looks like we got a customer coming."

"All right. I'm hurrying."

The buttons unfastened, Maude whipped off her skirt and stuffed it into a bag with the rest of the uniform for Jane to wash and iron for her that night. If Maude didn't have to tend to Jack's nightly needs and to giving Papa company and attention, she could do it herself. She'd figure out how later.

"Hey, Maude! I've rented out your horse and Jack's to some fellas from the Grand."

"Fine." It wasn't fine, but the mare and the gelding both required regular exercise.

She opened the wooden box, quickly pulled out her own garments, and then donned them. Thankfully the cedar lining and pomanders kept the horse scent from permeating the clothes. She dabbed rosewater behind her ears and then a generous amount on her décolletage before fastening her jacket.

Don't do this. Don't try to be something you aren't. Don't lie to your father.

Maude swatted at the air, as though the movement would dispel the admonitions. Guilt accompanied her as she sank down onto the box. Everything she thought would happen this summer had been stolen from her. *Why?*

"Maudie!" Stan's voice carried from farther away—somewhere inside the barn. "You got to get out of there. The gentleman who wants to rent the horses is here."

"Coming!" She unfastened the hairpins that fixed her curls to her scalp so that they were like a helmet. She ran her fingers through the ringlets as they cascaded about her shoulders. Not very ladylike, but it would have to do. She removed the loop from the nail and opened the door and stepped out into the stables. Fresh hay and the odor of horses permeated the air.

The stable door opened and a man slipped inside. Friedrich König. Alongside him ambled the hotel's most notorious womanizer, Marcus Edmunds. All the other maids had warned Maude never to be anyplace near Edmunds if she could help it. Why was Mr. König associating with him? Maybe Amanda was telling the truth about him, and the other maids were simply spreading rumors about him.

Maude froze, looking for someplace to hide. If she crouched behind a tack box, she'd be filthy.

"Good day, Miss Welling." Mr. König moved in her direction with a slow, easy grace.

What a supercilious man. He may have saved her brother, but he was someone very aware of his station in life.

"Mr. König." She gave a curt nod.

Unlike earlier at the hotel, when he'd not given her a second's notice, Mr. König smiled and slowly perused her from her curly head down to her newest lace-up boots. His grin revealed that he liked what he saw—unlike the pointed disinterest he'd shown when he met her as a servant. What a snob he'd been, not even bothering to glance her way in Mrs. Fox's office. And then berating her for being timid. Maude's gut spasmed.

"Perhaps you'd like to join me sometime, Miss Welling, for a ride around the island?" Mr. König's smile seemed genuine enough, but the smirk Edmunds wore showed just what he thought of the offer.

She'd not be fooled again. "A simple island girl like myself wouldn't be much amusement for a city fellow such as you, Mr. König."

Edmunds snorted then elbowed the taller man.

Stan grasped her arm and turned her in a half circle, away from his patrons. "Here, Maude, take the back door this time." None too gently he pushed her out the door.

❤

Why was the stableman shoving the lovely Miss Welling out the door? Ben squelched the urge to protest Stan's manhandling of the young woman. Such objections wouldn't be expected from the cavalier, wealthy, young industrialist he was supposed to be. Yet earlier, when Miss Welling's beautiful features had bunched in offense at his oafish leer, he'd regretted the behavior his job required from him. *Ach, what a* dummkopf *I am.*

Marcus elbowed him. "Say, she's a looker—too bad she's not staying at the Grand."

Ben gritted his teeth. "I think you have enough young ladies already chasing you down that long porch at night, ja?"

Edmunds laughed and buffed his nails against his tight vest. "True."

"You'll have to tell me all about those pretty women as we ride. Have you chosen one for yourself yet?"

"Gads, no!"

The stable manager returned. "Sorry about that, but my cousin needed to get home quickly."

"Your cousin?" Was Miss Welling related to everyone on the island? Ben relaxed his shoulders. His ribs, while still sore, had been re-taped. He hoped the ride wouldn't aggravate them.

"Yes, sir, my lovely cousin." The man's dark eyes narrowed slightly. *Challenging.*

"Yes." Ben relaxed his hands. "My friend and I wish to ride." He'd wanted a horse to ride around the island, away from the Grand, to interview Edmunds without all the fawning women who trailed his every move.

Danner cocked his head. "Have you ridden much before?"

"Ja, but it has been a long time." On Großmutter and Großvater's farm. In the countryside, in Bavaria, before so many illnesses and deaths changed their lives and sent them to this country. Before his aunt and uncle, who were to have allowed Friedrich's family to live on the estate between concert tours, unceremoniously expelled them from the property—their belongings all but destroyed. Jealousy had stolen his parents' livelihood and what was supposed to have been their home.

"You'll be riding the Wellings' horses today." He pointed to the nearby stalls where the two horses munched contentedly on hay.

These two were expensive horses. "Mr. Peter Wellings?'"

"His children's." The stable owner focused his gaze on Edmunds. "Are you a fair rider?"

"Steeplechase winner for Virginia in '93." The man's dimpled grin could even charm a man.

Danner's tanned face relaxed. "We'll put you on Jack's Thoroughbred and Mr. König up on the quarter horse."

If only Ben could jump on one and race after the lovely woman with the chestnut curls and amber eyes. Eyes that bore into his like the deep of night.

Soon the horses were trotting up Cadotte Avenue toward the interior of the island. "Very pretty out here, isn't it?"

"Too country-like for me."

Edmunds stopped beneath a huge maple tree. Drays and pedestrians made their way past, while the two horses munched on the grass. Ben used the opportunity to converse with the man and soon learned that Edmunds had prepared a list of his potential lady-loves ranked by "assets."

"And I do mean by income and property holdings." Edmunds winked. "Although feminine charms are a bonus."

What a cad. "I wonder if Greyson Luce had such a list."

"Looks to be too big of a hayseed to me. Seems to have lucked out."

A sleek black horse trotted toward them, a dark-haired man well seated in an expensive cordovan leather saddle. *Captain Swaine.*

Edmunds jerked his thumb. "Now there would be some real competition for us if he ever chose to pursue one of the young lovelies at the Grand. He's a bachelor."

"Do you know him?"

"Know of him. Swaine owns a very profitable shipping business. Nasty bit of goods though, with him having lost several ships recently. A fire on one in Detroit."

"I think I remember that one. Suspected arson." Ben hadn't been assigned the story.

"Swaine came away untarnished from the investigation."

The captain pulled his horse to a halt nearby. "Good day, gentlemen. Can I be of any assistance to you?"

Edmunds's horse raised its head and whinnied. "How do you mean?"

"Are you lost?" Swaine's mount whinnied back, but he held the beautiful Thoroughbred in place. "This area is where most of the year-round residents live. We call it the Village."

If that wasn't an invitation to bug off, Ben didn't know what was. "We're just out for a ride."

Swaine nudged his horse forward. "I gave this mare to Maude Welling. What are you doing riding these horses?"

The captain had gifted this expensive animal to Miss Welling. Even with a promotion and a raise, Ben would never be able to offer her such a gift. "We rented these fine animals from Danner's Stables. Miss Welling was there to witness our doing so. I suggest you ask her, sir."

"Rented?" he sputtered.

"Ja." Maybe she wasn't so taken with the captain.

"Would you care to examine the rental slip?" Edmunds set his jaw.

Swaine backed his horse up. "Pardon me. I just can't imagine why she'd. . ."

Why would she allow the animals to be loaned out? Was she that desperate for money?

"Apology accepted. I'm Marcus Edmunds, staying at the Grand for the season. And not a horse thief!"

What Edmunds planned to do over the summer was a form of thievery, but Ben schooled his features. "I'm Friedrich König, also at the Grand. Never a horse thief."

The captain grinned. "Jack's savior. Nice meeting you."

"Nein. Jack has only one Savior. But I'm glad to have helped."

"Well said." Swaine nodded. "Again, I apologize for jumping to conclusions. No hard feelings?"

"Treat me to a round sometime, Captain Swaine, and we'll be squared away." Marcus laughed, as though he were joking, but there was probably some truth to his words.

Swaine headed off toward Harrisonville and they turned back toward the Grand.

"Say that was clever, old chap, warming up to the captain with your talk of the Savior." Edmunds's mocking tone made Ben cringe.

"He seems a nice enough sort."

"Help me keep him away from my ladies, if you're a pal." Edmunds urged Jack's gelding into a trot.

Too late to keep Swaine away from the one Ben's heart yearned for.

Friedrich König was riding her mare. And with Marcus Edmunds. *Oh!* Maude clenched her fists and charged down the boardwalk toward home. Friedrich König was likely just as big a liar as Greyson was. How horribly unfair that in the course of a week she'd been abandoned by Greyson and now duped by Mr. König. And how confusing that it was the latter's affections she most mourned the loss of, even though she'd yet to experience them. She shook her head at herself and her silly notions.

Gentle breezes carried the sound of bells on harnesses as a carriage rounded the corner. A beautiful red-haired woman glared out the window at her. *Anna.* Shouldn't she be the one angry with Anna Luce, and not the other way around? She hurried toward home.

Maude ducked down the drive and toted her bag to the whitewashed laundry building, located behind the inn. Outside the building, the scents of starch and soap battled the rose- and lilac-infused air.

A bath would be heavenly. Inside, Bea stood over a steaming tub of water, stirring the soaking clothes. Maude handed Bea her bag of unwashed clothes. The girl's tiny features twisted in disgust.

"What did you do in these—chase Greyson around the island with a baseball bat?" The younger girl dropped the uniform into hot soapy water. Maude's mouth dropped open, but she couldn't manage a retort.

Jane emerged from the folding room in the back, her arms full of sheets—as Maude's had been earlier at the Grand.

She chewed her lower lip. This seemed wrong—knowing she was about to add to Jane's workload again today. The older woman eyed the bag.

The Irishwoman pushed Bea from the basin. "Here, let me do Miss Maude's clothes. I can get to it in a wee bit—soon as I get these sheets inside."

"I'll take the sheets." Bea held out her hands.

"Thank ye, lass." Jane passed the heavy basket to her. Bea didn't stumble under her heavy load as Maude had earlier at the Grand.

"Thank you, Jane." Maude smiled and caught a hint of a grin form on the servant's rosy lips.

Jane blinked at her. "Yer welcome, miss."

How many times had Maude taken for granted all the hard work done by Jane and Bea and the rest of the servants?

The senior servant took a scrubbing board and laid a shirt atop it then ran a cake of brown soap up and down the garment before attacking the underarms and neck collar with a vengeance.

"I'd try to help, but. . ." Maude displayed her red hands.

"Oh dear, Miss Maude. Ye should put some Bag Balm on." Jane wiped her hands dry on her apron and went to a nearby cabinet.

"What is that?"

"Healing ointment." She grabbed and opened a small jar. "Here, miss, try about a teaspoonful on yer cracked hands."

"Thank you."

The Irishwoman looked up with a faint expression of surprise. Had Maude never expressed her gratitude to the servants? She swallowed back the conviction she felt in her spirit.

"Ye go on up now and rest. Tomorrow will come quick enough."

Maude was tempted to hug Jane, but she didn't wish to startle the maid any further with her unusual actions. "I really need to take a bath."

Bea returned, displaying a box of magnesium salts. "How'd it go today?"

"Not too bad." Except that every muscle in her body ached. And her heart did, too, after her brief encounter with Mr. König at the stables.

"Guess you'll be needing this, then." The girl laughed as she set the box down on the counter. "Not so easy was it, Miss High and Mighty?"

"Beatrice Duvall!" Prickles ran up her neck. If she didn't need the help so badly and if the Duvalls weren't in such desperate straits, she'd be tempted to fire her on the spot. She could only imagine the look Bea would receive from Mrs. Fox if she'd said something so insolent.

"Sorry." Her tone was unrepentant and her eyes danced. Still, Maude could never stay mad at the spunky girl.

"We'll get your bath ready." Bea grinned her apology, her dimples flashing.

"I know it's extra work." She was beginning to understand the toll such physical labor took. "And I'm going to see if I can find us more help."

How absurd her words sounded. So she was working at the Grand trying to prove herself. Yet she'd cost the inn more money by hiring someone to make it possible for her to do so. And she was, at this very minute, making more work for their already overstretched staff. Maude hung her head. All she was proving was her incompetence.

"I'm awful glad for my job. Sadie's going up to the Grand tomorrow for an interview. Said she's sorry she's been too busy to get together, but between watching my little sisters and working for that mean cheapskate she's too tired to do anything."

Her friend hadn't even taken time to send a note. Maybe they'd be together again, soon, at work.

"I'll pray for Sadie." Maude patted Bea's shoulder. "We're glad to have you with us."

Bea's eyes watered. "I hope you can keep me on here."

"Why wouldn't we?"

"With your father talking about selling, and then. . ."

Dropping her hand to her side, Maude cleared her throat. "Then what?"

"There's rumors that some lady wants to buy the inn."

Her gut squeezed tighter, like clothes pushed through the fancy wringer washers at the Grand.

Chapter Ten

ane shoved a cup of Lion brand coffee into Maude's hands when she'd wandered into the kitchen a little before four in the morning. "Ya want the picture card from the tin, miss?"

Normally, Maude liked to look at the adorable little print cards the Woolson Spice Company tucked into their product, but not at this hour. "No, thanks. You take it."

"Has the most precious picture of a little girl clutching a doll—reminds me of my sister when she was young."

"She'll be coming to America soon, won't she?"

"Aye, she will." Jane added cream to her own coffee.

Maude drank the strong brew, grateful for its wakening effects.

The servant patted Maude's hand. "Do me and Bea a favor and give your earnings to the church—we've been telling your pa that you're out raising money for Mission Church."

"Certainly! I'm sorry you two have gotten dragged into this."

"Your pa will come around."

"I hope so." Maude headed out into the semidarkness. She rode her bike to Stan's stables and then hiked the hill up to the Grand.

Without the coffee, she'd not be able to keep her eyes open. After gathering her working materials, Maude pushed her cart into the long corridor. As she got to the midpoint, her immediate supervisor shuffled forward, fire in her eyes.

Mrs. Stillman wagged an index finger in Maude's face. "Mr. König aims to get my Amanda fired. You best watch yourself, missy."

Every pin poked Maude's scalp beneath her tight cap. "Yes, ma'am."

"That German is a wicked one." The woman's thin lips disappeared into a line.

Maude nodded, unable to stop her head's involuntary movement.

The matron turned to her cart and grabbed a pair of men's slippers. "Put these beneath that heathen's bed. His manservant requested them, but he'll not be in until later."

"Yes, ma'am."

Heading toward Mr. König's room, Maude's heart picked up to beat. Mr. König had gallantly rescued her brother. But he'd also been riding with that womanizer Edmunds. Were they two cut from the same fine wool cloth?

Friedrich König hadn't bothered Amanda. Surely not. Maude hesitated in front of Mr. König's chamber. He probably slept soundly, imagining all the young women he'd squired around Detroit.

Maude turned the key and entered the bedchamber. Men's cologne—a mix of cedarwood and spice—scented the large room. This was one of the premium rooms rivaled only by those reserved for shareholders.

Dense wool carpet sank beneath her heels. Thankfully the rug also masked the sounds of footfall.

I'm in a man's room. Heat built beneath her rough shirt. *Silly—you've been in men's rooms to clean, yesterday and at the inn.* But not *his* room. Ridiculous—he might be handsome and have a strong presence, but Mr. König was a snob. Arrogant. And perhaps even a cad. But he'd rescued her brother.

As her eyes adjusted to the dim light, a large mound on the other side of the bed came into focus.

"*Mutter? Ich bin jetzt fertig.*"

Maude froze. He said something was done. What was he dreaming about?

Friedrich König rolled toward her, his sheets dragging in protest. Then the brocade coverlet lifted as he rose up and thumped himself back on the bed.

Instinctively, she ducked. His broad hand flew over the side of the bed and dangled within inches of Maude's face. Warmth radiated from his hand to her cheek. She'd never been so physically aware of Greyson as she was of this stranger.

Fingers suddenly gripped her hat. Mr. König pulled. Maude quickly unfastened the pins from the white cap as he yanked it free.

"*Was*"—his bed creaked loudly—"is this?"

Maude ran to the door and out into the hall. Almost smack into Mrs. Fox.

Mrs. Fox grabbed Maude's shoulders. "What happened to your cap?"

Other servants passed by, murmuring, their expressions quizzical.

She spoke in a low tone, "He pulled my hat from my head. And he was talking—in German, in his sleep."

This was not the way Maude wanted to get the housekeeping manager's attention. Not at all.

Danke, Gott. Thanks be to God Mrs. Fox had believed Ben. Mrs. Fox had understood about sleep disturbances and had dismissed the episode as an accident. However, her assertion that perhaps the same had happened with Amanda was absurd. He hadn't wanted to, but he gave her the details of Amanda's "visit" to his bed, and she'd agreed that such a worker was a liability for the Grand.

Ray met him as he emerged from the housekeeper's office. "Sorry, sir, but no newspaper, yet."

Ben checked his watch. "I'll pick one up in town."

"You and Mr. Edmunds going, sir?" The servant's voice held subtle disapproval.

"No." Hanging around with Edmunds proved fruitful, but there was a physical and spiritual price to pay. While he now knew which women at the Grand Edmunds and Casey were pursuing, the pain from riding bordered on excruciating. He'd need to get back to the doctor again before their scheduled appointment.

"The taxi should be here in a few minutes, sir."

"Thanks. I should be back for dinner." And all the dreadful bore that entailed. If only Miss Welling were there, too.

The driver let Ben and several other men off downtown. Ben stopped in several shops. All three merchants asserted that Greyson Luce had deceived Maude Welling. But was Miss Welling not brokenhearted because she'd already found herself a ship's captain? Was there no real understanding between her and Greyson? Or simply no love? He preferred the latter to be the answer to his question.

He trod toward the makeshift newspaper stand—so shoddy it might blow away in a good heavy storm.

The newsboy shoved his cap back. "Can I help you?"

The kid reminded Ben of himself at that age. He allowed his eyes to drift down to the paper on the counter. His own newspaper.

"A copy of the *Detroit Post*." Ben tossed him the coinage.

The newsie handed him the latest edition. Ben froze. The front page featured article was written by that boot-licking toady Red O'Halloran, who'd been trying to elbow in on Ben's plum assignments for a while. Ben needed to get his story done and to his editor as soon as possible.

Ben stiffened and his back wracked with pain. He winced.

"You all right, mister?"

"It'll pass." He turned and strode to a bench near the docks.

Watching the boats and looking out at the gorgeous water were his two newest guilty pleasures. He'd miss the views here on Mackinac when he was stuck behind a desk in downtown Detroit. Only a few more weeks before the gig was up.

"Pssst!"

Ben looked around.

A shaggy head popped out from an alleyway. Jack Welling stood, two bicycles clutched to his sides.

"Say, can you help me ride Maude's bike back home?"

"Ja, I could." Ben rolled up the newspaper and stuffed it in under his arm.

"It's that one." The boy pointed to a black bicycle with a seat raised high enough that long-legged Ben could sit astride it. But surely not Miss Welling. "You're sure this is your sister's?"

The boy scowled. "Come on. Are you gonna help me or not?"

"Ja. I'll help."

Ben mounted and rode after Jack, peddling as fast as he could to keep up. After only one block, the boy turned right and Ben followed. At the post office, surrounded by deep purple lilacs and white roses, the boy stopped and dismounted his bike.

Jack fished a letter out from inside his shirt. "Want to come in?"

"Sure." Ben laid the bicycle gently on the grass, and the two of them entered the whitewashed wood-framed structure.

The postal clerk smiled warmly at Jack and then looked up at Ben. "Got a new friend, Jack, eh?"

"That's the guy who saved my cookies last week!"

The trim man glanced at Ben up and down. "Well, he looks none the worse for wear."

Ben's sore ribs contradicted the man's statement.

"What brings you to our island, sir?"

Subterfuge. Deceit. Getting a story that wasn't the story he was sent to get.

Jack waved his letter toward Ben. "He's a rich guy stayin' at the Grand."

The clerk rolled his eyes heavenward. "Jack Welling!"

The missive floated from Jack's hand to the post office's scuffed wood floor, and Ben bent to retrieve it. It was addressed to Steven Hollingshead, Esq., Attorney at Law, St. Ignace, Michigan. In the bottom left corner was written "*Urgent.*"

Were the Wellings in trouble? What could he do to help?

Chapter Eleven

aving cleaned rooms up and down the long corridor all day long, Maude shoved her cart inside the supply room then slumped onto a straight-backed oak chair.

The door opened and Sadie scooted inside the supply room. "Are you doing all right? I saw you duck in here."

Maude's cheeks heated. "I'm fine. Aren't you going now, too?"

Sadie rested her hand on a nearby shelf, covered with linens. "Why would I?"

"Because the position is only part-time. That's all Mrs. Fox had."

"It better not be." She placed her hands on her curvy hips. "I needed a full week's wages. She told me I'd have the normal six days a week."

Maude's jaw slacked. "She has me on a reduced schedule." Had Mrs. Fox lied to her?

"She said she needed a full-time worker because of Amanda."

"Oh." Maude exhaled in relief. She shook her shoulders, trying to ease the tension in them. Why hadn't the housekeeping manager offered her the extra hours? Not that she wanted them. After four days, she was realizing the toll this work took.

"I'll keep my eye on your Mr. König for you, when you're not here."

"He's not *my* Mr. König."

"I see how you sneak looks at him." Sadie laughed. "He's so handsome."

"He is." So was Greyson. Look where all those years had gotten her.

"Well, you better go before the onslaught of the draymen heads up the hill. You don't need any of them seeing you if you want to keep this from your father."

"Right." Maude sighed. "At least they're turning out to be my only nemesis when it comes to keeping things quiet."

"True. No one else comes up here from town. Not the islanders anyways."

"Why would they?"

"I don't know anyone who has come up here other than for the dog races. And that was just the men wanting to make bets."

A slow grin softened Sadie's tired features. "If I were to place any bets, it would be that Amanda is the one who caused the problem in Mr. König's room, and not him."

"Why do you say that?"

"Because I've been chatting with the other servants. And they say she shouldn't have been brought up here for the season."

"Oh?"

"Apparently she's done this kind of thing before."

The overwhelming odor of cleansers in the small space was making Maude light-headed. Or was it the relief she felt?

From the hotel's front porch, the straits of Mackinac's brilliant blue water and the rosy streaked sunset enticed Ben to stray down the hill to the shore. Today he'd spent time with Edmunds and the sycophantic women who surrounded him. Edmunds's obvious scheme sickened him, and now all he wanted was to get free from the hotel. He'd never been so lonely in his entire life. Cut off from the support and camaraderie of his fellow journalists, Ben felt adrift.

When he got to the boardwalk, he removed his shoes and socks and edged toward the water, cool night air tickling his hairline. He sucked in a breath of fresh northern air.

A woman's soft exclamation accompanied the sound of water splashing off the jetty. Near the jagged rocks, a lone figure pushed off in a canoe and continued out into the water.

Paddles dipped into the water and flashed silver droplets into the air as a canoe pulled free from the rocky alcove. A single person clad in a white dress that clung to her left no doubt as to her gender. Ben watched confident arms move back and forth, guiding the canoe across the water as the sun sank lower in the sky, pink streaks of light disappearing on the horizon.

Alone. But whoever she was, however foolish her venture, Ben would wait to make sure she returned safely.

Drowsy, Ben propped himself against the rocks and waited, the night air chilling him. If he was a betting man, which he wasn't, he'd wager the young woman would return soon. He'd wait. The sound of the waves lapping against the shore soothed him. Fatigue claimed him, and he drifted asleep.

❤

Alone. Maude sighed in relief.

Paddling solo in the canoe and headed to Lookout Pointe toward Aunt Virgie's place—all was right with the world. But it wasn't. Sadie needed the job, and she didn't. If rumors among the staff were true, one of them would need to go. The thought made her heart feel as if a wet rag had settled on it and been squeezed, just as she had wrung rags so many times that day. Her raw hands stung from the abuse she'd given them toiling at the Grand.

She'd not been surprised to learn from Sadie that Greyson may have been after her family's money—after all, he did need money to keep his family afloat and to care for his mother. Maude needed to forgive him—God required she give mercy as He extended it to her. If only there was some easy way that order could be restored to her world. It felt as if someone had smashed a framed portrait and all the glass shards had been picked up and returned to the frame, obscuring the photographic image. She sighed then picked up her paddle and dipped into the water.

Moonlight glittered on the lake like so many diamonds tossed across blue velvet as Maude aimed for the jetty near the inn.

❤

Ben tried to rouse himself. With the moon illuminating the woman's form, she could have been an angel. He wiped sleep from his eyes.

"Is that you, Mr. König?" Maude's melodious voice carried like a perfectly tuned piano.

"Ja." He rubbed his head. "Why are you canoeing at night?"

She placed her fists on her hips. "What are you doing sleeping on the beach?"

He shrugged then located his socks and shoes.

"Isn't your room at the Grand comfortable?"

"Not always." Such as when he was thinking of her. "Why are you paddling about in the dark?"

She sighed. "My family has been canoeing in these waters for over a hundred years."

"I worried earlier, when I saw a young woman alone on the water. Didn't realize it was you." He wiped sand from his left foot and pulled on a sock and shoe then repeated the process with the other foot.

Standing, he turned toward the street. A carriage, with its lamps lit, rounded the corner.

Maude giggled. "Looks like Stan is giving some love-struck couple a moonlit tour—up to Arch Rock no doubt."

"I've never seen it." He placed her arm in the crook of his elbow.

"It's beautiful."

"Perhaps you'd like to see it with me sometime?" He coughed, clearing his foggy mind. "With your beau accompanying us as well."

"My beau? What do you mean?" Her voice held accusation.

"Ach, forgive me, but I saw you in an embrace with a man."

"Saturday?"

"Ja. By the docks."

Her laugh peeled out like silver bells. "You mean Robert." Then she snorted in a most unladylike manner.

"He isn't your beau?" Sweet relief flooded him. He once more had a chance with her. What was he thinking? He had no chance. He hadn't enough income to support a wife, much less a family. Still. . .with her so close, hope rose in him, and he'd not squelch it.

The moon lit her beautiful face and he could have sworn moonbeams had twinkled in her eyes. "I've known Robert all my life and I can assure you, I've never ever considered him as a possible beau."

The captain appeared to be at least a decade older than Maude, but that wouldn't stop some from pursuing a romance. But apparently it did her, given her derisive snort. A sound that warmed his bones.

He took her hand.

"That's really not necessary, you know." But neither did she pull her hand free.

They moved carefully across the cool sand.

"I don't want you twisting your delicate ankles in the dark." While the streetlamps provided good illumination along the walk, here near the beach the gas lamps shed little light.

She laughed. "These delicate ankles have never been injured going to and from my canoe, I'll have you know."

With her damp skin pressed against his arm, Ben felt her shiver.

"You're cold." He paused and removed his jacket. "Here." He draped it around her shoulders then drew her back beside him, linking her arm through his.

"Mr. König, if anyone sees us together at this hour and this location, they may make some very wrong assumptions."

"What can I do to spare you aspersions on your character?" He reached across with his other hand to enclose the small hand resting atop his arm.

"The only people who would think anything ill of me would be the summer people. And I care little for their prattling tongues." She yawned.

"The summer people?" He led her across the street toward her home.

"I'm sorry—I spoke out of turn."

"Ah, I see, for I am one of those summer people, am I not?"

"Afraid so." They stopped at her gate. She slipped inside and then closed it, locking him out.

Chapter Twelve

ou can't do that, Maude! You could tip the cart." Sadie's stern voice roused Maude as she slumped over her cart, leaning onto the heavy wood handles for support.

She must have been dozing off. "I only slept four hours."

"Is that why you had that towel disaster earlier?" Her friend scowled at her. "Were you falling asleep?"

Maude cringed. Luckily no one had seen her when she'd toppled an entire stack of pristine white towels onto the floor in the finicky Burroughs's room. Sadie had helped her brush them off and get the towels all back in order again. "No, I was awake for that. Pure clumsiness."

A covey of ladies swished silently toward them.

"Aren't you pushing this a little too far, Maude? You have no idea what you are in for working as a maid. I've been your friend a long time."

Sadie dipped her chin as the matrons neared and kept her eyes downcast. Maude couldn't help staring at their outlandish exercise costumes. Didn't the hotel have a rule against bloomers? Apparently with enough money, it didn't matter.

When one of the women narrowed her eyes at Maude, she averted her gaze downward. Her face blazed at her failure to display appropriate subservient behavior.

"Such impudence from the household staff," the blond with the massive bow affixed at her narrow hip bones huffed.

How long would she keep this position?

Maude sighed as the women rounded the far corner to another corridor.

"I told you, I'm trying to prove that I can do this."

Rather than allowing the conversation to escalate, Maude slid the key into Mr. König's lock and turned it.

"I'll help you. I've got time." Sadie pushed the cart into the room.

Maude inhaled the unmistakable scent of men's hair pomade and a woodsy cologne. Her lips twitched upward. Just breathing in the man's fragrance warmed her as had his presence last night after her canoe trip. He'd cared enough to wait to ensure that she'd gotten back safely. And his behavior had been completely gentlemanly.

Sadie removed a stack of papers from atop the typewriter. "What's he got on the desk? Looks like every newspaper edition we have on the island."

"Probably has to keep up with the latest in industry."

Sadie said nothing in reply—instead pored over the papers.

"Hey, I thought you were going to help me, Sadie, not read the news." Maude fluffed the pillows.

"Does he usually have these thrown out each day?"

"Yes." She straightened the silken bedcovers. "But I pass them on to Mrs. Fox—you know how she loves to economize."

"As long as she doesn't save money by eliminating my position." Sadie bundled the newspapers and stuck them on the bottom of the cart. "Stillman is spreading rumors that Mrs. Fox intends to cut one of our positions."

Maude ceased straightening the bed. Was she that incompetent? Was the manager going to fire her? "Do you believe that?"

"I don't know." Her friend dusted off the desk, using a feather whisk on the keyboard.

"I wonder why he needs a typewriter if he's on holiday."

"Maybe he's sending in reports?" This was her only diplomat room. "Don't the other suites have one?"

"I only have one I clean, and it doesn't." Sadie ran the Bissell sweeper over the carpet, moving back and forth in fluid motions.

Maude dusted the side tables, knocking Mr. König's mechanical clock to the floor in the process.

"Oh, Maude, you're not cut out for this kind of work."

"At least it's not as bad as me knocking over all Zeb's shoes on the delivery rack." She bent and retrieved the clock, recollecting her previous day's mishap.

After dipping a rag in diluted ammonia, Maude wiped the looking glass. As she leaned forward, her vision seemed to blur as her ashen face and severely pomaded hair, covered by a cap that wasn't quite straight, filled the side of the mirror. *What am I doing here?*

Sooner or later she'd be found out for the fraud she was.

After finishing the room, Maude pushed the cart out into the hallway. She delivered the newspapers to Mrs. Fox's office.

"Maude, can you please get me a dozen maps from the concierge's desk?" The diminutive woman sighed. "Some of our guests think I have his job as well as my own."

"Yes, ma'am."

Maude hurried to the main floor and entered the elegantly decorated hallway. As she neared the registrar's desk, the clerk's voice carried around the corner. "Welcome, Mr. Cadotte."

Perspiration broke out on her upper lip. Maude ducked behind a huge potted palm—as if that would hide her. Which relative was at the Grand?

"Robert Swaine, actually. I own Cadotte Shipping, but my surname is Swaine." Uncle Robert's baritone voice startled her, and she froze to her spot.

"Excuse my error, sir. I only had Cadotte Shipping for the reservation."

A deep laugh accompanied Uncle Robert's voice. "We shareholders for the shipping line require a rest now and again. But I don't plan to stay long at the Grand."

Maude cringed. What was he doing here? And shareholder—what did he mean? She pressed against the plastered wall. She needed to get past him to the concierge. Peeking around the corner, she saw her uncle's head bent over the register as he signed in. She hurried past the desk, tempted to break into a run.

Her uncle wasn't staying at the Winds of Mackinac inn. Nor at Grandmother Swaine's beautiful home up on the cliffside by the Grand, nicknamed "the Canary" for its bright yellow hue. What was he up to?

Deep in thought, she strode toward the concierge's desk. A man rounded the corner and with a long stride stepped onto her foot.

"Ow!" Maude bit back a howl of pain. She peered up into Mr. König's blue-gray eyes.

Recognition flickered.

"Miss Welling?"

Maude turned and dodged several couples as she ran all the way down to the servant's closet.

♥

Needing to work off some steam and quiet his mind, Ben changed into his sporting clothes and headed for the men's gymnasium. His ribs felt better, and he didn't want to lose his stamina. After seeing Maude Welling dressed in a maid's costume, he needed to work out how he would approach this problem. And exercise often helped him focus.

He opened the walnut-stained six-paneled door and entered the small room. The man in the corner, attired in a sleeveless shirt and mid-calf pants and lifting weights, appeared to be about Ben's physique, but he stood a few inches shorter. "Captain Swaine?"

"We meet again, Mr. König."

Ben gave a slight nod and took his place on the mat near the weights. Dr. Cadotte had recommended that Ben begin slowly and work his way back up to the amount he used to lift before the injury.

The dark-haired man eyed Ben. "You look like you're moving slowly."

"You could say that, ja." With just the two of them in the stark white-painted room, it was hard to ignore the other man, but he tried. Which was foolish. This was exactly the type of man ladies would flock to—especially if he was wealthy. "Just got the tape off my ribs."

"Might want to start out at half lift unless you are some kind of strongman." The captain hoisted a hundred-pound globe weight-lifting barbell over his head. "The barbell in the corner is just over fifty pounds."

"Danke." So now not only had the good captain bested Ben by providing a horse for Miss Welling, but he'd displayed his prowess, too. He'd not felt this puny since he was a newsboy on the streets of Chicago. He lifted the barbell with only a twinge in his ribs.

"I hear you're a businessman."

"Ja—I'm in business. . . ." Newspapers were business, weren't they? "What about yourself?"

"I travel the Great Lakes, and although I'm not a businessman per se, I own. . ." The man frowned then lowered his barbell to the floor. "I possess a number of businesses, but I only run the shipping company." He ran his thumb over his lower lip.

The man was holding back something. "Ja, so you have others who do the oversight for you?"

"You could say that." Swaine walked across the heavily varnished wood floor and removed the jump rope from the wall.

He began to jump. After finishing twenty lifts, Ben decided to join in. He went to the rough plastered wall and grabbed the other rope that hung from a peg.

When he stopped, so did the captain. "You all right? Your face is pale."

Ben bent over, his hands pressed against his thighs. Sweat dripped from his face. "I'll be fine." He had to be.

The door to the gym opened, and two maids pushed a cart in.

"What are you doing here?" The curvaceous blond chambermaid shook a finger at the captain. Fire sparked from her eyes.

A smile twitched at the captain's lips. "I believe I could ask you the same question." The captain's slow easy gaze traveled the woman from head to toe.

The blond swiveled on her heel and left the room.

Arms akimbo, Maude glared at the two of them then focused on Ben. "You aren't supposed to be overexerting yourself."

"Still the bossiest gal on the island." Swaine laughed.

She glared at him. "This man saved Jack's neck, literally, just this past week, and he fell by the rocks across from the inn."

Swaine winced in sympathy. "Took a few falls there myself, but I was climbing on them at the time."

"Well, now you both know I'm working here, Robert. And Mr. König."

"Not for long, you won't be, dear girl." Swaine frowned. "Nor Sadie, either, if I have anything to do with it."

By the man's smug expression, he was clearly smitten with Sadie. And thought he had some control over her. So he wasn't enamored of Maude. Ben couldn't help the grin that spread over his face like honey on a hot piece of toast.

"Why, you. . .you. . ." Sputtering, she followed her friend's example, spun on her heel, and departed.

Jerking his thumb toward the slamming door, Swaine sighed. "They'll both get themselves dismissed if they keep up that kind of behavior."

Ben could have sworn he heard genuine satisfaction in the man's voice.

❤

One more hour. That was all Maude had to last. Sixty blessed minutes, and her first week would be finished.

She stepped on someone's foot, and then she slammed into a solid wall of muscle. Maude startled, rocking back from the tall man but not before inhaling his scent of sandalwood and light hair pomade. He grasped her shoulders, the warmth of his hands seeping down to her own. She daren't look up but somehow knew Friedrich König was holding her.

Her heartbeat skittered. "I'm sorry."

He laughed. "Don't be. It's not every day I have a young lady literally run into my arms."

She craned her head back to look up at him. Although his handsome face reflected genuine pleasure, he didn't have a cocky look like some men might have.

He grinned down at her and raised a finger to his too-perfect lips. "Won't utter a thing if you wish to keep up your work as an actress."

"Not doing too good at my charade, am I?" Maude waited for him to release his other hand, but he didn't. And somehow, she didn't want him to do so.

"Or are you spying on the Grand to pick up their secrets?"

With that comment, she pulled free. Maude opened her mouth, but no words formed. She clamped her lips back together.

"You wouldn't be the first hotelier to do so, you know." He slacked his hip. "The elusive and reclusive Mrs. Adelaide Bishop has been known to take a menial position at hotels she's considering acquiring or investing in."

Maude had read scathing articles about the woman, who was America's wealthiest but most eccentric lady. Every picture of her seemed a little uglier, as though the journalists wished to have an image that made her appear to be the crone they described her to be. Or maybe that was what money did to someone. It obviously didn't have the same effect on this man.

She found her tongue. "What I do with my time is no business of yours, sir."

He arched an eyebrow at her and chuckled. "I'd like to make it mine."

Cheeks heating, she turned and scurried down the hall to finish out her shift. And then to get home. Where she belonged. But in the position of running the inn.

Chapter Thirteen

s he biked toward Maude's home Saturday morning, Ben couldn't stop wondering what on earth Maude Welling was doing working at the Grand Hotel. Was she scoping out a wealthy husband? Or had her family fallen on such hard times that she had to work? Or did they send her there to spy on their competition?

Ben tugged at his tie with one hand as lake breezes blew through the gap between the shirt and its detached collar. He had sent ahead a note requesting permission to meet with Peter Welling, and the inn owner had agreed, even though Ben hadn't offered an explanation.

What would his editor, Banyon, say if he knew? "Why, Bennie, what are ye thinkin' my lad—ye don't need an island hotelier tellin' ye what goes on in town."

Ben swept away the unwelcome nagging sensation and continued on, pumping his legs hard and dodging slow-moving drays. What he really wanted to know was more about Welling's daughter. Why hadn't she married? How could half the merchants in town claim to be her kin? Why did she paddle around by canoe at nighttime? This last question he dare not inquire about for he was certain her father had no idea that she did so. And now—why on earth was she working as a maid at the hotel? And why had her father sent word to an attorney—were they having legal difficulties?

All along the left, beautiful homes with carefully tended gardens bespoke the wealth of the owners, many of whom were nonresidents. Yet, many were Mackinac Islanders' homes.

"Yoo-hoo!" A stout woman waved at Ben from behind her arched front gateway.

Ben slowed his Sterling and pedaled in her direction. "Yes, madam?"

The lady, perhaps in her sixties, clutched her hands together almost as though in prayer. "Are you the young man who saved Jackie?"

"Jack Welling?"

She giggled like a schoolgirl. "Such a precious boy. I want to thank you—as one of the Wellings' neighbors."

"That's unnecessary." But here was a golden opportunity.

"I'm Mrs. Glenn. I'm having tea and cookies if you wish to join me."

Ben looked past her where an ornate silver teapot sat atop a small round wrought-iron table with two chairs. A platter of cookies did indeed rest there as well.

"Peter told me he expected you to call on the hour, so you should have time." She turned and moved toward the house remarkably quickly, for a woman of her girth.

Ben pulled out his watch. He still had thirty minutes. He opened the gate and crossed the lush green lawn.

Mrs. Glenn sat and poured tea into a blue gilt Bohemian glass cup nestled in a matching saucer.

The teacup reminded him of one his großmutter preferred and that he'd never been allowed to use. A wave of sadness washed over him.

"Have a seat."

"Thank you." From the street, the sounds of carriages rolling by competed with a low foghorn.

The matron poured Ben's tea. "I think Maude needs to move on and not let this dreadful business with that poor Luce boy slow her prospects at a better marriage opportunity. Is that why you're meeting with Peter?" She smiled beneficently.

So the lady already had Ben married off to Maude? "I wished to introduce myself to him, ma'am."

"He's been ill. But I think he's just heartsick over losing his wife."

"It must be difficult."

"She passed away over a year ago." The woman added five lumps of sugar to her small teacup. Ben watched in fascination that she could drink so sweet a tea.

"A shame."

"I wonder if Peter will be leaving the island now that he has no reason to stay."

No reason to stay? When she offered him the plate of cookies, Ben selected a madeleine and a lemon wafer. "He has his daughter and son here."

"Pish posh." The woman waved her hand as though dismissing the notion. "He's been longing to return to his family's farm downstate in Shepherd. Only a matter of time till the poor man may have to."

"Oh?" Ben tried not to sound too eager. He nibbled on the wafer.

"That mother-in-law of his was a real harridan. The inn belonged to her, as did all the other properties that her daughter and son-in-law managed. I was surprised Peter didn't sell off half of them after she died, just to spite her memory."

Ben sipped his tea and nodded, hoping the busybody would continue.

"You mark my words—someone wants to buy that inn—and Peter will be gone just as fast as that boy of his runs. I believe Peter Welling has been running over to St. Ignace to see the attorney so he can sell." She waited expectantly, eyebrows raised.

"Mr. Hollingshead?"

She lifted her chin and grinned in satisfaction. "That must be the one."

He exhaled. So this biddy didn't know—she was fishing for information from Ben. He almost laughed at the absurdity of it. But what *did* she know?

"Mrs. Glenn, do you believe the Wellings are having difficulties?"

She frowned and cocked her head to the side. Sporadic birdsong announced the presence of a great many avian friends. "Oh, yes, I'd say so. With Robbie Swaine not even staying with them this summer. Simply unheard of. His sister, Peter's wife, kept him in her household all those years after their mother died. There must be some bad blood between Robbie and Peter that I haven't heard about. I do know they aren't speaking to each other."

"Captain Swaine is Maude's uncle?"

"He's been more like an older brother to her." The woman's beady eyes darted right and then left, as though she thought someone might be listening. "My drayman swears he saw Maude working up at the Grand Hotel. Can you imagine? I insisted he cease spreading such rumors, or there shall be consequences."

Ben coughed to stifle a laugh. This woman wanted to keep others from gossiping?

"You haven't seen her there, Mr. König, have you?"

He took a long drink of his tea. "My dear Mrs. Glenn, if I had seen her

I'd have been the soul of discretion, like you—I'd keep that to myself and urge others to do the same."

"I knew you'd understand. You see, islanders try to protect their own, and when my drayman started in with such an absurd tale, I silenced him immediately." She gave a quick nod of her head to emphasize her words.

A foghorn sounded, followed by a toot from a boat in the harbor. The mist had thickened even as they'd sat chatting.

"I must keep my appointment with Mr. Welling, and I fear I must depart."

The matron smiled. "A pleasure to meet you."

"And you as well, ma'am. Good day." He departed and closed the gate behind him.

Walking the Sterling, Ben rounded the curve to the Winds of Mackinac. In front, the groundskeeper deadheaded the roses and clipped the lilacs. A fringe-topped carriage slowed to a crawl as fog crowded the roadway.

As Ben leaned the bike against the fence, the gardener's wizened face appeared behind a pink rosebush.

"Don't leave it there."

"Why not?" Seemed a perfectly reasonable spot.

"Jack'll take it."

Ben shrugged. "It isn't his bike."

The elderly man scratched his head. "His new prank is to ride off with a bike and leave it down at the docks."

"At the docks?"

The gardener resumed snipping. "Young people and their bad hearing—I said docks, and that's what I meant."

"Ja."

"Before that, he was taking them from town and leaving them at the island post office. Heard he even got you to help him with one of those trips."

"Me? I helped Jack take Maude's bike. . ." Her very masculine bike with a seat raised high enough for a tall man. "I see. I was duped."

Mr. Chesnut cackled. "Yup, you were duped by a kid." His scrunched-up face sneered up at Ben, but he supposed he had it coming.

"Do you know why Jack would do such a thing, sir?"

The gardener's white head popped up again. "Sir am I now? I see. Yes." He straightened, though it didn't much improve his height. "Believe I know."

Ben waited.

"Jackie's hoping to go to the mainland—poor boy hasn't been the same for a while. Not since his mother died." Sadness flitted over the wrinkles in the man's weathered face.

"And that is why he takes bicycles not belonging to him and deposits them at the wharf?" Some kind of cryptic message for his father, no doubt.

Two hazy blue eyes raked his face. "He's not a bad boy, but he's cooped up on this island." A gleam of moisture shone on the man's eyes.

Ben couldn't do anything about Jack's mother—knowing from experience the pain loss could bring even when assured that one would be reunited with loved ones in heaven. But if he wanted a trip off the island, that he could arrange. "I could take the boy with me when I go over in a few days."

Mr. Chesnut extended his hand. The two men shook and Ben caught the scent of chewing tobacco.

"Ya probably ought to stop jawing with me." He gestured with his trowel toward the inn. "You'll find Mr. Welling in the office."

Ben tipped his straw boater at the man and hustled up the steps and into the lobby. Every piece of metal gleamed—from the brass fittings on a leather trunk to the gas-lamp fixtures and the doorknobs. A sumptuous emerald green carpet covered the entry hall.

A girl dressed in servant's garb whisked with a feather duster at the dark wood bannister railing. Beeswax scented the air. "Can I help you, mister?"

"Ja, Friedrich König here to see Mr. Welling."

"The one who helped Jack!" The girl moved toward a nearby mahogany-stained paneled door and rapped several times.

The door flew inward and a disheveled man stood there, his hair mussed as though he'd been awakened.

The girl bobbed a curtsy. "Mr. Friedrich König, the one who helped Jack, here to see you."

"Thank you, Bea. Tell Jack to come down."

"Yes, sir." The girl practically flew up the nearby stairs.

♥

"Come in." Folders and ledgers covered the rectangular black Eastlake desk.

"Thank you."

"Have a seat." He pointed to an upholstered chair on the opposite side of the desk.

Through the nearby window, a brief break in the fog gave Ben a view of the lakefront. Small boats ducked in and out of the waves.

"I want to thank you for saving my son." Welling followed Ben's gaze and rubbed his chin. "Rough out there."

"I only did what any man would do in the situation, sir."

Thick brows drew together. "Shame I had to hear it from the local gossip and not from my own daughter."

Above and behind the man, four pictures hung side by side from a picture rail. The first two were framed tintypes of dark-haired men in army uniforms but with different hues and insignia, the third a beautiful young woman attired in a frothy gown from about two decades past, and the fourth a sad-eyed young man with chubby cheeks.

Ben pointed to the pictures. "Are these your family?"

"No." Welling turned and pointed to the woman. "My wife."

"Beautiful lady."

"Yes." He cleared his throat and pointed to the left. "Her older two brothers, killed in battle in Virginia."

"During the war?" Ben perused the tintypes again. One man wore Confederate clothing while the other was attired in Union. Now there was a story he'd like to know more about. He pressed his fingers to his lips.

"Yes, I never knew them—they were more than a decade older than my wife."

"And the youngest?" The man's clothing was similar to that worn by Ben when he'd come to America, so he couldn't be much older.

"My mother-in-law was blessed in her grief with yet another son. He's actually closer to Maude's age than to my wife's."

"Ah, that must be Captain Swaine when he was young."

Ben's only sibling, his older sister, had perished on the journey over from Germany. She'd be thirty now, had she lived. Perhaps God spared her the humiliation he and his parents had endured.

"Why do you want to talk with me, Mr. König?"

"Sir, I'm here to. . ." He was about to request an interview about Greyson Luce, but instead, he said, "To ask permission to court your daughter."

"Maude?"

"Ja, she is your only daughter, right?" Ben laughed, but Welling frowned.

"She's had her heart broken by a young man. I don't think she's quite ready."

"Her heart is broken?"

"She's been mooning around the house. Disappears all day—probably out doing good to anyone on the island she can visit her attentions upon. I just hope they aren't tormenting her over Greyson."

Might Maude be "mooning" over him? Might Ben presume such a thing? "Ja, sir, perhaps it would be best if I was her friend?"

Welling's lower lip bulged, and his eyebrows drew together. "Yes, she needs a companion. With Greyson abandoning her, and her uncle—"

Three long foghorn blasts were followed by a quick toot from a boat and then another.

The screeching of metal upon metal carried through the office's open windows. Ben sprang to the one facing the jetties. Through the haze, he discerned the shapes of two boats.

"Oh, Lord," Peter Welling moaned as he, too, looked through the window. "Come on, we've got to help. I'm on the rescue brigade."

Welling pulled off his jacket and threw it across his chair. Ben did, too.

"Your shoes, too—leave them here and come on. Can you swim?"

"Ja."

"You able-bodied enough to help, König?"

"Ja—I'll try." His ribs argued otherwise.

"Mr. Welling!" Bea called out as they ran past her. "Be careful."

He heard the girl's sobs as bells began to clang in the distance. In the street, carriages and drays were pulled aside and parked at the curb as men stripped down to their undergarments and ran to the jetties.

Mr. Welling pulled a whistle from his pocket and blew it. A dozen men of all ages encircled him within minutes. "Form a line. We'll have the women tie the shirts together, and I see Ned has got us the rope, too."

A middle-aged man dropped a heavy-looking reel of rope to the ground and began to unroll it toward the shore. "Arrange yourselves from youngest to oldest, healthiest first, and go!"

The smell of hot metal gagged Ben, but he followed the others into the frigid water. Cries of the injured carried across the water. Another day long ago came to mind. They had to save whomever they could. Finally up to his shoulders in the cold water, his ribs feeling fine, Ben swam steadily out toward the two sinking ships. The new lighthouse, being built on Round Island, wasn't yet completed, and there was no light to pierce the fog.

Every reporter's instinct within him urged him to memorize what was happening and get the story down. But the pitiful moaning and the bloodied injured were real. As were his reactions. Back at shore, he spied rowboats being pushed off. The cacophony of noises emanating from the boats made his hair stand on end. With such thick fog and the waves unrelenting, would he or some of the other rescuers soon find their own watery grave? He couldn't think of such things. A dark-haired man sliced through the water toward two little girls who clung to a trunk that inexplicably floated on the water.

Spurred on by the man's heroism, Ben released the rope and swam to where a young mother with her infant continued to slosh against the side of the hull, as she clung to a large cleat. "Take my baby. Don't let her drown." The woman sobbed as Ben reached her.

"Take your shawl and put the baby in—like a papoose is carried." Ben had seen some of the Chippewa women on the island carrying their infants secured to their chests in such a manner.

Ben held the baby while the woman removed her light wool shawl and tucked her infant inside. "Tie the corners and drape that over your head."

Soon he had pulled the woman and child to shore. Women had set up fires with kettles of water and had brought stacks of blankets, which they distributed.

"Thank you, sir. We were coming here to see my father—he's right there."

She pointed to Dr. Cadotte at the same time that Ben collapsed to the sand in agony, his ribs burning in excruciating pain. But he had to keep on.

"Father! We need help."

❤

Maude wished she could have soaked in the new porcelain tub Father had had installed inside the inn, but she'd not risk walking into the house smelling as foul as she did. So she'd washed in the laundry house out back after she returned home each day from the hotel. Although they sometimes heated water over a fire in the building, Cook had taken to heating Maude's water on the woodstove, inside, before she arrived home. Quickly she dried off and dressed. But the entire operation from donning her corset and pantalets to buttoning her shirt consumed almost a half hour.

She moved to the rotary washer and began loading her own work clothes to save the servants the task. She'd determined to cease her habit of changing for every activity of the day. Instead of a morning walking suit, a dress for afternoon tea, and possibly even a change to an evening dress, she vowed to pick an ensemble that could make it through the day's typical activities. At the Grand that morning, she'd been forced to assist a young woman who'd donned seven ensembles before she'd settled on the very first one Maude had suggested. Had she been so inconsiderate of others' time? Yes. But no longer.

A strange crashing sound rent the silence in the room. The water in the tin bathing tub sloshed over with the reverberation. Maude grabbed a mop and sopped up the mess, lest anyone slip on the brick floor, then headed outside. She moved through the foggy air to the right side of the house, where all manner of men were tossing aside their bikes and disrobing to their undergarments. She raised a hand to her mouth as the mist broke and she spied two vessels near the jetties.

Bea stormed through the back door, her face crimson. "Oh, Maude, oh. . ." She ran into Maude's arms and buried her head in her neck.

Maude stroked the girl's head.

Bea pulled free. "Two ships crashed together in the fog, and your father and Mr. König went down there."

Maude stiffened. "Father and Mr. König?"

"Yes."

Might both men be gone before the day was over? Chills slid down her arms as she pulled the girl close again. "We need to pray. And we need to be useful. Let's gather blankets and towels, and get every available servant to help with heating water."

Jane stumbled out the back door. "Miss Welling." Her face had gone ashen.

Bea and Maude turned to face her. "Please get out all the blankets and towels you can find, and we'll need to heat the water ourselves. Those survivors will be chilled to the bone." If there were survivors.

An hour later, bone weary, Maude, Jane, and Bea gathered on the front porch. Maude crossed her arms and clutched them close to her body, shivering from the chill fog. Survivors were being driven away by carriage and even dray, just to get them to someplace safe and warm.

Jack rode into the backyard and threw his bike down. "They've found them all!"

Bea ran to him and grabbed his arms. "Your pa didn't go out in that water, did he? I couldn't stand it if he drowned. He's been so good to me."

The girl raised her apron to her face and wiped her wet cheeks.

Maude joined them on the front lawn as Mr. Chesnut brought lounge divans and cushions around from storage in case they had anyone who would need to recline on the porch after the ordeal.

Jack tapped Maude's shoulder. "Dad says get Uncle Robert's room ready."

"He's coming here?"

"He ain't comin' here, sis. Mr. König, that German guy who saved me, is."

"What?" Her heart pounded against her ribs. "Why?"

"He got hurt rescuing Doc Cadotte's daughter and granddaughter."

Maude gasped. "They were on board?"

Jack scowled. "No, they just swam out there to look at the wreckage, you silly girl!"

Bea whacked Jack on the arm. "That isn't funny."

"Neither is Mr. König being hurt again, but he's real bad off this time."

All the air seemed to have been sucked from Maude's lungs.

"He'll be all right." Jack slapped her back so hard, she thought he'd rammed her corset boning into her rib cage. "But you two best go get the room ready."

"When will he arrive?"

"All them folks are all right because of our men saving 'em. So I think they're gonna tend to Mr. König and bring him over soon."

Within twenty minutes, Bea, Jane, and Maude had tidied the room and put fresh sheets on the bed. Jack's distinctive footsteps pounded up the stairs.

"Stan, Dad, and Friedrich are here now." He stood in the doorway, panting.

Maude sank onto the bed. Her breath caught in her throat. With the excitement, her breathing had become difficult. But she had to calm herself. *In. Out. In. Out.* She willed her breathing to slow.

"You all right, Muddie?"

"Maude!" Her cousin Stan's voice carried up the stairs. "We're gonna bring Friedrich up."

Mr. Roof, their handyman, held Mr. König up on one side while the other arm was draped around Stan.

Maude's heart raced. "He's so pale." She quickly pulled the bedcovers back.

Friedrich groaned.

"He's also mighty big." Stan and Mr. Roof turned and positioned the injured man so he could sit on the bed.

Maude pressed back against the wall. How was she going to put her feelings aside and help him recover?

"We'll get him situated, daughter. François will reexamine Mr. König in the morning."

Chapter Fourteen

The Lord's Day. Gott sei Dank. He'd survived and rescued the mother and baby. Something wet trickled down his cheek. The door to the room opened.

"How are you doing today?" Maude leaned over him, the scent of rosewater and soap carrying with her.

"Fine." He turned his head to the side to wipe the moisture from his cheek.

"Let me fluff your pillow."

Ben groaned as he leaned forward, and she quickly puffed up and rearranged his pillow. When he rested his head again, she pressed a cool hand to his forehead.

"You're a little warm."

With her in the room, ja, he was getting a little warmer.

If he wasn't in so much pain, Ben would be thrilled to be in this position—lying in a comfortable bed under the same roof as Maude. She'd sat beside his bed most of the night, despite her father's admonition that she get some sleep.

Jack ducked his head in the doorway. "Doc is here."

"Good." Maude squeezed Ben's hand. "He'll take good care of you. I imagine he's worn out after checking on everyone injured or who'd swallowed water yesterday."

Staccato footsteps brushed up the steps. Dr. Cadotte entered the room, placing his bag on a nearby empty plant stand. "Reinjured, I hear, but I cannot fuss at you, Mr. König. God bless you for saving my daughter and granddaughter. I can never repay you for your kindness."

"We all were eager to help. Glad to do so."

Cadotte grasped Ben's hands in his own and pulled. "Let's get you up."

The pain, while still present, had calmed. Was he so seriously affected that he required continued care in the Wellings' home?

"I think I will be fine, Doctor."

But this could be his chance to find out what was going on in the Welling household. Perhaps if he stayed he could help Maude.

"Nonsense. Let me check you."

He'd not lie. Perhaps he might emphasize his pain. But when Cadotte began jabbing at his ribs, Friedrich yelped. No feigning anything there.

"Maude, help me get his shirt off."

He'd slept in Peter Welling's nightshirt when they'd been unable to find pajamas that were long enough for him.

"Me?" Her voice squeaked.

"I made your father lie back down—his heart is out of rhythm again."

Ben noticed a look of concern cross her face, but then she tilted her chin up as if fighting off fears.

"What happened last night?" she asked. "Do they know?"

"Two ships didn't see each other. The foghorn sounded, but it wasn't enough warning."

"I'm so glad no one perished, but were there many serious injuries?"

"Thank God, Dr. DuBlanc from the Grand came to help and Aunt Virgie rode down with her herbs and remedies. She was especially useful when it came to treating the children who'd swallowed a great deal of water."

"Oh my."

"And Rev. and Mrs. McWithey put up a dozen families at the church last night. The island ladies are feeding them this morning. There will be a short service and prayers, but the pastor felt the best thing parishioners could do today was to help these folks get settled into their lodgings and to try to bring whatever can be spared for those who've lost almost everything."

"That sounds like our logical pastor." A faint smile flickered on Maude's beautiful lips. "Father sent word last night to the dray drivers, asking them to work today, and they agreed."

"Yes, and all the shop owners save one have opened for those who need to purchase goods.

"It could have been so much worse," the doctor added. "There could have been much loss of life had the men hesitated at all. Your father ran that group like a drill sergeant with the army. Brought back my memories of all those soldiers up there at the fort."

"And Father overdid it?"

"Of course. You know him."

Cadotte squeezed Ben's shoulder. "Can we get you up? We need to make you more comfortable, and I'm going to need to re-tape your ribs."

Maude and the doctor helped him stand up, but then Ben released their hands. He tried to unbutton the sleep shirt, but any movement brought searing pain.

"Help me get that off," the doctor ordered.

Her cheeks bloomed pink. "But he's wearing no pants."

Cadotte rolled his eyes. "If he had them on, you'd take those off, too."

From her horrified expression, Ben wondered if she'd never seen a man bare-chested, much less in his birthday suit. "I have sleeping shorts on, Miss Welling."

♥

When Maude hesitated, François glared at her. "Cadotte women do their duty. Duty over modesty, my dear. Don't forget that."

Had she ever in her life forgotten this maxim? She and her uncle began to disrobe Friedrich. She tried to be careful as she unbuttoned the front of his shirt. When she glanced up at his face, he was observing her from beneath heavily lidded eyes. Her heart skipped a beat.

When they'd gotten him down to Father's undershirt, which strained against his back, she hesitated, mesmerized by the dark tufts of hair that covered his broad chest at the base of his neck. François lifted from the back and she pulled up in the front, blushing deeply when she saw that his entire muscular chest, down to his trim waist, was covered with thick dark hair. She felt like covering her face and running from the room.

"Stay while I examine him, Maude."

She swallowed as he quickly poked and prodded Friedrich, turning away when he cried out.

Finally he stopped. "You've reinjured your ribs. I'd like you to rest here for another day or so, eh?"

"Ja."

Friedrich's pallor concerned her. "Can you leave something for the pain?"

François gestured to the bed. "Let's get him back to bed, and then I'll give you some laudanum."

After they got Friedrich settled and covered up, François went to his medical case and pulled out a corked glass bottle. "I'll need for you to give this to him and then sit with him for a while."

Maude repeated for him a mandate she'd received growing up: "Cadotte women don't abandon their posts."

"Exactly." He gave her a half smile and winked as he left. "They're practically perfect. Or are supposed to be, anyways."

She exhaled a huff, but he laughed.

When her uncle finally left, Maude collapsed into the chair beside the bed. Tears threatened to spill over her cheeks. She was exhausted by dealing with this new and intriguing man's injuries. And being forced into what felt like an intimate situation drained what was left of her emotional reserves. But she must be strong.

Friedrich reached for her hand. "Is there anything Cadotte women cannot do?"

Apparently Father didn't believe Maude was capable of running the inn, but she bit her tongue. She forced a laugh as she wiped away a tear. "François sounded just like my grandmother and mother. He's only repeating what he was brought up hearing."

"This Sadie, is she a Cadotte, also?"

"No." In some ways her friend was lucky that there had been no expectations of her.

Friedrich's hand heated hers. She began to pull away, realizing how chapped her palms and fingers were. But he wouldn't release her hand.

"The jig is up, as they say." His blue-gray eyes searched hers. "I know you're a maid at the Grand, as does Captain Swaine, and it won't be long before Mrs. Fox hears."

His thumb traced a circle over her palm, which had the effect of unnerving her further. He smiled but then flinched.

Maude pulled free and stood over him. "Are you all right?"

Sweat trickled down his brow. "Ja." He closed his eyes and leaned back on the embroidered pillowcase.

She stroked his forehead, covered with streaks of soot. She needed to get him cleaned up. "I'm so sorry you were reinjured."

He pressed his eyes shut tight. "I'll be all right."

"I pray you will be."

"Ja, pray for me like I pray for you."

He prayed for her? She couldn't help smiling.

She glanced around Uncle Robert's room, with its collection of mariner-related objects. Tiny bottled ships lined several shelves. An old wooden captain's wheel mounted on the wall had pegs hammered into it so Robert could hang his hats. Somehow she pictured Mr. König's own bedroom in Detroit as large, with a collection of books and art. "I know this isn't the Grand Hotel, but we'll try to make you comfortable here."

"I am most comfortable in this bed—especially with the feather ticking on top." A grin tugged at his finely formed lips. "How long has this inn belonged to your family?"

"This was my grandmother Swaine's inn and my great-grandmother Cadotte's before her, so several generations now." *But no more, if Father has his say.*

"And you obviously love it."

"Yes, I do. . . . I always thought I'd be in charge here one day." But her efforts at the Grand to prove herself may have been for naught.

"Why not now? Has something happened?"

She puffed out a breath of air as she sat back down. "I was supposed to marry my childhood sweetheart, and we'd run the inn together. But he married someone else."

"I'm sorry. No—that is not honest, I'm not sorry." His eyes lingered on her mouth. "But why should you not be able to run the inn? I'd think a father who allowed you to canoe unaccompanied at night wouldn't be opposed to you running the inn."

Should she tell him? With the laudanum her uncle had given him, he'd likely not remember in the morning, anyway. "My father believes he is protecting me. His mother died when he was a little older than Jack. He blamed hard work for his mother's death. And now with my own mother gone. . ."

She sniffed back her tears.

"I'm sorry. I don't mean to upset you."

"It's all right. Since my mother died, he's been acting so odd. Now he's saying that he'll sell the inn—but both my mother and grandmother led me to believe I'd own the inn." She bit her lip. Mother and Grandmother also said she and Jack would split the remaining businesses but that her father would assist until Jack came of age, unless Maude agreed to run them all. Now none of that seemed to be happening.

♥

When Ben awoke, Maude was gone, and he had a new visitor.

Mr. Welling lowered himself into the wooden chair adjacent to the bed, setting his arms squarely on the armrests. "Thank you for helping."

Ben attempted to lift his head but then allowed it to flop back onto the rose-scented pillow.

Was his boss sending more work O'Halloran's way? He knew how things worked. Someone was gone and another journalist tried to take their place, jockeying for a new position.

"Well, I've been running a number of businesses on this island for some time." Mr. Welling stroked his jaw.

"I see." He didn't.

"And it's been thankless work." The man harrumphed.

His journalist's mind urged him to focus. "What types of businesses?"

Welling settled back into the chair. "Drays—hauling, carriage rentals, and a few other businesses that my wife and I. . .managed."

"Many." Not just this inn.

The man rubbed his eyes. Ben's vision was too blurred to tell if he might be crying.

"I worked hard for all these years, and now I see Robert Swaine coming in to take all that away from me."

Must stay awake. "How so?"

"If Maude had married, it wouldn't have been an issue, but now. . ."

"Maude is lovely." The words slipped past his lips before he could restrain them.

"I think so." Welling pulled a handkerchief from his pocket. "I don't know why I'm telling you all this, Mr. König, but for some reason I trust you."

"Danke." He trusted a man lying to him. This was wrong.

"I wish my wife was here so I could talk with her." Welling blew his nose. He was weeping.

"I am sorry." Morpheus was pulling Ben down further into a quilt-covered sleep.

"I have to think there was something she could have done about the codicils her mother placed upon her will."

"A legal matter?" Ben's mouth felt stuffed with cotton.

"It's more than that—my mother-in-law as well as my wife convinced my daughter that she should remain on this island. I fear it is becoming like a prison for my son. He must leave to obtain further training and I intend to accompany..."

Sleep overtook him as Welling's words faded out.

Chapter Fifteen

Another day, another disaster. The other maids commandeered their carts down the hallway, but Maude lingered behind. She sunk onto the low upholstered bench behind the door in the linen room. Empty. Thank God. She wiped her wet cheeks with the back of her hands.

The scent of fresh linens and starch surrounded her, reminding her of wash days with her mother in the winter—when the two of them would fold and put away sheets and blankets in the linen closet. *Mother—I miss you so much.*

A sharp rap at the door caused Maude to flinch. Mrs. Fox entered and locked the door.

"Listen, I know something isn't quite right."

Maude sniffed, and Mrs. Fox handed her a square of cotton cloth to use as a handkerchief.

"Young lady, you don't belong at the Grand." The older woman settled beside her on the bench.

Fresh tears welled in Maude's eyes. "I know, but I'm learning."

"You can't keep up with the other girls, which they're starting to notice."

"I'll try harder."

"Very good." Mrs. Fox stood, unlocked the door, and left.

The rest of the morning passed in a blur, but Maude had finished all of her rooms on time.

Sadie wheeled her cart down the corridor toward Maude. "Miss Ada wants to see you in her office."

"Thank you." Swallowing, Maude pushed her trolley against the wall.

Compassion softened Sadie's lovely features. "She said pronto."

Panic built in Maude's chest, tightening her lungs. Was she being fired? She prayed as she pushed her work gloves into her pocket and then set off.

She entered the parlor outside the chief housekeeper's office and tapped on the open door.

"Come in, dear."

Dear?

Only Mrs. Luce called her dear. Maude missed the sweet lady—she should go visit her. She hadn't seen the infirm woman at recent church events. Without the Wellings carrying her to and fro, Greyson must not have reassumed his responsibility to bring her to services.

"You needn't bother with Mr. König's room today—he's staying elsewhere for a day or two." Behind those silver frames, Mrs. Fox's eyes steadily searched hers. "I hear he was quite the hero, during the ship rescues."

Maude smoothed out her apron and averted her gaze.

"Also, you've been reassigned to the front parlors."

Hadn't she been satisfactory in the rooms?

The housekeeping manager tapped a pencil on a diagram of the hotel's layout. "We've had complaints that the front parlor and the smoking rooms aren't being cleaned properly."

The sensation of tightly knit yarn wound round her lungs began to unravel, and Maude breathed more easily. "Those rooms are the most important. First impressions count."

Mrs. Fox's smile grew broader. "I knew you'd understand."

Maude shifted her weight. "When do I make the move?"

"Now."

Today?

Maude stopped herself from opening her mouth to protest. The black Ansonia mantel clock on her supervisor's desk read half past ten. "Did Merry do the early morning cleaning?"

The smile slipped from her supervisor's face. "Unfortunately, no—which is why I need your help. I only just discovered she'd gone missing today. Mrs. Stillman brought it to my attention."

Mrs. Stillman. Why did she take notice of everything? It wasn't even her area to supervise. Sadie needed her job.

"Is there something you wish to ask, Miss Welling?"

"Yes, ma'am. My friend Sadie is most diligent."

Mrs. Fox's brown eyes narrowed ever so slightly. "Are you making a request?"

The woman's knowing eyes always undid her—reminded her of her mother's ability to see through any pretense. How she missed Mother. "Sadie is supporting herself and her younger sisters." She left off that Sadie's sister Bea was employed by her inn.

"I'll see what I can do for your friend." Ada Fox leaned forward. "Be discreet in the parlor."

"Yes, I won't be underfoot."

"Good girl. You surely understand from"—Mrs. Fox's eyes held Maude's a moment too long—"working at the Winds of Mackinac, how important social rooms are. Critical even. Slip in and tidy up as quickly as possible."

"I'll do my best, ma'am."

The woman chuckled. "I'd bet a silver dollar that you would."

Maude looked up. Ada Fox knew. And was enjoying Maude's discomfort.

"Be on your way, now—before I dock the pay that you so *desperately* need." Her tone wasn't unkind, but her supervisor's words accused Maude to her very core. Her cheeks flamed.

"I..."

Mrs. Fox raised a hand. "It's my intention to meet with the proprietor of the inn soon."

A hot ball of boiling maple syrup seemed to have dropped into Maude's gut. She opened her mouth, but no words came out.

"Please tell Mr. Welling that I have been remiss in not paying my respects earlier."

Maude couldn't even swallow her own spit.

"When I heard Peter, that is, Mr. Welling, assisted in the rescue yesterday, I knew I should wait no longer." Were those tears glistening in the manager's eyes? Mrs. Fox turned away.

Peter? Mrs. Fox must be acquainted with Father. "Yes, ma'am." Maude bobbed a curtsy. How did the housekeeping manager know her father?

Maude scurried down the corridor to the main rooms. In a large alcove near the registration desk, she paused to watch the shoeshine man work and to catch her breath. A ruddy-faced man, a coal-mine tycoon, was seated in the chair. His daughter was an absolute tyrant and had sent home her personal maidservants. Thankfully, Mrs. Fox had put her foot down and sent no more staff up to assist the girl after she'd slapped a senior staff member. Most of the young women vacationing at the Grand had been kind enough to Maude. She'd rather be ignored, though, than attacked by someone.

Maude continued on to the parlor. Teacups and saucers littered the mahogany side tables, and crumbs covered the carpet in front of the three velvet chaise longues. "Oh my."

Soon, Maude had everything shipshape. She beamed with pleasure at the scent of beeswax and lemon oil. Nary a dust mote in sight. Maude set her pail down and propped the mop against the dark walnut-paneled walls.

Sadie slipped into the hotel parlor wringing her reddened hands. "They're making cuts!"

Maude pulled Sadie behind the tall potted palm, so no one passing in the corridor would see them. "I spoke with Mrs. Fox earlier, Sadie. I believe she'll keep you on."

Sadie gave her a quick hug.

Gretchen, one of the lower housemaids walked by, her eyes and nose red.

"What's wrong?" Sadie called out and pulled the young woman toward her and Maude.

"They fired me! No severance even. How am I to get home to my family?"

Maude gasped. "Miss Ada did that?"

"No—that supercilious Mrs. Stillman had the night manager fire me. But I didn't do anything wrong. Someone came behind me and messed up all I had done."

"Stillman probably made the mess herself," Sadie mumbled.

Gretchen nodded, her white cap flopping loose. "My thoughts, too."

Sadie offered the other servant her handkerchief, but she refused it. "Well, I have to get back to work. But I'll be praying for you." Sadie swiftly moved toward the main floor.

Gretchen sobbed. "What'll I do?"

Maude wrapped her arm around the younger woman. "Don't worry. I know a place that needs a hard worker like you." Jane and Bea could use extra help.

"Where?"

"I'll hire you to work at my father's inn."

"Your father's hotel!" The girl's loud voice carried, and two matrons raised their eyebrows as they marched by toward the exit to the porch, their walking suits perfectly pressed and their gold jewelry glistening.

"Shhh! You have to promise to say nothing to anyone."

"I won't. You have my word." The girl made an *X* over her lips.

Maude pulled a piece of scrap paper from her pocket and wrote the address for Winds of Mackinac on it. "Meet me there when I get off."

"But that's hours from now."

She pulled a coin from her apron pocket. "Go to Al's Soda Shop in the center of town and get a phosphate. Tell him Maude sent you. He might not charge you anything. If he does, give him the money. Then go to the wharf or the park. Like the tourists do. Go watch the boats come in."

Color drained from the young woman's face and her brow puckered. "Why are you doing this?"

"It's the right thing. And what I said is true—I know you work harder than anyone else."

Lips pressed together, she nodded, and two tears trickled down her cheeks. "Thank you."

♥

Noise carried through the inn's thin walls, waking Ben early. After taking a dose of laudanum, he drifted back to sleep. When he awoke, he dressed himself without assistance. Examining his whiskery face, he considered shaving. How long had he hidden behind his beard in Detroit? When the barber had shaved him in Detroit, he'd revealed the strong König aristocratic features he'd inherited. Although his hair had been cut shorter, he still had recalcitrant waves in his brown locks.

A woman could dye her tresses. Ada Fox reminded Ben of Adele Schwartz, who managed Detroit University's most notorious fraternity house. In one year, the woman had brought the men all under control—save perhaps Greyson Luce. Mrs. Schwartz sported a reddish loose chignon, which may have been henna-tinted, and wore no spectacles. She'd quit shortly after an article was published about her success with the college students in Detroit. And in the one glimpse he'd had of Mrs. Schwartz at a fraternity social event he covered, she may be the woman now calling herself Ada Fox.

Another possibility had come to him. Was Mrs. Fox actually Adelaide Bishop, the wealthiest woman in America but also a notorious tightwad and a hermit? Rumors surfaced that she'd begun taking menial jobs in establishments in which she hoped to acquire a financial interest. Would the housekeeping manager, with her hair fluffed closely around her face, resemble the one picture he'd seen of Adelaide Bishop? He'd search the island library's archives to see if they possessed the copy of *Collier's* magazine that printed a picture of the recluse after the death of her second husband. He needed to refresh his memory.

He rubbed his chin—Mrs. Bishop's first marriage was to an executive from Battle Creek. Her second marriage was to another skinflint like herself. The third husband made a fortune in iron ore. She was connected everywhere there was big money, despite living like a pauper herself. Reportedly she'd shown up at several of the Forhams' society events, when Ben was there for an article—and keeping an eye on Anna. The miser sat on a number of boards and was rumored to have a keen mind for business. Ironically, Mrs. Bishop had been refused admission at several meetings across the country, when staff believed her to be a servant or, worse yet, a vagrant.

Could Ada Fox be Adele Schwartz and Adelaide Bishop? Perhaps she hoped to invest in the Grand Hotel. Maybe Banyon could send him up some information, or the island newspaper editor might have heard something. But that might raise the island journalist's suspicions about who Ben was. Unless he couched his concerns as exactly what they were—whether the woman wasn't quite as she seemed. But really, what business would that be of his if he was simply a guest at the Grand Hotel?

Ben rubbed his temple. This masquerade was doing strange things to him. Maybe this was all just wild imaginings. But he trusted his gut. And his journalist's instincts told him there was a connection.

Footfalls sounded loudly on the nearby stairs, followed by a rap on the door.

Ben shook out his shoulders and turned. "Come in."

Jack opened the door. He glanced at the bed, which Ben had made despite the struggle it had presented. He'd been so drowsy he'd reverted to his old habits.

"Whatcha do that for?" Jack pointed to the bed. "You're just gonna get back in it after breakfast. That's what the doc said."

"I feel better—except for the medicine he gave me."

"You want to eat with us, then? Dad and I are ready for breakfast."

"Ja, and I can smell bacon on your breath. Did you sample?"

He frowned. "Of course! And I told him Maude slept in, but she ain't in her room."

"She isn't?"

"Nah, she's pretending to be a maid at the Grand." He crossed his arms.

Ben forced his features into an expression of surprise. "Why do you think she's doing that?"

Jack's features scrunched together. "Don't know—I wondered if she was spying on you for some reason."

"Why would she do that?"

The boy shrugged. "I think she likes you. Besides—who can understand women?"

Ben laughed but brought the action to a quick halt when his ribs complained.

"Come on, there's some girl downstairs waiting to talk to Maude. She asked Bea what it was like to work here."

"Isn't Bea rather young to be working here?"

"Kinda, but her pa is gone and her ma is dead—like mine."

The boy's matter-of-fact words seared Ben's heart. Despite Jack's display of bravado, the child had to be hurting.

Ben stretched. "Ja. I forgot—I've been wanting to ask you to accompany me off the island sometime. Perhaps to St. Ignace?" Where the *Rechtsanwalt*, Mr. Hollingshead, her attorney, had his office.

"You'd take me?" The boy's chin began to quiver.

"Ja."

Two wiry arms wrapped around his torso before he could stop them. Ben stifled his groan of pain and allowed the boy to rest his head on his chest.

He pulled away and wiped his nose with his hand. "Thanks, Mr. König. When we going? What about this afternoon?"

"Maybe tomorrow. Or the next day, depending on how I feel."

"Okay. Come on—let's go tell Dad."

Bone weary, Maude arrived home as Winds of Mackinac guests, the women attired in tailored walking dresses and the men in day coats, exited the inn in pairs. At the end of the queue, a young mother and father pushed a pram down the sidewalk and toward the street.

Drawing in a deep breath, Maude approached the Taylor family. "Good day."

Dark circles ringed the young woman's eyes.

The husband offered a sheepish grin. "I hope our baby isn't disturbing the other guests."

Mrs. Taylor's curls bobbed as she bent over her son. "I think he has a tooth coming in."

"We're taking him on a private carriage ride around the island tonight before bedtime." Mr. Taylor's face reflected the satisfaction of being a good father.

"We're hoping the fresh air tires him out." The young mother leaned in toward Maude.

"I know that worked with Jack." She'd treated him like he was her own baby, she and Robert taking him for rides.

Mr. Taylor laughed. "If only we had Jack's energy!"

If only Maude did, too.

The family walked off, parents smiling at each other, obviously very much in love. What would it be to have someone look at her that way? Greyson hadn't.

A sudden shiver coursed through her, and Maude rubbed her muslin-covered arms. The lace at the bottom of the wide cuffs rippled in the breeze.

The porch was empty save for one very handsome man. Friedrich must have slipped outside while she was talking to the Taylors.

"You're looking lovely."

"Thank you." She felt a blush creep up her cheeks. "How are you feeling?"

"I'm fine. The doctor will check me again in a little while, and then I believe I'll be free to return to the Grand."

"Oh." She frowned.

"You're sad that I am well?"

"No." Maude nibbled on her lower lip.

He rose as she approached him and took her hands. "Might I hope that you prefer to have me nearby?"

His firm hands held hers, and he ran his thumb across her knuckles, stirring delight. She looked up into his eyes, seeing the same longing she felt. Birdsong rose from the garden as the scents of peonies, lilacs, and roses mingled aloft on the breeze.

His head tipped closer to hers.

The door opened.

Friedrich drew back, and Maude sucked in a breath.

"You've hired another maid?" Father peered at her.

Behind him, Gretchen cowered.

"Sorry, I forgot to tell you she was here," Friedrich murmured.

"Gretchen is a hard worker." Maude tried to keep the edge out of her voice.

Her father frowned. "And you know this how? She says she worked at the Grand."

Maude opened her mouth, but when Friedrich nudged her she closed it.

"Mr. Welling, this chambermaid is one of the best. The Grand Hotel's loss is your gain."

Father rubbed his jaw. "Come inside." Soon the three were seated in the office, with Gretchen waiting outside.

"Father, we've more visitors—hence more work. And if we want to keep our guests happy—"

"I'm not criticizing—I simply wonder where you've found them. The Grand has scooped up our best workers. Despite paying them less and terminating them before the season is over."

No islanders, save for Sadie and Maude were in the Grand's employ, but she dare not disclose this to Father lest he ask how she knew. Furthermore, the pay exceeded what Jane was earning at the inn, something Maude wished to rectify.

"Well," Maude wrung her hands, "I did hire this young woman away from the Grand."

The door swung in and Jack stomped into the room, lightly kicking the door closed behind him. "Al says to stop sending him your sob-story friends, Maude."

"I sent Gretchen to Uncle Al with money for her refreshments." She made a face at Jack, and he made one back at her.

"Yeah, well, he says stop sending people in off the streets." Jack blew a large bubble from his gum and popped it.

"She's not off the streets."

Father shook his head. "Your sister has a soft heart—like her mother."

The boy came around and wrapped his arms around Maude's neck.

"I love you, Muddie."

"Love you, too, silly boy."

Father opened his drawer and pulled out a medication packet and poured it in his water glass. "Maude, you do as you see fit with this young woman. Gretchen, is it?"

"Yes. We have a room for her upstairs." Maude rose and went to his side. "Thank you, Father."

He squeezed her hand. "It's a busy season, after that economic down-turn last year. We can use the help."

What help had she been? Instead of pitching in, she'd run off to prove herself.

Jack threw the door open. "Come on, Gretch, and I'll show you where you're gonna be stayin'."

Chapter Sixteen

ill I pass muster?" Ben began buttoning up his linen shirt.

"No mustering out on Mackinac Island, anymore," Dr. Cadotte joked. "Not since the military left. But you do pass my physical examination."

"I need to get back up to the Grand." He'd already been gone three days, and he had to monitor Edmunds and the progress he was making in his pursuit. Casey Randolph had already shown Ben the diamond he planned to offer his intended target—a lovely old-fashioned diamond in rose gold that had been his grandmother's during the family's better times, which Casey hoped to enjoy again once he'd married into wealth.

The door opened, and Peter Welling and his son peeked in. "I insist that you not take a bike nor walk back, Mr. König."

"Aw, Dad, I wanted to race him back to the hotel." Jack groaned. "You're gonna be all right, ain't ya?"

Scowling at his son, the man shook his finger. "Diction, young man, diction."

Dr. Cadotte secured his medical case. "Best if you take the carriage."

"Aw." The boy scrunched his nose up.

"Son, go ask the driver to bring it around."

Ben had never conversed with the aged driver, who usually sat in the Wellings' carriage house behind their inn. He was kept busy with providing transportation to the guests. Jack ran off, his footsteps clattering down the stairs.

Ben gathered his belongings, bid his adieus, and was soon inside the spacious coach. Light rain misted the island as the driver of the Wellings' personal carriage brought Ben back to the Grand. Dark clouds piled up, portending a downpour.

The driver directed the pair of bays to pull up by the central stairs to the hotel's main entrance. Ben got out as the rain increased in intensity. Quick-stepping, he ducked his head and mounted the entrance stairs two at a time.

The early summer deluge hammered the canvas overhang and dripped down to splash off each side, some onto Ben. The door swung outward.

"Welcome back." The doorman held the entrance door wide for him. "We heard of your heroics, Mr. König."

Just what he needed—calling attention to himself—a fraud. Hopefully word of his participation in the rescue hadn't spread through the hotel. He didn't need anyone looking too closely at him. Ben cringed as the door closed behind him.

"Excuse me? Don't I know you?" Someone tapped Ben's shoulder. He slowly turned to face one of the journalists from the *Lansing Tribune*.

Danny Williams's exuberant smile yanked a grin out of him in return. "Thought that might be you, Steffan. You sure clean up well!"

Morris, the clerk, raised his head and glanced in their direction.

Ben grasped Williams's elbow and angled him toward the exit to the porch. "Friedrich König is my pseudonym here."

Pulling his arm loose, Williams shrugged free. "Fine."

"Let's head to the porch."

"Should be fine as long as we don't get too close to the rails."

"What brings you here?" Ben asked.

"Holiday with my parents."

The two journalists passed through the wide, heavily glassed doors and onto the Grand's famous porch. Breezes carried up hints of the pine trees below. Beyond the lawn and trees, heavier rain fell into the straits. Rainfall pounded the porch roof, performing an ominous percussion prelude.

Ben nodded as several couples strolled by opposite them, arm in arm, one of them Marcus Edmunds, who quirked an eyebrow at him.

Ben leaned toward the other journalist. "So you've been here before, Dan?"

"I take it you're not a newspaperman on this gig, Ben. Am I right?"

"True. I'm a German aristocrat and American industrialist."

Williams threw back his dark head and laughed. "That's you, then—I've been hearing about the mystery gent up here. Keep an eye on me this week and I'll show you how these rich girls want to be treated."

"I thought you were finally getting married, Dan."

"I'm not dead yet, am I?"

"No, but after that stunt in the balloon, we all wondered."

"Yeah, well..." Williams gave a curt laugh. "I covered a story at the 1889 State Fair in Michigan, where they had the thing tethered, but some crooks made off with it."

"For the *Free Press*?"

"Yeah, so I'd wondered what it might be like."

"Probably not the best thing to do with the boss's daughter." Anna Forham had been willfully disobedient of her mother's request that she not go up in the balloon. Williams had paid the price, too.

"Nope. But I'm enjoying Lansing." He grinned. "And I met my fiancée."

They moved toward a bench, on which two young women perched against the porch's back wall, away from the possibility of rain.

Dan stretched out a hand to the first girl. "Nadine? I believe you grow lovelier each year."

"You're mistaken, sir." The brunette's Gibson girl hairstyle bobbed as she craned her neck back. "My name is Evelyn Stanton, of the New York Stantons."

The journalist grasped her hand and brought it to his lips. "I apologize, dear lady. You're far lovelier than the fair Nadine. Many pardons."

Ben held himself aloof, observing the little scene.

Marcus Edmunds strolled back by, the daughter of a wealthy investor on his arm. He winked at the young ladies, eliciting giggles. He and his lady strolled on.

Miss Stanton extended a slim hand toward her lithe blond friend. "And this is Gladys Matelski."

"Daniel Williams at your service, and this is..."

Ben clicked his heels together and gave a short bow. "Friedrich König."

Gladys waved toward two empty seats, one on either side of them. "Do join us, gentlemen."

Dan pulled out a chair for himself. Ben reluctantly sat down beside him. If only he could have followed Edmunds and listened in on his conversation. He needed that backup story for the paper.

"What brings you fellows to the island?" Another downpour hammering the roof almost drowned out Miss Stanton's words.

"Here to meet someone." Williams grinned broadly. "And I heard about the wealthiest young woman on Mackinac Island cavorting with a Detroit journalist. Wondered if he was after her money. Figured if it would make a good article."

Ben swallowed. He feared the lengthy porch might sink in and suck him down with it. He wiped at the sweat that had broken out on his brow, the fine linen handkerchief yet another reminder of the fraud that he was, the tiny embroidered crown mocking him by digging into a cut from his too-close shave. Moisture continued to billow in, seeping through his jacket, which he yearned to remove.

"You don't say?" He had to stop this young man from pursuing the story further.

"And I heard a better rumor." Dan leaned in, his elbows pressed against the table, his jacket straining across his back.

"What's that?" Gladys cocked her head sideways.

"That the skinflint Adelaide Bishop is here and intends to buy an inn." Dan laughed. "My money's on the Winds of Mackinac. It's an island landmark."

"Adelaide Bishop!" The blond leaned forward. "The wealthiest woman in America and she's here on the island?"

"That's what I heard, and I intend to find out." Danny's handsome face split in a grin. "Just look for the lady reusing her tea bags all day and dressed in the shabbiest clothes. I heard she was denied admittance to the last railroad shareholders meeting because the guards believed her to be the washerwoman."

Over the next hour, the rain ebbing and flowing in fits, Dan flirted and cajoled the young women until they were fawning over him. Ben recollected a time when his uncle would do the same. Right in front of his wife and usually at one of his parents' orchestral events. Had Uncle Friedrich been trying to embarrass them?

The blond leaned closer to the table, her elaborate chain necklace swinging against her lace-covered bodice as she met Ben's gaze. "What do you think about Mrs. Bishop being here?"

"I would wonder why she was here. A woman like her doesn't do anything without a purpose, ja?"

Her friend elbowed her. "Wouldn't you like to know what her secrets are?"

Friedrich shook his head. "It is no secret when one lives like a pauper, has no children to tend to, and is a miser, then. . ."

The two shrank back. He'd been too severe in his assessment of the woman. He raised his hands. "I apologize—but I feel sorry for a woman whose only joy in life seems to be profiting from the misery of others." Who might be attempting to profit from the Wellings' situation.

"Well said, Stef. . .er, Mr. König." Dan scooted his chair away from the table. "Excuse us, ladies, but we're going to resume our walk."

Ben likewise rose and bowed to the two demoiselles. Then he and Dan resumed their stroll. The cool mist seemed to bank and roll onto the porch, chilling Ben.

Ben had to help the Wellings keep their inn. Bishop was known for swooping in like a bird of prey and devouring assets that were in trouble.

Maude's family must be in trouble.

Face washed and powdered, Maude descended the stairs to the inn's lobby just as Uncle Robert opened the front door. He tucked his umbrella into the stand and removed his coat, hanging it on the oak hall rack.

Where was Bea? She was supposed to be monitoring the front parlor and entryway. She could have assisted him.

Maude moved toward him, expecting a hug. "Uncle Robert, I'm so glad you're looking so well today—what a fright yesterday must have been."

When she reached him, however, he didn't even kiss her cheek. His wavy hair curled around his white collar, moisture making it appear even darker than usual.

"Maude." His clipped tone and unsmiling face chilled her.

She took a step back.

"I've come to discuss some things with your father."

"Like why you aren't staying with us?" She crossed her arms.

"It's complicated."

"But Winds of Mackinac has been your home for the past ten years." Since Grandmother died.

"Let's take this conversation into the office."

Maude stepped around him and opened the door to the office, Father's stale cigar smoke greeting them. She took a seat, and Robert sat in the chair adjacent. "Father is resting."

He shoved a hand back through his thick hair. "I need to speak with him."

"Then you'll be waiting quite awhile because I'm not waking him up."

Raising his hands in surrender, he shook his head. "You're almost as stubborn as he is."

"Probably more so."

He laughed.

"Since you're here, I wondered about the Canary."

His bright hazel eyes widened, and he stood and paced to the window. "What about it?"

"We've always rented it out in summer, before. . ." Before Mother died.

He whirled around, his eyes hard. "Yes, I've allowed your mother to rent my house out, but make no mistake—it is *my* home to decide what I wish for it."

Maude swallowed hard. She'd just been put in her place. It had been Grandmother's home and one the Wellings had lived in during the winter months when there were no guests.

The office door opened and Bea, attired in a frilly blue gingham dress, entered. "Is it okay for me to come in now?"

Robert's eyes widened. "Not now, Beatrice. Wait for me on the porch."

"Why aren't you in your uniform?" Maude frowned at the girl. "And who is watching the front parlor and desk?"

"I don't work here anymore." Bea rocked back. "You've got that new girl now."

Maude stared at the girl slack-jawed.

"She thinks she was going to be let go—sent me a message at the Grand." Robert clasped his hands together.

"She isn't dismissed—I've simply hired another girl." Why was Bea turning to Robert for help? "For now, Bea, please attend to your duties."

Bea bobbed a curtsy. "Yes, Miss Maude."

Robert cleared his throat. "Before I forget, I need to tell you that Sadie asked if you could work second shift at the Grand tomorrow."

"What?" Was her best friend seeing Robert? Maude's face heated at the thought.

"Sadie has permission to take tomorrow off. But she swapped with the second-shift parlor maid."

Maude swallowed hard. "And Mrs. Fox has said what?"

"As long as you are agreeable, you'd need to stay on in the parlor area until after dinner."

That long? How would she cope?

"I wish you girls would stop this nonsense."

"Sadie has sisters to support."

Robert opened his mouth but then clamped it shut.

"And if I could get Father to see reason. . ."

"That's one reason I'm here." He scratched his chin, now bare but normally covered with a thick black beard streaked with premature silver. "Your father has had his head in the sand ever since my sister died."

She sighed. "Tell me about it! He's refused to allow me to run the inn."

"So that's why you're at the Grand?"

"I'm trying to prove to him that I don't need Greyson beside me to run the inn. Cadotte women have run businesses on this island for decades." Granted, Father had done most of the inn's management for Mother.

Robert huffed out a breath. "Maude, what has your father said to you about the will?"

"Nothing."

"And that's the problem. He refuses to sit down with me and the attorney in St. Ignace to address specifics."

Maude frowned. "I thought he had at least read it."

"Oh, he read it all right—but he doesn't believe what it says." Robert shifted side to side in his oxford tie-ups.

"Why not?"

"Well, if you had worked as hard as your father has, running these island businesses, would you accept that upon your wife's death you owned none of them?"

The wind seemed to have been sucked out of her lungs and off to the Mackinac straits.

Chapter Seventeen

Cumulous clouds dotted the robin's-egg-blue-colored skies Wednesday morning, and the previous day's rain had vanished. The changeable June weather perfectly suited Ben as he set off to the docks with Jack.

They boarded the boat bound to the Upper Peninsula with only a handful of islanders.

"I'm doing my shopping in St. Ignace, Mr. Christy," a red-haired woman told the bearded workman seated beside her. "What brings you to the mainland?"

"I'm going to see my sister. She runs a bakery over here." The man tugged his slouch cap lower. "And I could use a little break from all that work at the Grand and at my wife's tea shop."

Jack needed a break from the island, too, and Ben was happy to provide it, especially since he also needed to make the trip.

Soon the schooner crossed into the north side of the straits, skimming with the breeze, through the waves. The boat carried Ben to the Wellings' attorney and Jack away from the island. Jack leaned out as far as he could from the side of the boat.

"Come over here by me, Jack." Ben patted the bench. This boy could end up being his brother-in-law one day, if God blessed him with Maude as his wife. How, though, unless he got his promotion and raise? Today would be only a slight detour on his route to getting a stellar story for the paper.

Scrunching his face, the boy returned to his spot. "What's it like living in Detroit?"

Ben shrugged. "Busy place—lots of traffic, lots of exciting things going on." Social events he covered as a journalist. He dragged his hand across his jaw.

"Me and Dad are gonna move downstate, soon as we can sell the inn."

Ben raised his eyebrows. "So your family owns the inn?"

"Of course we do." The boy sighed. "Well, Grandma owned the inn and Great-grandma Cadotte before her."

"Cadotte?"

"Yeah."

Maude was a Cadotte. Williams's words sluiced through his mind—a journalist chasing the Cadotte heiress.

Jack grinned. "But the inn is Dad's now."

Or was it?

"And we need money for my training for the Olympics."

"But I think your sister wishes to stay, ja?" Could she care enough for him to leave the island behind?

The boy picked up a flyer for a musical show in St. Ignace and wadded it into a ball. "Dad says she's free to do what she wants."

"But what if she wants to run the inn?"

"Greyson married up, so that ain't happenin'." Jack crossed his arms over his thin chest. "Dad has someone interested in buying."

"Do you know her name?"

Jack's eyes dimmed. "Nah."

This smelled like Adelaide Bishop's tactics.

"Hey, I want to run after we get there."

"I thought you might want to." Good thing, because Ben planned to visit with Mr. Hollingshead. He had to find out what he could do to protect Maude and her family.

♥

Gilded letters on the black door announced "STEVEN HOLLINGSHEAD, ESQUIRE." Ben glanced through the glass. A young woman sat with a child on the floor. He went inside and stepped onto the wide-planked, unfinished floor, which creaked as it bore his weight. The heavily pregnant mother stood and wiped her hands on her wrinkled gray skirt.

"Can I help you?" She moved toward a small oak desk angled in the front corner of the rectangular office.

"I'm here from the island to speak with Mr. Hollingshead about the Wellings."

A tousle-haired man emerged from an office to the left, hastily tying his floppy bow tie. "I was wondering when someone would finally come."

Finally?

The toddler jumped up from the floor and threw his arms around the man's pant legs. "Go to Mommy now, Johnny."

The young woman pried the child's fingers loose and picked him up. "Almost time for your nap."

"Take him upstairs, dear."

She shuffled down the dark narrow hall, and in a moment footsteps ascended a back stairway.

"This is normally a paperwork day." The attorney shrugged. "But my secretary quit, and my wife has taken over her duties."

One would never see this arrangement in Detroit. "Friedrich König."

Hollingshead shook Ben's hand firmly. "So you represent the Wellings?"

Do I, Lord? Maybe not like this man meant, but when Ben opened his mouth, "Ja" came out.

"I'd given up on Mr. Welling coming to see me."

When Ben said nothing, the man waved him forward.

"Well, come on in, then, and let's go over the specifics." He went to a tall oak cabinet nearby and pulled out a large folder. *Jacqueline Cadotte Swaine and Heirs*, was written on the front. "I got the letter, by the way."

"We mailed it from the island." Jack had. Didn't that count?

"Mr. Welling must realize that, despite his personal feelings, we're dealing with a binding legal document, does he not?"

Ben shrugged.

"Well, I guess he intends to object or he'd not have sent you." The man sighed and sat down in his cane-backed chair and pushed forward to his desk. "I'd hoped he was simply venting and didn't plan to contest the will."

Hollingshead pointed to a seat across from the desk. Ben sat, the five journalistic *W*s always in his mind. "What would you do in his situation?"

Hollingshead's light eyes widened. "If my wife knew of these contingencies, I'd be furious that she didn't inform me when her mother died and she'd inherited."

"Ja." Ben swallowed. "Why do you suppose Mrs. Welling didn't share the information?"

The lawyer laughed. "My wife tells me things all the time, and I don't listen to her if I'm distracted by business—daily."

"So maybe Mrs. Welling did talk with him, and he's not remembering."

Hadn't Mother told Großmutter and Großvater that their son, her brother and the heir to the title, would run her off the land as soon as they were laid to rest? And both scoffed.

The attorney shrugged.

"Who else knows about the provisions?"

"Your client's brother-in-law, Robert Swaine, of course. He's tried to set up several sessions for me to meet with Peter, but he was unwilling to come over from the island."

"At least he sent the letter. . . ."

"Yes, in which he also threatened me if I showed up at his inn uninvited!" The attorney barked out a laugh. "If I were his attorney, I'd have advised him the same thing."

Ben forced a chuckle.

Hollingshead flipped through a file atop his desk.

"Welling has been overseeing half the businesses for about ten years, maybe longer." Hollingshead whistled. "I'd be mad, too."

Perhaps he could answer his journalistic question of *where* by offering a statement that the attorney could confirm or deny. "And all are on Mackinac Island."

"Exactly. So he couldn't abandon them until this transition had taken place. But Welling won't even respond to Robert's requests. At least you're here now. Why don't we go over the main points again, and I'll explain why I think your client won't win if he takes us to court."

"Ja, very good."

"And may I remind you, the first point is that the judge on this circuit drew up this will and codicil for Mrs. Cadotte fifteen years ago. Thus, he's unlikely to overturn his own handiwork."

An hour later, Ben's mind was reeling. All of the properties Mr. Welling oversaw had belonged to his mother-in-law. Since his wife preceded him in death, per the codicil, Peter Welling didn't inherit anything his wife received from her mother's estate. All of a sudden it was like being back in Germany—his uncle having been tasked to care for his mother and her family. Then they were evicted from the property almost as soon as Grandmother was buried, and their belongings, what few his uncle allowed them to keep, were unceremoniously dumped on the ground in front of their home on the estate. Mother screaming and crying. Father begging. Sister despondent. And Ben in shock.

He wouldn't allow this to happen to the woman he was falling in love with. Ben could admit it now. Leaving the island without her would be like giving up breathing.

"What will happen to Miss Welling?"

The young attorney's eyes narrowed. "Since she is of age, I'm unable to discuss her situation with you, of course."

The man stood, and Ben realized he was being dismissed. He rose.

"Might I have your card?" The lawyer slid the file into his drawer and turned the lock then pocketed the key. "I'll contact Miss Welling to obtain permission to speak with you."

He had a card all right. It said "Ben Steffan, Reporter," not "Friedrich König, Faux Attorney, Fake Industrialist, and Generally Nosy Person." He patted his pockets. "Afraid I don't have one with me."

The man shoved a paper pad and pencil toward him, atop the desk. "Give me your information, then, so I have it on file."

Fraud. Had he just committed an illegal act? No doubt he had. He scribbled his full name so that it was almost indecipherable.

A child's wail interrupted the silence. "You can let yourself out, Mr. König. I think my wife needs help."

Ben departed, stepping onto the plank sidewalk. All along Main Street, bustling new shops touted their wares. Tobacconist, butcher, druggist, clothier, and a newspaper office. He was tempted to duck into the newspaper office, but he needed to find Jack. He checked his pocket watch. They were to have met at the Timber Pines.

Seagulls ducked and bobbed, some squawking over a piece of roll a lumberjack had dropped near the bakery. The tempting smell of sugar cookies almost drew Ben into Jo's Bakery, but he needed to fetch Jack.

When he arrived at the cedar-sided barnlike building, Jack was seated at a table near the windows. He waved. "Come on—they've got the best whitefish here. I already told the lady to bring us some."

"How was your run?" Ben slid into his seat.

"Well, I went around Robin Hood's barn and was all the better for it."

Ben smiled at the quaint expression. "So all around, then? But you didn't get lost?"

"Found some kids my own age, and we had a few races." Jack wadded his faded cotton napkin into a ball and tossed it into the air, leaning back in his chair so that it opened and landed on his lap.

Ben chuckled at the boy's antics and picked up his own napkin. "And?"

"Well, I licked 'em all, so that wasn't much of a challenge."

The coffee hostess, a rail-thin woman, poured Ben a cup of coffee.

"Me, too!" Jack pointed to a spot in front of him.

"What does your dad say?" The waitress pursed her lips.

Ben folded and tucked his napkin so that it formed a sailor's hat.

The woman raised an eyebrow. He looked up, realizing the woman meant he, Ben, might be the boy's father.

Before he could correct the woman, Jack leaned back in his chair and announced, "He ain't my dad."

The woman shook her head but poured the boy a mugful.

He and Ben reached for the creamer at the same time. "You drink coffee at home?"

"Yeah, Maude started drinking it about my age to help with her breathing. So I get to drink it, too."

"What do you mean for her breathing?"

"The doc said the coffee might help with some of her breathing spells. That's why she can't come with us to the farm." The boy grabbed the sugar tongs and dropped ten sugar cubes into his coffee.

"Maude won't go with you?"

"Nah, she don't do so good around farms—'specially if there's any hay growing."

Ben sipped his coffee. *Strong.*

How could her father be so cold? "What will she do?"

"Don't know." He rubbed his eyes. "But I'm gonna miss her."

Did the boy really not know about his family's tenuous situation? Did Peter Welling even realize that he couldn't sell the inn? That because of the entailment, the codicil on the will, Robert Swaine stood to inherit all. In fact, at this point in time, Robert controlled the entire Cadotte fortune.

"Jack, how does your father get along with your uncle Robert?"

The boy scowled. "They used to be great pals. Uncle Robert used to live with us. Since Mom died, though. . ." When Jack's eyes began to fill with tears, Ben ceased his questions.

A different waitress stopped. "Everything all right here?"

Ben handed the boy his handkerchief. "He lost his mother last year."

The round-faced woman squinted at Jack. "Aren't you Robert Swaine's nephew? Saw you in here once with him."

Jack blew his nose and nodded.

The waitress harrumphed. "I'd be crying, too, if I was you."

The child looked up at her, his head cocked.

"Did he already put you out of your home, boy? I can't imagine he'd be that hard-hearted, but you just don't know with some men."

Ben shot her a look that would have silenced the toughest Chicago thug, but she just shrugged at him. She departed and Jack frowned at Ben.

"Why did that lady say that stuff, Friedrich?"

"A busybody prattling on. Probably *verrückt*."

Jack cupped a hand around the side of his mouth and whispered, "Ya mean crackers?"

"Ja. Pay her no mind, Jack." If only he could do the same.

Stifling a yawn, Maude finished dusting and wiping every surface in the Ladies' Parlor. After extinguishing the lights, she crumpled into the low overstuffed chair inside the private sitting room. Here the ladies sat and chatted about their children and grandchildren and compared vacation locales. With this parlor housing the best piano besides the ballroom, some ladies also kept up their skills by entertaining the others.

She should never have agreed to stay and take this double shift. Maude pressed her head back against the velvet cushion of the chair and sat in near darkness, with only the light from beneath the doors lending its glow. *God, give me the strength to get home tonight.* Although Father had assured her he was fine today, his skin had an ashen quality to it. She wanted to get home and check on him before he went to bed. And she'd have some explaining to do as to where she was. She needed to resign. Her family needed her.

The door to the room creaked open. A slit of light pierced the darkness from the hallway and then widened to a path of pale gold on the crimson carpet. She cringed. Maybe she shouldn't have shut the parlor down so early. But it was after nine o'clock.

One charcoal pants leg was followed by another as a tall man eased into the darkened room. Sulphuric scents bit at her nose as he lit a match and one by one ignited the tapers in the candelabra. She stiffened as the flare of fire lit his handsome features. *Friedrich.* Here in the dark corner, could he see her? What was he doing in the women's parlor, in secret? Mesmerized, she watched him, not wanting to startle him. Should she speak?

With only the pool of light to guide him, he slowly moved toward the piano, setting the candelabra atop it. He lit another short candle set in an old-fashioned brass holder and placed it in the receptacle on the side of the keyboard. He pulled the padded bench back from the piano and lifted the cover from the keys.

Was the man going to bang out one of the silly songs the men enjoyed in their smoking room? If she heard one more rendition about Casey dancing with his strawberry blond, she'd scream and reveal her location. She leaned forward. She'd slip from the room once he began playing. He gently pressed on several of the keys. It was the beginning of a piece she knew well—one of Mother's favorites. Maude relaxed back into the seat, holding her breath.

Friedrich's fingers seemed to barely brush the keys, yet soon *Moonlight Sonata* softly, gently, filled the room. Not a popular ditty.

Instead, the soft notes sent chills up her spine. Maude straightened, as she always had when her mother played it for her. His fingers caressed and lifted the song with skill. With the music's decrescendo, tears covered her cheeks.

Friedrich's rendition of the piece then turned, the staccato notes climbing an uphill celebratory sequence. She rubbed her tingling arms.

As though sensing her presence, he stopped. *"Wer ist da?"*

"It's Maude...." She raised her fingers to her mouth.

He was the finest pianist she'd ever heard—and the island had been blessed to have virtuosos perform at their music house. She began to cough.

"Are you all right?"

"Yes..." She raised her handkerchief to her mouth.

Confident steps brought him to her side. He knelt on the floor beside her and took her hand. "What are you doing here so late, my *liebchen?*"

Hope filled her. "Am I your sweetheart?" Longing lit in her heart, and she pushed a lock of hair from his forehead.

His warm, masculine hand brushed against her hands and brought her fingers to his lips. One by one, he pressed a kiss to each finger of each hand. The warmth and the tenderness sent jolts of pleasure through her. Then he turned her hands over and gently kissed her wrists, the warmth sending heat through her blood. Her legs began to tremble beneath her petticoats. Friedrich set her hands in her lap and covered them with his own. He leaned in and pressed his forehead against hers. He smelled of spice and clean linen, intoxicating. Faint peppermint was on his breath as he leaned in closer yet. She leaned forward to meet him. His lips met hers, warm, firm, and inviting, and felt like nothing she'd ever experienced before. She wanted it to never end. This felt so right. She tugged her hands free and wrapped them around his neck grazing the tendrils of hair that covered his collar, drawing him closer, but he placed his hands against the armrest and held himself back from her.

"Maude, I have something I must tell you."

She wanted another of those amazing kisses. "Yes?" Her voice came out husky and didn't sound at all like herself.

"I love you."

He loved her.

"And I must tell you some other things, too, my darling."

The door to the hallway opened, framing Ada Fox. "My, my, isn't this cozy?"

Chapter Eighteen

*B*en awoke with dead certainty. He was in love with Maude Welling, but he'd just gotten her dismissed from her job. And sometime in the night, he'd worked out in his dreams that Ada Fox was Adelaide Bishop. Which meant she may be the one working with Robert Swaine to take the inn from Maude's family.

After breakfast, he made his way to the housekeeping manager's office and rapped on her door.

"Who is it?" Mrs. Fox's tone was brittle.

Instead of answering, he opened the door and allowed himself in. Ignoring her imperious gaze over the top of her teacup, he closed the door behind him then settled into the chair opposite her desk.

"I know who you are, Mrs. Bishop."

She set the cup into its saucer with a clink. "Mr. Steffan, you have ferreted me out."

"What brings you here to the island?"

"As you can see, I'm managing the staff at the Grand. And doing quite well, if I don't say so myself." She chuckled with satisfaction.

"Agreed." He quirked an eyebrow at her.

The lines between her brows relaxed as she poured herself another cup of fragrant tea from the teapot nestled between a long yellow ledger and a small tray of muffins. "Tea?"

"Yes, please."

"No, 'ja, danke,' then?" She laughed then opened her desk drawer and retrieved a matching cup and saucer, marked with the Grand Hotel insignia.

Ben tugged on his tie. "German is my native tongue, but, ja, I normally only slip into it when I'm not thinking." Or stressed, or in his sleep.

"Cream and sugar with your tea?" Adelaide Bishop acted as though she'd invited him for this express purpose.

"Two sugars, please."

She added two cubes of sugar to the cup, stirred it with a silver teaspoon, and passed it to him. Not even one crumb from the pastries marred the surface of her desk.

"Danke."

"You are most welcome." She raised her teacup to her lips and peered at him over the rim. "Have one of those poppy seed muffins you're eyeing, Mr. Steffan."

He shook his head, not wanting to lose his focus. "I do wish to apologize for kissing Miss Welling." He wasn't sorry. "Well, for kissing her here while she was at work."

Her dark eyebrows rose behind her glasses. "So you've had contact with her outside of the Grand?"

He gritted his teeth.

"Tut-tut. Now what would your editor say? Mr. Banyon isn't a very forgiving man. Thought he'd have me drawn and quartered when I made a bid to buy the newspaper."

Ben refused to be goaded. America's wealthiest woman rose, looked at the watch on her chatelaine, and turned toward the window. "Why don't we get right to the point?"

"Agreed." Ben set his cup back in its saucer and slid it onto the corner of the desk. "Stay out of my way, and I'll stay out of yours. *Verstanden?*"

He'd not meant the words to come out so harsh, but if she got in his way, he may lose his story and his promotion.

She nodded, as though approving his tactics. "I understand perfectly. I'll assume you're not here for an article about me or else you'd have been pestering me and the staff with questions, instead of dogging those horrid young men and simpering young women."

"True." And in his heart, for some unfathomable reason, he was glad Banyon didn't know Adelaide Bishop was managing housekeeping at the Grand. "I have another target."

"An islander."

"Perhaps."

"You might be interested to know Greyson Luce was one of the young men under my care at the University of Detroit." She drew in a deep breath. "And I'm afraid I did Miss Welling a great disservice."

He frowned. "How so?"

"Can you believe it of me, the great manipulator of industrial boards, that I was naive? And at my age, no less." She removed her spectacles. The eccentric woman probably didn't need them. How old was she really?

"Not from everything I've heard, but. . ." He splayed his hands and shrugged. "Anything can happen, right?"

"I'll be paying a visit to Peter Welling today."

"Please, Mrs. Bishop, you mustn't say anything about Maude and me—it would upset him."

"Are you more concerned about Maude or yourself?" She clasped her teacup in both hands, rocked it gently, and then looked down—almost as though reading tea leaves.

"I've asked permission to court her." He set his cup into its saucer. Of course, Peter Welling hadn't said Ben could court her—he said Maude could benefit from a companion.

"As yourself or as this König person?"

His shoulders slumped, and he exhaled loudly. "If I can get a scoop on Greyson Luce and Anna Forham Luce, I have a shot at a promotion. I don't think my other stories are going to stir enough interest—they aren't scandalous enough."

"Well, I think we can both benefit from me sharing what I know about the matter." She inclined her head.

"I'm listening."

❤

Maude didn't awaken until after eleven. Thank goodness, Mrs. Fox insisted she take the day off. Or was it to be a permanent thing, as in fired? She cringed at the humiliation she'd suffer if Father discovered she'd failed. Bea came in and pulled back the drapes and opened the shades so that bright sunlight streamed into Maude's eyes.

"Get up, sleepyhead."

Maude stretched, unleashing a string of muscle pains from head to toe. "Oh." She relaxed her body back into the feather bed, like a marionette suddenly released from performing. But whose tune had she been dancing to? Not God's. *Lord, forgive me.*

"Come on and I'll help you." Bea sighed as she began to pull back the coverlet.

"No, I'll be all right."

"Suit yourself, but that good-looking Mr. König is downstairs waiting for you."

Maude tossed off the rest of her bedclothes and hopped from the bed.

Bea bobbed up and down on the balls of her feet. "Thought that might put some rise in your shine!"

She had so much child in her, still. She didn't belong here working away what was left of her youth. What could be done?

"And guess what?"

Maude pulled off her nightgown then moved to her armoire. "What?"

"Your father's got a visitor, too."

Searching for all her undergarments, Maude inhaled the scent of dried lavender that lay beneath the drawer liners. "Oh?"

"A lady."

Maude swiveled around to look at her. The girl's eyes sparkled in merriment. "Are you going to tell me who?"

"Old friend." Bea scratched beneath her cap.

Those pins itched terribly—how well Maude knew. "Come here. Let me help you."

She plucked a half-dozen pins from strategic places on Bea's scalp. "You've jabbed them in too tight, Bea."

The girl patted her head and accepted the hairpins from Maude. "Thanks."

"Any time."

Maude returned to her quest to gather all the items needed for her ensemble. Stockings, corset, petticoats. Maybe she did need assistance if she was to get ready quickly.

"What's the woman's name?"

"Mrs. Wolf?"

"Wolf? Wonder who that is. Bea, I hate to ask, but, yes, I do need help."

Maude gazed at the lovely pink vase of pink and raspberry peonies that Jane had placed on the bed table the previous night. They were the most perfect specimens that had ever grown in Mother's garden. And Friedrich was the most perfect specimen of man she'd ever met. And his kiss. She pressed two fingertips to her lips, remembering the response he'd stirred in her. Was God moving her in another direction? But to Detroit? She wanted to cough just thinking about the stale air she'd be forced to breathe there. But if they lived in a grand home out in the country and didn't farm. Then maybe.

Bea helped her into her undergarments and pulled the laces on the corset gently tight. Thank goodness, she knew to not constrict Maude's lungs overmuch.

"Oh, Fox, not Wolf."

Maude stiffened.

"Ada Fox?" Oh, no. What did she intend to tell her father? Maude jerked upright as Bea pulled in the last section of the corset.

"Sucking in your breath to get a smaller waist?"

Maude exhaled. "No. Please loosen it."

"Sure."

With a rushed toilette, Maude would be able to head downstairs, before the clock struck again. "I'll wear the navy gabardine with the dropped waist." Perhaps the demure day dress would be best—especially if Mrs. Fox was there to dismiss her or expose her secret.

"That's a plain outfit."

What if Friedrich were coming to ask for her hand in marriage? He had kissed her and embraced her—and they'd been seen. No—a rich man from the city, a cultured man like him, he probably kissed many girls. But he said he loved her. Did he tell them all that? Greyson's betrayal rose up like a hissing serpent, taunting her. She went to her jewelry case, atop her chest of drawers, and opened it. She found the bracelet Greyson had given her at Christmas. Wearing it would remind her to guard her heart.

"Hurry, miss, they're waiting for you." Bea sighed loudly.

Maude fiddled with the clasp, finally turning to the younger girl for assistance.

"There you go."

"Thank you." She pretended to tweak the girl's nose as she passed her and headed into the hall and downstairs.

At the landing, the sweet sound of piano notes carried down the hallway, reminding Maude of the days before Mother had died. The music ceased as the song ended. A man's deep laugh accompanied her father's and a woman's low chuckle.

Was Ada Fox truly his friend? But if so, why hadn't she come to visit earlier? It had been far too long since Father had welcomed friends to the inn. What would Mrs. Fox say? And Friedrich? Her heart hammered against her new Coronet corset, which didn't seem as flexible as the advertisements touted.

Hesitating in the hallway, Maude heard Mrs. Fox. "Peter, doesn't this remind you of the old days?"

Pressing a hand to her pleated bodice, Maude strained to hear her father's response.

"Oh, Ada, it surely recalls those jolly days in my parents' parlor." Warmth coated Father's words.

Entering the room, she found her father and Ada seated together. And at the piano—Friedrich König.

Maude almost didn't recognize her supervisor. Dressed in a pale yellow skirt and blouse, the woman appeared thin and delicate—her hair upswept into a fluffy chignon. She looked far younger than Maude thought her. The silver-rimmed glasses that either perched on her nose or hung from a chain around her neck were noticeably absent. A heavy gold locket dangled on her Alençon lace–covered bodice.

Friedrich rose from the bench, and bowed. "Miss Welling."

Father gestured toward her supervisor. "This is my old neighbor, Ada."

"How good to have you in our home, ma'am." At least for Father.

Maude moved toward Friedrich, sensing his discomfort and feeling her own escalate rapidly as Mrs. Fox cast her a quick glance. Of warning?

He drew her hand to his lips and kissed it gently. Comfort surged through her. Suddenly it seemed as though she had an ally. And while Greyson had been her friend through thick and thin, this type of succor was qualitatively different—like comparing their inn to the Grand Hotel. Lovely, sturdy, and long-lasting—versus new and larger than her dreams could have imagined. But the jangling bracelet taunted her.

"Sit down, Maude." Friedrich slid over on the piano bench and gestured for Maude to join him. She hesitated. What would Mrs. Fox think? Or Father?

When Friedrich flashed a toothy grin, she pulled in her skirts and sat beside him, his warm shoulder pressed against her own. If she moved back, she'd fall off the edge, and he had nowhere left to move. Looking up into the man's eyes, she could see the flecks of gold in his blue-gray eyes, and her mouth went dry. He was so close. Her lips warmed as though expecting him to lean closer and... *Stop it right now!*

Mrs. Fox cleared her throat. "Mr. König, would you please play Stephen Foster's 'My Old Kentucky Home'? It's one of Peter's favorites."

"Oh, yes, Ada—my mother loved that song." Father sounded more excited than he had in a long time. "Do you remember the swing we had on the old oak tree?"

"Right outside the window of your mother's parlor. Yes, indeed, and we could both fit on it then." Mrs. Fox laughed. "Like your daughter and Mr. König are sitting now."

Maude's cheeks heated at the thought of Father having sat so intimately with Mrs. Fox. What else didn't she know about the woman?

"Are you ready?" Friedrich glanced down at the music and placed his hands over the keys.

But while she had to periodically glance at the sheet music, Friedrich did so only when she turned the page, smiling gently at her and then continuing on, playing the tune from memory.

They spent a good hour or more, with the wealthy industrialist playing requested songs without music, when they didn't have it. But when he was complimented, he dismissed each comment, shrugging as though his abilities were nothing.

"Let me excuse myself. I should be going." Friedrich's gaze accused her, but of what, Maude didn't know.

She slid to the side of the bench and then stood, pulling the wrinkles from her skirt.

"Good to visit with you Mr. Welling. Mrs. Fox." Friedrich bowed curtly. He was obviously uncomfortable, but Maude didn't understand why.

Father came to them and clapped a hand on Friedrich's shoulder. "Nonsense, König, stick around! Stay for lunch."

"Nein, I must be going." The wealthy bachelor's face contorted as though he'd asked for plum pudding but had been offered pickled herring instead.

Ben's nerves were frayed like jammed paper that had gotten stuck in one of the printing presses, shutting the entire operation down until it was removed and discarded. He didn't trust Adelaide to keep up her end of the bargain. Would she reveal his identity? Or that Maude was her employee? Would she disclose that he and Maude were locked in a passionate kiss the night before? By the way a twitch had started near her left eye, Mrs. Bishop might be as distressed as he was.

He hoped Ada Fox, or Adelaide Bishop, wanted his silence enough that she'd keep their secrets. But watching her with Mr. Welling, he was reminded of a black widow. Was this sweetly feminine front she conveyed the method by which she'd snared her three previous husbands? Had she swooped in on her first husband and then the next two and relieved them of their assets when they died?

The eccentric woman, Adelaide Bishop, had been written about in numerous newspaper accounts, but every report varied, and so the compilation made no sense. A good journalist wanted truth and confirmation, of which there was none for Adelaide Bishop's memoirs. He'd sit, he'd watch, and he'd put up with his roiling stomach if it meant he could help Maude. On the other hand, Mrs. Bishop had nothing to gain since the man hadn't inherited his wife's estate.

Ben tried to relax, but with Maude pressed close to his side, her rose-and-lilac perfume delicate and lovely, his efforts failed. Under the gaslights, gold and copper hues shimmered in her gently waving hair. Tendrils had worked loose all around her face, giving her an angelic look of innocence. This close, her pink lips beckoned him closer.

Maude leaned her head back. "Please don't go yet."

He drew in a deep breath full of her floral essence. Lost, hopeless—he had nothing to offer her. "Ja."

"You don't have to continue to entertain us, Mr. König." Maude's leg bumped against Ben's, sending a sensation of pleasure through him. Her limb then moved away far too quickly for his liking. He shouldn't be thinking these thoughts. Soon he'd be back at his desk or on the streets of Detroit, chasing stories. He should go. But he couldn't seem to get up.

Her father took his seat again. "With any luck, we'll be seeing more of you, Ada, now that I know you're here." Mr. Welling's voice held the same hope Ben felt in his heart.

"We need to invest time and renew our old friendship." Mrs. Bishop certainly knew about investing with largesse—she'd gotten in on the railroads and transportation north to the very hotel at which she now worked.

Maude's father laughed. "You make it sound like a banking transaction, Ada."

When she cringed, Mr. Welling covered Adelaide's hand with his.

"Maude and Friedrich, come, you two—sit over here and relax." Mr. Welling pointed to the chaise lounge across from them.

Ben stifled a grin of satisfaction. Her father called him by his first name.

Progress. Maude eased from the bench, and Ben rose, following her to the chaise.

"My husband Jonathan so enjoyed to play. But he died last year—apoplexy." Mrs. Bishop raised a handkerchief to her eyes and dabbed.

"How tragic." Maude's wide eyes reflected genuine concern.

"Where had you settled, Ada?"

"Oh. . ."

Someone rapped at the door.

Welling rose and went to the door. The scent of baked ham wafted in from the kitchen, tempting Ben to take up the offer of lunch.

Beatrice bobbed a curtsy. "Excuse me. A boy from the Grand sent a note for you."

"Did you give him a tip from the jar?"

"No. He's waiting for a reply."

"All right." He turned to face his guests. "Excuse me, while I handle this."

Eyebrows drawn together in consternation, Welling departed.

Mrs. Bishop offered Ben a tight smile. "We lived in Lansing and later in Detroit—where you live, I believe."

"Detroit? Ja." Was she baiting him?

"I worked at a university fraternity house."

Maude sat straighter. "My former fiancé lived in one of those."

"Yes, Greyson was one of the young men who lived with the fraternity where I served as house mother."

"Really?" Maude frowned.

"He was fairly quiet. It was understood he had a young lady he planned to marry upon return to the island."

Maude's cheeks glowed scarlet.

"But all manner of rumors circulated among the young men—you know how they can be."

"Ja." Ben did know, but he wasn't of that ilk.

"Some try to pass themselves off as something they are not." She arched a brow. The faux housekeeping manager was definitely baiting him.

He swallowed back bile. "Sometimes for good reasons."

"Sometimes not." A smirk tugged at Mrs. Fox's lips. Dressed so femininely, she showed how handsome a woman she was. Attractive enough to catch the eye of her old friend, or possible beau? At the hotel, she always appeared so dowdy, and her clothing today concealed her slim figure.

Peter Welling reentered the room, scratching his chin.

"Father?"

"Hmm?"

"Are you all right?" Maude leaned forward as if to stand, but her father gestured for her to remain seated.

"Request for your uncle Robert to come by sometime for a chat."

Ben drew in a fortifying breath. "I believe I should be going soon. I have an appointment myself."

Mrs. Bishop also rose. "Myself, too—but, Peter, I so wish you could accompany me to the theater. I have tickets available to me for any of the presentations."

"I don't know, Ada. I'm barely out of mourning."

Mrs. Bishop held out her hand. "As old friends? Might you escort your widowed neighbor to see *The Gondoliers?*"

"Father, tomorrow night is Islander Night at the theater. It might be a good time for Mrs. Fox to get a feel for the island flavor."

"Exactly what I was thinking." Mrs. Bishop grinned like a newsboy who'd just sold his last paper for the day. "And Miss Welling, you and Mr. König might enjoy watching the performance reserved for guests of the Grand. I believe that takes place a few nights from now—perhaps Monday."

"A grand idea, Mrs. Fox. If Mr. Welling permits." Ben nodded toward the man.

Welling harrumphed. "About time Maude got out of the house again for social events instead of running around raising money for the church."

Mrs. Bishop's head dipped, as she looked sideways at Maude, much like a bird about to pluck a worm from the ground. "You don't say? I imagine you worry, Peter, over her wearing herself out with these endeavors!"

"I do. Indeed, last night she didn't return from her rounds until very late."

Ben clenched his jaw and watched Maude's face pale.

A slow grin grew on Adelaide's face. "Perhaps both your daughter and I have a confession to make—and Mr. König, too?"

What a devious woman.

When neither Ben nor Maude responded, the matron popped open the fastener on her clutch, from which she retrieved a silver coin. She held it out to Maude. "For your charitable efforts, dear."

Peter Welling began to laugh. "Don't tell me she actually was at the Grand Hotel, too!"

"Yes, I was, Father." Maude's lips rolled together. "Last night."

"Oh, how could you?" Welling scowled. "Soliciting for Mission Church up there?"

"I'm sorry."

Mrs. Bishop snapped her reticule shut. "Happy to part with my money for a good cause, Peter."

Ben reached into his pocket and Mrs. Bishop glared at him. "I understand Mr. König has agreed to play the piano at church sometime."

"Ja, I'd be glad to do that." He exhaled slowly and pulled his hand from his pocket.

Mrs. Bishop tugged at her gloves. "If only all young people would search their consciences."

"Ja." A schnitzel-sized lump formed in Ben's throat.

Adelaide took Maude's hand. "It's amazing what can happen when one seeks to do God's will instead of insisting on one's own way about things."

What about him? Was journalism his way of insisting on his will and avoiding the talents God had given him? Music wasn't what had ruined his life—his uncle's behavior was what had sent them away from everyone they'd known and loved. And cost Friedrich his sister.

Mr. Welling took Ada's elbow and guided her from the room. "I'll send the carriage for you at seven o'clock tomorrow, then, Ada?"

"Perfect." She smiled up at Welling but then turned her direction to Maude. "And Miss Welling, I hate to have to tell you this, dear, but we shan't be expecting you back at the hotel again unless it is purely for social reasons."

Maude's lower lip trembled as she gaped at the woman.

A smile twitched at the wealthy recluse's lips. "I'm sure you understand, don't you?"

"I understand perfectly."

As did Ben. Maude was fired—but in the nicest way possible.

Chapter Nineteen

A swath of local color highlighted Ben's Friday afternoon agenda. Determined to wear his own clothing, even if it meant acquiring a few stares, he dug through his trunk for his tweed jacket and tan trousers. He could always tell people that he was going for a hike.

Feeling his nubby jacket's texture reminded him that the life he was playing at was borrowed rather than owned. He drew in a deep breath of the cedar-lined trunk as he located his pants. He'd wear a linen shirt the newspaper had paid for, though. The sound of the trunk closing caused an ache in Ben's chest. It was as though his whole life was compartmentalized into that one leather trunk.

Today, Jack Welling was Ben's "appointment." The two of them would head down to the Chippewa encampment near the water. Checking his pocket watch, Ben realized it was time to go. He cleared his desktop and slipped his notes about his active story leads into the dresser drawer, beneath his undershirts.

Someone pounded on the door. Ben startled. "Who is there?"

"Hey, Friedrich! It's me!"

Ben opened the door, two matrons shooting him wide-eyed stares as they marched past.

Jack gave a crooked grin, and Ben reached out to muss the youth's hair. "You ready?"

The housekeeping manager rounded the corner. "Good day, gentlemen."

"Mrs. Fox." Ben bowed in her direction.

She glanced between the two of them. "Does your father know you're here, Jack?"

"Yeah."

Ben bent closer and whispered in the boy's ear. "Yes, ma'am. Say 'yes, ma'am,' not 'yeah.'"

The boy straightened. "Yes, ma'am, my father knows I came up here. Gonna show old Friedrich where the Indian stuff can be bought."

The woman raised her eyebrows. "I see."

Delicious scents wafted from the food cart a servant rolled by.

Jack appreciatively sniffed the air. Quick as a flash, he lifted the cover from a dish. "Umm, smells good!"

Mrs. Fox placed a hand over the boy's and pressed the lid back down. "Are you hungry, child?"

Rubbing a hand over his midsection, Jack nodded.

Why would he be hungry? The family enjoyed sumptuous meals in their private dining quarters.

"Cook told me not to eat if I'm late to the table."

Ben frowned. "What does your father say?"

"Dad sleeps a lot lately, or he looks at the books and sighs at his desk. Sometimes he naps outside on the porch, so the gardener and I put a blanket on him so he don't get cold."

"Merciful Father." Mrs. Fox's eyebrows rose into two inverted *v*'s.

"He's that, for sure." Jack's constrained smile indicated that he misunderstood the woman's retort as literal. "Well, we better get going."

Offering a tight smile, Mrs. Fox strode off down the hall.

"Whew, thought I was in trouble." Jack elbowed Ben as he locked his room and pocketed the key.

"I was going to meet you down by the bike stand."

"I was here early."

"So how did you find me?"

Jack winked and touched the side of his head. "I've got a few brains in my noggin."

Ben chuckled then followed the boy down the hall and outside. "I'll get you some lunch, okay?"

"Thanks." Jack pointed to the bike lying on the ground. "Had some trouble getting Sis's wheels to fit in right, so I laid it in the grass."

"I'll walk it down the hill for you."

"Gee, thanks."

"Why didn't you ride your own bike?"

The boy's freckled cheeks grew rosy. "Dad said I couldn't ride my bike for a week."

Ben chuckled. "So you think that means you can ride your sister's? I suspect your father meant no riding whatsoever."

Jack hung his head.

"Say, are you ready to accompany me to the Indian settlement?"

His tawny head shot up. "Let's go!"

After carefully walking downhill with the bicycle, dodging horses, carriages, and pedestrian traffic, Ben and Jack approached the Indian settlement near the point where Lakes Michigan and Huron met.

All along the encampment were lined stalls of vendors and picketed horses. Ben purchased sandwiches for the two of them, and they sat watching some of the women performing leatherwork.

When he was done, Jack shot up. "Come on."

The boy led Ben to a squat woman with tanned and withered cheeks. She smiled warmly at them.

Jack jerked a thumb toward Ben. "Miss Lulu, this is my new pal, Friedrich."

She motioned to him, her long dark braid bobbing. "Come. Sit." She patted the wood bench across from her.

Ben caught the subtle scent of maple and corn bread emanating from the woman. He hoped he and Jack didn't reek of the liverwurst and cheese sandwiches, mounded with hot onions, they'd just ate. But they probably did. He sought peppermints from his pocket and offered one to the boy.

In a basket at the woman's feet lay jars of trinkets, spools of thread or wire, clips, scissors, small boards, and rows of multicolored beads.

Maude's brother plopped down at the woman's feet. "Whatcha makin', Miss Lulu?"

She pressed her lips together. "Nothing for you, Jack Welling."

Lulu laughed, bent, and retrieved a square-shaped interwoven basket filled with berries. "Go rinse them, Jack. Blueberries from the mainland. Picked them ourselves."

The boy grasped the basket and headed toward a pump spigot nearby.

"He a good boy, that one. His sister has hands full, though." She bent and chose a bottle full of tiny red beads and sat up, poured them into her lap, and began threading them onto the needle.

"What are you making?"

"A rose for the church fund-raiser. The Mission Church has been friend to my family all my life."

Ben warmed to this topic. "Ah, I believe Miss Welling is also trying to raise funds."

"Ha! She supposed to do that, but she not make anything for the bazaar this year. Too busy at hotel." Lulu's dark eyes speared his.

He didn't want to betray Maude's confidence.

Lulu turned and spit on the ground. "Grand Hotel maid. She shame her father."

"I don't believe that was her intention."

The woman smiled and looked him up and down. "She up there for you? At least you look like real man—not like that boy she not marry."

Ben felt his face heat. "No. She wasn't there for me."

Jack returned, the basket empty and streaks of dark blue around his lips. "Thanks, Miss Lulu."

"Nice meeting you, ma'am."

A shy smile flitted across her face, but then she leant her full attention to her beadwork.

Jack sprinted off. Ben followed him past tents and canopies, under which tables piled with goods enticed visitors to splurge on Chippewa or Odawa handmade items. Tiny dolls attired in deerskin dresses attracted two little girls attired in matching white sailor dresses.

Jack turned and jogged back to Ben and grabbed his hand. "Come on. Let's go into town and get a Coca-Cola at Uncle Al's."

Soon they'd reached the docks and the main part of town.

Couples and families crowded around a demonstration in front of the emporium. Ben smiled at a towheaded boy being hoisted up onto his father's shoulders. In a few short years, Ben'd be thirty. Would he ever have a family of his own?

"Ugh! I don't know why anybody'd want to watch demonstrations of all those baby things."

At the front of the observers stood a titian-haired woman and a blond man. Anna and Greyson.

❤

After he dropped Jack off at the inn, Ben developed a splitting headache. Banyon wanted that story as soon as he could get it and as salacious as possible. Now all he wanted to do was get to his room and lie down for an hour or so before he and his typewriter got busy. He entered the hotel's side entrance and hurried up the steps and into his hall, heading straight for his room.

Not allowing her dark bombazine skirts to slow her pace, the head of housekeeping strode directly toward him, a determined look on her face. "Mr. König, I have a telegram for you."

"Mrs. Fox, delightful to see you." As soon as he spied her quirked eyebrow he exhaled. Not the thing to say to the housekeeper. His boss would be berating him if he could hear what Ben had said. Thankfully, the hall was empty save for a young couple lingering on a chaise longue. The Grand's orchestra had an afternoon performance, and that likely attracted many guests.

She handed him the telegram. "I'm looking forward to hearing you play again, at the Wellings' church." She looked up at him. "Before you return to Detroit, that is."

Had she looked at the message? He scanned it. *Needed back at the office soon. Finish story pronto.* He scowled.

Touching his hand lightly, the older woman met his gaze. "Mr. Steffan, I'm not sure you're cut out for what it takes to be an editor at the *Detroit Post*."

If she meant drive, she was wrong. "I've worked hard for this."

"Mr. Steffan, you are a virtuoso. There simply is no other word to describe your talent. I have traveled the world over, as you know, and I don't make this pronouncement lightly."

Such musical talent amounted to nothing but ruin for his family. He half-closed his eyes, trying to shut out the sudden memories of his uncle screaming at them to get out. "I love my profession. I just don't love what it takes, sometimes, to bring in a story."

"And you don't have that passion for music."

"No."

She took a quick look at her watch. "Dear me, I've got to get ready for the show."

"I hope you find it enjoyable."

"I'm sure I will." Her smile was genuine and her eyes sparkled behind her silver glasses. "I've never had anything but a good time with Peter, ever. Now his mother—that's another story."

"Oh?"

"She has affected both our lives. I just pray it isn't permanently."

Chapter Twenty

Maude closed her bedroom windows to the chill morning rain. She lowered the wood slat blinds and closed the heavy velvet drapes. Today she'd organize her wardrobe herself, instead of asking the servants to help. Three raps sounded on the door.

Bea entered carrying a wide House of Worth dress box. "Delivery here, Miss Maude."

"Just call me Maude. No more of this 'Miss Maude' business." The box, banded by a wide ribbon, was stamped with the name of Detroit's premier clothier—Botentorte's.

"Sure thing. . .Maude."

Together they set the heavy box atop Grandmother's old leather trunk. "You should have let Jack help you, Bea."

Maude didn't have to ask who'd sent it. Uncle Robert had ordered dresses in the past for special occasions.

"Is Uncle Robert downstairs now?"

"Yes, in the parlor, but your dad said no interruptions. That includes you."

"Surely not."

Maude waited until Bea departed and then descended the steps, praying she'd get to talk with Robert.

She stood outside the office, listening.

"I'd like to know what's going on." Father's voice rose.

"Nothing, with you stonewalling!"

"What do you intend to do?"

Jane emerged from the kitchen, balancing a teetering silver tray covered with sweets in one hand and the coffee service tray in the other.

Maude swooped toward her. "Let me help."

"No, miss, I've got it."

Maude grasped the handle of the coffeepot before it slid precariously to the tray's edge. "There—I need a good cup of coffee, too."

Jane's cheeks reddened. "Sorry, it's just that yer uncle is here, and—"

"You'll do no such thing!" Father's voice carried into the hallway.

"Miss Welling, I wouldn't go in there, if I were ye." Jane bit her lower lip and bowed her head.

Carrying the silver coffeepot in one hand, Maude threw the office door open with the other, just as her uncle finished saying, ". . .what my mother wanted."

The two men stood in the center of the office, only a foot or so apart. Father whirled on her. "Get out!"

His hand was raised as though he might strike her. His cheeks took on an odd purplish hue.

Maude gasped and pressed a hand to her chest. He'd never hit her. Behind her, Jane hastily set down the pastries and the coffee service tray before fleeing from the room.

"Were you invited in?" Father wiped spittle from around his mouth and lowered his hand.

With trembling hands, Maude turned and set the pot down on the tray then swiveled back, meeting her father's stony gaze. Maybe he hadn't taken his medicine.

Robert took several steps toward her and pulled Maude into his arms. She could hear Robert's heart pounding in his chest, echoing her own. He released her and faced her father.

"You have no business treating her so brusquely, Peter."

"She's my daughter!" He lowered his head toward his left shoulder.

Something was definitely wrong with him. Maude pushed past Robert.

"Maude is an adult, and because she is your daughter she deserves your respect."

She tried to get past her father to go to his office, to check his medication vials, but he grabbed her arm, squeezing it so hard she cried out.

"Get out of my house!" Father abruptly released her and crumpled to the floor, clutching his chest.

"No!" Maude sank down beside him. She couldn't lose him, too.

♥

Ben entered the Winds of Mackinac inn's lobby. No servants were in sight, not even Beatrice.

A loud thud reverberated from farther down the hall—near the family's personal quarters.

"Father!" Maude's cry set a fire under Ben.

He hotfooted it down the hall.

"Muddy, what's wrong with him?" Jack's voice carried from the family parlor.

Inside he found Mr. Welling lying on the floor, Maude holding his head in her lap, and Robert Swaine standing over them.

"Was ist falsch?"

Swaine gaped but gave no explanation of what was happening.

Mr. Welling shivered, his color ashen.

Ben pulled off his coat and laid it atop the man. "Go get the doctor, Jack!"

The boy met his eyes and nodded, but didn't move.

Using a calm tone, Ben slowly but firmly urged the boy, "Ride your bicycle to Dr. Cadotte's and tell him to come quickly."

Maude sniffed and stared up at Ben. "It's his heart, I think."

"Does he have any medication?"

"In his office drawer."

"Get it." When she flinched at his brusque command, he softened his tone. "Please."

"Oh, God, I cannot lose Father, too. I cannot." Sobs wracked Maude's frame as she departed.

Swaine shoved a hand through his hair. "I didn't mean for this to happen. We just needed to clear the air."

"Looks like you've done more than that." Ben saw Welling's eyelids flutter, but the man didn't move.

Soon Maude returned with a glass vial. An apothecary's label affixed to the front read "DIGITALIS."

"Mr. Welling, can you take some medicine now, ja?"

The man opened his eyes and looked up at his daughter. Maude opened the container and administered a dose to her father, smoothing hair from his brow. Her uncle shifted back and forth, a tremor visible in his hands.

Ben pointed to the divan. "Swaine, should we settle him over there?"

"Yes." The captain moved and took one side while Ben took the other.

Mr. Welling was a bulky man, but with the sturdy captain's help, Ben hoisted him up and carried him carefully toward the divan.

"Let me put a pillow behind his head." Maude tucked an overstuffed chintz pillow under her father's neck.

"Good." Ben glanced at her worried face.

Maude's father groaned.

"Sir?" Ben leaned in.

Welling shook his head. "Oh. . ."

"Father!" Maude pressed her ear to his chest.

Ben pulled a chair close to the sofa so Maude could sit.

"I'm going up front to watch for Jack and the doctor."

Welling strained to sit up. "Perhaps it is Robert's duty to go do that." He practically spat out the words then began to cough and reclined back onto the chaise.

"I'll keep an eye out for Jack." Swaine departed.

"Stay, Friedrich, please." Maude's gentle shake of her head urged Ben to not ask any questions. "Father, try to rest now. Just close your eyes."

Her father groaned but pressed his eyes shut. In a short while, he appeared to be entering sleep.

Maude leaned in and whispered, "I think it's best if my uncle Robert leaves."

"Ja?"

She mouthed, "They were arguing."

He nodded and took two steps before she grabbed his hand. "Can you see if Jack has returned?"

"Ja."

Closing the door gently, Ben scanned the hall for Swaine and found him at the reception desk, speaking with Beatrice. He motioned for the captain to come aside with him, and the girl departed.

"Captain Swaine, your niece thinks it might be best. . ."

The man raised his hands, effectively cutting Ben off. "I'll go. But send me word immediately about what the doctor says."

"Ja."

"I wish my brother-in-law wasn't so darned rigid. If only he'd. . ."

Jack flew through the front door, his face pale and wet.

Ben grasped the boy's arms gently. "Your father is resting well."

"I've got to see him." Tears coursed down the boy's face as Ben moved a restraining hand on his shoulder.

Swaine grabbed his hat from a nearby peg. He'd not even spoken an encouraging word to his nephew. Ben tamped down his frustration and tried to focus on the boy's immediate needs.

"You'll see your *vater*, your father, in a moment. But, for now, you must be calm, ja?"

Jack's starry eyelashes, so like his sister's, blinked furiously, but he nodded.

"Your father and sister are counting on you to help keep calm in the house. Can you do that?"

The boy wiped his nose with the back of his hand. Ben fished his handkerchief out of his pocket and offered it to him. Jack blew loudly.

"Let's go back outside—get some fresh air."

As they stepped onto the porch, Dr. Cadotte, atop a shiny black bicycle, rode up the street, dismounted, and set his bike against one of the gardener's prize rhododendrons.

The physician strode up to them. "Jack, I need you to take Maude to the office and preoccupy her while I examine your father, all right? Don't let her in."

"Yes, sir, I can do that." The boy stood an inch taller at the command.

"Mr. König, I'll need your assistance if we must move Mr. Welling and get him to his room. Undressed and such."

"Glad to oblige."

An hour later, after Mr. Welling had been situated in his own bedchamber and had fallen asleep, Dr. Cadotte took Ben aside.

"I've got to get him to the mainland to a specialist. If you have any influence on Maude, please use it to get her to accompany him."

"Why wouldn't she take her father?" From what Maude had said, she wasn't the problem—her father had been obstinate about going.

The doctor's eyes widened, and he held Ben's gaze. "You really don't realize the extent of her fears, do you?"

Maude's fears? Who wouldn't panic if they had asthma and couldn't breathe in certain locales? "Are you one of Freud's followers?"

"No." Cadotte laughed. "I'm just a country doctor. But I have known Maude Welling all her life. And I've been her physician. Some of her avoidance of leaving the island has to do with the breathing attacks she's had. But I'm not convinced that some of it isn't psychological."

"Oh?" The man may not be a follower of young Dr. Sigmund Freud's theories, but Cadotte was sounding like the growing group of psychiatrists who liked to expound on why every ailment was in the psyche. Like the men who became concerned over King Ludwig.

Maude didn't need Cadotte giving her a problem in her mind, when none existed. Ben would be sure to watch the man's influence over her. Yet how could he, when he was leaving soon?

♥

Only a few hours had passed since Friedrich had left, but it felt like she'd sat in her parents' room for days. Not just because of Father's illness, but because she sensed her beau's absence keenly. No wonder Mother and Father had wanted her settled and married. Father slept peacefully, an arm draped over Mother's pillow, as if she might yet be with him. She rose and quietly slipped out of the bedchamber.

Descending the stairs, she fingered the smooth bannister, which had known the touch of a Cadotte woman for over a hundred years. What good would living here be if those she loved weren't with her? Paintings of the island's spectacular views lined the stairwell wall. She would now be running the inn. By herself. Father in bed. Greyson married to Anna. Every one of her ideas for her life altered.

She quickly met with the entire staff to give them an update and assure them she'd be assuming stewardship of the inn. Whether Father liked it or not. But, oh, what a predicament. She'd never wished for him to grow sicker.

When Maude was finished, Bea raised her hand. "Do you want tea in the office now?"

Cook eyed the hall grandfather clock, and Maude shook her head.

Jane caught her eye. "Will ye be in the office, then, miss?"

"Yes, but feel free to come get me if you need anything. And thank you all for your attention."

Gretchen remained behind as the rest scattered in different directions to their duties. "Where do you need me tonight?"

"Could you please sit with my father until after dinner?"

"Of course." Gretchen bobbed a curtsy. "And thank you for the chance, miss. I'd be on the street if it wasn't for you."

When tears sprung up in the young woman's eyes, Maude pulled her into a quick hug. "Thank God you're here to help us, Gretchen."

They parted ways and Maude settled into her father's chair in the office. She'd not be able to attend services on the morrow, so she sought time alone with God. She studied the Word and reflected before entering a time of prayer. Prayers hadn't saved Mother, nor had good works. What, then, other than the will of God, would save Father? Maude's Bible reading convicted her that she'd been selfish, thinking of herself and wanting to remain on the island with Father and Jack with her. They needed to go. No wonder Father couldn't get well—everywhere he looked he was reminded of Mother. Tears streamed down her face. Father had to get better and then leave. And the rift with Uncle Robert must be resolved.

Jane peeked her head in, her white hat askew. She adjusted it. "Almost dinnertime."

At this time last week Maude had the luxury of being home, after working herself to the bone for hours already. "What time did you start your workday?"

The servant's pleasant features scrunched together in puzzlement. "I think 'twas eight o'clock this morning."

"It's already six." Maude ran her hand over her chin. "Tomorrow I'll work on the schedule and adjust the hours."

Jane's stricken look prompted Maude to add. "Same pay, maybe even a raise if I can manage it. Jack and I can serve ourselves."

"I better bring the food in, though, miss—you know how Cook is."

"Yes. I better get permission to be in her kitchen first. Please warn her that in the future I might do so."

"Yes, miss." Jane smiled and then headed down the hall, humming an Irish melody.

Footfalls battered down the stairs, and Maude cringed. Jack arrived at the office, his face pale. "Do I gotta go to service tomorrow, sis?"

She drew in a deep breath. "Mr. König agreed to teach my Sunday school class."

"He did?"

"Yes." She hoped he could manage the children.

"I should go, then."

"Yes, but for now let's have our dinner."

After shoveling down his meal of whitefish, corn bread, and wild asparagus, Maude's brother ran off.

Jane carried in a peach cobbler.

"The whitefish was superb."

"Sorry Jackie is missing out on dessert. I saw him run down the hall."

"Hopefully to the bathroom, to brush his teeth and comb his hair."

"I don't think so, miss." Jane pointed toward the window as Jack sped past on his bicycle.

Maude sighed and then met her gaze. "Just call me Maude."

"Yes, miss. . .Maude, that is." Jane dished out a serving of the cobbler onto a small blue floral china plate and set it before her.

"Thank you. It smells heavenly."

"Georgia peaches. Your uncle sent them over when he heard about your father."

"How good of him." Probably half the island now knew of her father's troubles. She took a taste of the peaches. Perfectly sweetened and with a hint of ginger and cinnamon.

"I hate to ask ye a favor, but. . ."

Maude looked up into Jane's pensive face. "What is it?"

"My sister has arrived in New York."

"That's wonderful." Maude grinned up at the Irishwoman. "At last—you'll have family here."

The servant blinked away tears. "I was hopin' ye had a position for her, but with Gretchen coming on now, I didn't know."

"Of course we'll find a place for her, Jane."

"Thank ye, miss, Maude. And I'll keep prayin' for yer father. He's been kind to me."

"We're grateful we have your help, Jane. Even if I don't always tell you. . ." Had she ever told her? "I appreciate all you do."

Jane's cheeks bloomed as pink as the peony on the table. "Thank ye, miss. . .that is—Maude."

"I want Gretchen to start training under you once Father is better. Beginning on Monday, you'll be our senior housekeeper." Maude would examine the books and find money for additional staff and raises.

"I don't know what to say."

"There will be a raise, but I'll have to tell you later what that amount is."

"Thank you." Jane bobbed a curtsy. "Anything else, Maude?"

She smiled at her. "Yes. You can take the carriage to church tomorrow with Jack. It's Gretchen's turn to stay home since she's the new girl. You'll be able to claim the Sundays from now on unless you have to accommodate the schedule. You just let me know."

"Aye, Maude."

After she'd finished her cobbler and Jane had cleared the dishes away, Maude checked on her father. He was resting well, and his color was good.

She headed back to the office.

Settled at her father's desk, Maude pored over the books, checking for discrepancies. She could tell exactly when Mother had stopped making entries in her fluid feminine hand and Father had taken over. After an hour, she got up to stretch and check on her father again.

Bea stopped her in the hallway. "Your pa is sitting up eating dinner, and he's fine. Said he doesn't want to be bothered."

"Bothered? Is that what he calls it?"

"His words, not mine." Bea chuckled.

Chapter Twenty-One

*T*he sweet scents of lilacs and peonies mingled with the roses' fragrance in the side garden, where Maude settled onto a stone bench. With only a week left in June, soon her favorite flowers would be gone. The last lacy lilac blossoms would tumble from the trees and the peonies' silky petals would fall from their tall stalks. She opened her Bible to the book of James.

Voices carried from up front. Bea was arguing with someone. Sighing, Maude rose and returned to the back entrance.

Bea ran up the hallway as Maude reached the top of the back wooden stairs. Eyes wide with alarm, the girl grabbed Maude's leg-of-mutton sleeve and pulled.

"Maude—I couldn't stop her!"

"Who?" Maude pulled the frantic girl's hands from her sleeve, now a wrinkled mess.

Bea pointed to the office, where the door was opened wide. Maude turned to the right and stepped closer. A woman bent over Father's desk, red curls trailing from beneath her silk-rose-covered bonnet. More alarming than seeing Anna Luce at the inn, though, was the fact that Father's books were all open on the desktop. Where Maude had left them.

Maude strode into the room, closing the door a little too firmly behind her.

Anna flinched but remained rooted by Father's desk as though she had every right in the world to be there. Immaculate in a mint-green walking suit with lace appliqué, Anna looked more suited to a prominent social call in Detroit than to calling at a small-island inn.

"What're you doing?" Maude met Anna's cool gaze as she propped her matching mint silk sun umbrella by the desk.

"I thought it was time I paid your father a visit."

Maude's heart galloped. Oh, no—could it be that she was the woman rumored to be planning to buy the inn? Although Bea had already brought the coffee cart in, Maude had no intention of encouraging this woman to linger.

"He invited you?"

"Not exactly." Anna ran a finger along the top of the cabinet. "Where is he?"

Sucking in a breath, Maude moved between the intruder and her father's desk. What should she call this woman? She couldn't call her Mrs. Luce. Maude was supposed to have been Mrs. Greyson Luce, and Greyson would be running things with her right now were it not for Anna.

"My father is ill, and I'm in charge of the inn." For now, at least. She swallowed. Maude would also provide oversight for the other businesses. She was an excellent bookkeeper, but previously she'd only been tasked with keeping up with Uncle Al's shop. Having examined the books, she was daunted by the ledgers from the number of businesses that her parents had taken over after Grandmother had died.

The woman's eyes narrowed. "How convenient. The very day I wish to speak with him he's suddenly ill."

"Mrs. . ." Maude couldn't say it. And she'd not share that Father may have suffered a heart attack last evening. "This is Sunday, and you've confessed you've not been invited."

The woman had the decency to blush.

"Suffice it to say that I'm in charge for the foreseeable future. Whatever you need to say to him can be addressed to me."

Anna took two steps toward the front windows. "I imagine you know why I'm here, then, since your father finds you so infinitely trustworthy."

Twin hammers began to pound on Maude's temples. "Are you here to purchase the inn, then?"

Never mind that Grandmother Cadotte as well as her mother had always said the inn was to be Maude's and her husband's. She had no husband. But Friedrich König's handsome face suddenly came to mind.

"This inn?" Anna's scoffing tone left no doubt as to what she thought of the Winds of Mackinac. "Hardly."

Maude's cheeks burned. "Then why are you here?"

Anna lifted Father's prized Eiffel Tower clock. The two-foot-tall reproduction of the Eiffel Tower featured lacy cutwork metal completely gilded, save for the clock rim. It had arrived this Christmas. Father said an old friend had sent it to him.

"My father's friend owns one exactly like this."

Maude could not care less about Mr. Forham's wealthy friends. She didn't keep up with society columns.

"Adelaide Bishop. The mysterious and fabulously wealthy recluse?" Greyson's wife smirked. "You've probably heard of her, even up in this rural area."

"For your information, St. Ignace has several newspapers, Mackinaw City has theirs, and the island has one, as well." The straits bustled with activity, and that meant news. Hadn't the *St. Ignace Journal* run a brief article about the infamous Adelaide Bishop? Maude rubbed a spot on her temple, trying to recall.

"This image of the Eiffel Tower reminds me that my father promised us a Paris honeymoon."

If only Mr. Forham had—and Greyson and Anna hadn't come here.

Anna giggled, as though she realized her gaffe. "But I imagine you don't want to hear that, since you were supposed to marry Greyson yourself."

Slumping into Father's chair, Maude gestured to the seat opposite. She needed an ocean between her and this woman, not this cluttered desk. One by one she closed the bound books: Cadotte Ice, Cadotte Island Shipping, Cadotte Firewood, Cadotte Carriages, Cadotte Hauling and Delivery.

Deftly arranging her layered silk gown around her, Anna lowered her elegant form into the chair. "Greyson and I have been here several weeks already."

"Yes, you may recall I met you at the docks." Maude compressed her lips tighter. Anna's eyes cut to one of the ledgers still open and Maude flipped it closed with one finger.

Three taps preceded Bea into the room. "Pour your coffee now, miss?"

Before Maude could respond, the uninvited visitor waved an imperious hand. "No, thank you. I'll be leaving shortly."

When Bea turned to leave, Maude cleared her throat. "I'll take my coffee with cream and three lumps of sugar, please, before you go."

The girl swiveled and bobbed a little curtsy.

Anna folded her hands in her lap. Her ecru crocheted gloves were edged at the cuffs with tiny ruffles that fitted her dainty hands. Maude glanced down at her own work-roughened hands. She'd earned every callus. What had this woman ever earned on her own?

"As I was saying, we've been here and settled in, yet your father still hasn't put Greyson to work."

To work?

The filigreed pink Bohemian glass cup Bea held clattered into its saucer. "Sorry!"

Maude gave Bea a tremulous smile. "Just bring it to me, please."

Bea set the coffee before Maude. "Please try it, Miss Welling. And make sure I got it right."

Wonderful! Now Anna was going to think the Wellings never had their servants wait on them. Maude took a mouthful of the sweet creamy beverage.

"Fine, Bea. Thank you."

Anna lifted her pert nose. "Greyson expected to be put to work at one of the Cadotte holdings."

Bea's mouth dropped open. Maude took another sip of coffee. *Lord, give me patience.*

"After all, being a Cadotte descendant, it's expected of him, isn't it?"

Maude's mouthful of coffee flew past her lips and spread over the books. Bea quickly strode forward, lifted her apron, and blotted the ledgers dry. Thank goodness, Maude had closed them.

"He ain't a Cadotte nothing, miss!" Bea blurted.

Face twisted in outrage, Anna half-rose from her seat. Did she intend to strike Bea?

"Mrs. Luce!" Maude said pointedly, and the woman scowled.

"Your maid has insulted my husband."

Maude waved her hands toward the door. "Bea, you're dismissed."

"I ain't fired, am I?" The girl's emerald eyes filled with tears.

"Just go." She'd talk with Bea later.

As she left, Bea gave wide berth to Anna.

Jack bounded in.

"Aw, it's her—the stranger Greyson up and married. Whatcha doin' here, lady?"

Anna twisted in her chair and craned her neck back to look up at Jack, attired in a navy-and-yellow-striped running suit with matching blue socks.

"I could ask you the same thing, Jack." Maude made a shooing motion.

"I'm goin' for a run up Grand Hill."

"All right." Maude continued to wave him away.

Transfixed, he gazed down at Anna in adoration. "You sure are pretty."

To Maude's surprise, a beautiful smile lit the woman's face, and she raised her hand. Except that Jack didn't bend to kiss it. Instead, he pumped it vigorously.

Then he left, calling out, "For a redhead, that is!" He cackled, and the door closed behind him.

Anna's features tightened into a mask of rage. Maude closed her eyes momentarily. Jack had been rude, but he'd also given the woman a back-handed compliment.

"Mrs. Luce." There, she'd said it. "Had Greyson told you my father offered him employment?"

"No, but. . ."

She measured her words. "Has he *ever* said to you that he is part of the Cadotte family?"

"Not exactly, but. . ." Anna lifted her chin.

"I didn't think so." After she pushed her coffee cup aside, Maude rested her elbows on the desk and steepled her hands together. "Who has made these claims?"

Straightening in her chair, her silk roses bobbing on the brim of her hat, Anna frowned. "Greyson has been saying for years that he'd be running many Cadotte businesses because of his family associations."

"For years?" While he was courting her? She cocked her head, awaiting Anna's reply.

She averted her gaze. "To his fraternity brothers and so on."

"Did he now?" Maude began to chuckle.

"Why is that funny?"

"Because Greyson *was* supposed to have run the inn with me after we were wed. That would have been his family association—via marriage into my family." She met Anna's green glare.

"But, but. . ." The redhead waved her gloved hand toward the desktop. "Was he not heir to the other businesses—the Cadotte holdings?"

Maude gritted her teeth, her head now at a full pounding boil. It was none of this woman's concern what her family owned on the island.

"I don't think that's any of your business."

Anna stood. "It is if my husband is being deprived of his inheritance."

Maude shook her head then pushed back her father's chair. "I may be related to half the island, because so many of us are Cadotte descendants. But I can assure you: Greyson Luce is not one of them!"

"And you are?" Anna's voice came out almost a whisper. "You're the Cadotte heir—no, you're the heiress."

Maude didn't answer, unsure what Greyson's wife meant.

Anna's features altered to a knowing, almost catlike visage. "Well, that's certainly worth knowing, now—isn't it?"

A chill coursed through Maude.

"I now understand what Benjamin sees in you." Anna rose, a sly grin on her face. "Or should I call him Friedrich?"

"How do you know Mr. König?"

"Benjamin and I are old friends." Smirking, she strode from the room.

The coffee she'd drank rose acid-like in Maude's gut. No—more like arsenic that this woman had surreptitiously added.

Benjamin? Who was Anna talking about?

Like a genie from Aladdin's lamp, Bea appeared in the office doorway. "Well, I got rid of one, miss, but now there's another lady here."

Maude procured a headache powder from the desk drawer and poured it into her glass of water. "Who now?"

"Mrs. Fox from the Grand Hotel. Say—did she fire you, Maude?" Bea clasped her hands together.

"Bring her in, Bea, and stop your prattle." Maude gulped the bitter water down. *Please work quickly.*

Attired in a trim-fitting navy-serge walking suit edged in white grosgrain ribbon with a matching sailor hat, Ada Fox joined her in the room.

"Come in, Mrs. Fox."

"I heard of Peter's spell, and I wanted to come see him, but I wished to check with you first."

"I'll send one of the men to check on him and let us know if he feels able." Maude rang the bell on her desk.

As Anna had done, Mrs. Fox took several steps toward the windows and Father's collections. The woman's eyes lighted on the Eiffel Tower clock. "Oh, my."

"It's lovely, isn't it?"

Mrs. Fox beamed. "I'm so glad Peter gave my gift such a prominent spot in which to be displayed."

The bell slipped from Maude's hand and clattered onto the desk and then to the floor. She bent to retrieve it and remained bent over, in an effort to recover her shattered nerves. If the clock was as expensive as Anna implied, how had Mrs. Fox afforded one? How might she have come by it?

Surely she'd not have stolen in her previous job or the Grand wouldn't have hired her. Or was it possible Father's friend was Adelaide Bishop? Was she then the one after the inn? And was that her point of renewing her friendship with Father? Maude exhaled slowly and sat up, trying to squelch her imagination.

Shuffling footfalls announced their flat-footed porter, Russell James. "Miss Welling?"

"Please ask my father if he is up to visiting with Mrs. Fox."

"Yes, miss."

With a quarter turn of her chair, Maude faced her former supervisor. The woman's face as she touched the gilded clock was all expectancy, her lips slightly parted, her eyes wide like the children at Al's Soda Shop when their ice cream was being dipped. But if this was Mrs. Bishop, was her excitement more the thought of obtaining an asset from someone in difficulty, at a fraction of its price? Would Father want to sell out just to get off the island?

"Have a seat." Maude gestured to the chair.

The woman's eyes started to tear up. She fumbled with her reticule until she found her handkerchief. "I hate for you to see me like this. And I don't want to distress you or your father. Perhaps I should come back later."

Maude ground her teeth together. Perhaps she should.

"I have made such a mess of so many things. But this is something I wanted to do right." Mrs. Fox sniffed.

"What do you mean?"

The woman shook her head. "You never knew your grandmother Welling, Maude, but the day you walked into my office I knew you were Peter's daughter. You're the very image of her."

"Thank you." Grandmother's portrait and tintypes of the family reflected a lovely woman. "Father never said much about his mother." Other than saying she'd worked herself to death.

"A very charitable woman. I lived next door to your father and his family." A twitch started near her eye.

"Father misses the countryside and farming life but has said little about growing up in Shepherd."

"Nor about me, I'm sure." She gave a curt laugh.

"I'm afraid not."

When Mrs. Fox's gaze strayed to the clock, again, Maude corrected herself. "I was wrong."

She stood and touched the top of the Eiffel Tower effigy. "He shed some tears over this—said his best friend from home had sent it. He was happy the friendship hadn't been forgotten."

Mrs. Fox's eyes brightened. She wiped at the tears rolling down her face. "Did he?"

"Indeed. I'd assumed his pal was a man."

"We were two peas in a pod." Mrs. Fox fingered the lace on her handkerchief. "Sometimes I think he saved my life. I owe him."

Maude wanted to test her hypothesis about the housekeeping manager. "Anna Luce was just here."

"Oh?" The smile disappeared from Mrs. Fox's face, and she blew her nose.

"Anna said her father's friend has an identical clock. She was curious about who'd sent it."

The woman's eyes widened. "Did she say from whom her father received it?"

Russell tapped on the door frame and then entered. "Mr. Welling will be ready in a few minutes."

Mrs. Fox rose, her face flushed. "I should come back another time."

"No, ma'am, he's very enthused about your visit."

Enthused? When was the last time Father had been enthused about anything? "Please stay, Mrs. Fox. Let's not disappoint him."

The servant departed.

"Well." Mrs. Fox sighed and shrugged in the puffed shoulders of her jacket. "This inn is lovely, Maude. A gem."

Maude tapped a finger on top of the ledgers. Was that her motivation? "Have you ever considered running an inn?"

She laughed. "Certainly—especially when someone like Mrs. Stillman is constantly in my shadow, nipping at my heels."

"Mrs. Stillman?"

"She was in line for my position and never loses a chance to remind me."

"She's insufferable."

They both laughed.

"I don't understand why you came up to the Grand Hotel, not exactly."

Maude blew out a breath of frustration. "When you knew him, did my father object to women working outside the home?"

Mrs. Fox's features dissolved into a face of stony resolve. "Apparently not. I believed he was quite fixated on me attending secretarial school." Another round of tears coursed down her cheeks. "Forgive me, I'm just overwrought at the idea of finally renewing my friendship with your father and then the thought of him, well. . ."

What would happen to them if Father died? Mrs. Fox's display of emotion rattled Maude more than she cared to admit. Obviously, she and Father had been very close. Possibly sweethearts.

Heavy footsteps echoed from the staircase. Maude gasped as her father entered the office, fully dressed, his hair brushed.

"Should you be up?" Mrs. Fox voiced the question running through Maude's mind.

He made a beeline to the petite, slender-appearing woman and took her hand in his, raising it to his lips. "Just knowing you'd come by is the best medicine I could have had."

"Oh, Peter, I'm so glad you're all right." Ada Fox stood.

For a moment, Maude wondered if the two would embrace.

Father offered his arm. "Let's go out to the garden."

When the two departed, Maude sat in the chair, blinking. She could imagine everything now—Father selling the inn, possibly remarrying, and leaving the island with Jack. No genie had appeared. But the rest of her future seemed to be going up like a puff of smoke in the air.

Chapter Twenty-Two

*A*nother spectacular lunch at the Grand—served with a generous dollop of gall. Ben had dined with Casey and Marcus and acted as though he was cut from the same cloth as they were. Soon this farce would end.

With what he now knew about Anna and Greyson Luce from islanders and Adelaide, this story would get him not only a promotion but also a substantial raise. And his other piece, on Marcus Edmunds's pursuit of the society girl from Boston should also sell well. But with Edmunds and Miss Clancy, daughter of a wealthy banker, not from such prominent families, the article would publish more as a novelty piece. Casey was ending up being more of a bootstrap type of fellow than a gold digger. He was a man with lots of business ideas but no capital. Still, Ben could get a story out of Casey and Myra's romance.

He picked up his shoes, polished to perfection by Zeb, from the stack on the cart around the corner from the shoeshine chair and headed back to his room. His tuxedo would be sent up later, before the theater engagement with Maude. How could Greyson Luce have abandoned such a lovely young lady?

As he strode down the hallway to his room, he observed Mrs. Stillman standing outside at his door.

"Sadie, you need to get your other rooms cleaned." The supervisor barked these orders into Ben's room.

The sharp-tongued woman walked inside. "Put down that notebook this instant and straighten the bed linens."

His throat constricted as he followed the woman. Had Sadie seen his article about Maude, Greyson, and Anna? He pressed his eyes shut and sent up a quick prayer.

"Mr. König is here."

Ben entered the room. The blond maid reminded him of a press boy who'd fallen asleep on the job and awakened to find papers sliding in all different directions.

His red notebook lay on top of his typewriter, not to the side. Had Sadie been snooping? "Ladies?"

Fire burned in his gut. This woman could ruin it all between him and Maude. Although he'd recorded Maude's name in all the accounts about Greyson, he'd not intended to directly name her in his article. Sadie wouldn't know that, but she'd surely wonder why he was writing things up. Had she gone through his drawers and found his business card and his telegrams from the newspaper?

Dear Lord, please guide me.

He needed to prepare and dress to take Maude to the theater. He didn't have time to address Sadie now. He intended to get right with Maude and be honest.

"Miss Duvall?" He evoked a warning's cutting edge.

She averted her gaze and fled the room.

Quickly opening his notepad, he found nothing missing. He'd been careless leaving it out, but he'd been so tired. Hopefully, Sadie had only moved his notes to clean. He'd reveal his identity to Maude after the play.

A brisk breeze stirred the leaves of the oaks and birches in the side yard where Maude and her father sat, taking an early afternoon tea.

"I'm glad you were able to see the performance before your episode, Father."

"Good show." He tapped his foot against the lush green lawn. "*The Gondoliers* plays at the Maximillian Theater tonight, too."

"I wonder if Mr. König remembers."

"I should think so—he sent flowers for you."

She set her pink teacup back into its saucer. "Where are they, then?"

"I put them in the hall. You forgot to order a fresh arrangement."

She feigned mock horror. "You put mine on the lobby stand and didn't even tell me?"

He laughed. "Correct."

"I can't believe you did that."

"I'm a practical businessman." He shrugged. "No one ordered more flowers, and the others were dead."

Maude couldn't help laughing. "Then you owe me another bouquet."

Jack ran past them as he circled the inn. Father needed to get him off the island and someplace where he could compete with other athletes of his caliber.

"Ada said the guests at the Grand have been raving about the performance." Father served himself a piece of lemon tart. "I can see why—they were superb."

She cut herself a wedge of the treat. "Our visitors have praised the show, too."

Father took a bite of his dessert and Maude followed suit, savoring the lemon tart's tangy sweetness.

A carriage with the familiar red covering and gold fringe rolled by. She didn't need to see the initials "*GH*" on the bonnet to know from where it had come. "No doubt the Grand will employ every single one of their carriages tonight."

Father sipped his tea. "And require Stan's help, too, I believe."

What if someone recognized her? Or worse yet—actually pointed out that she had been a maid there. A tiny flutter began in Maude's stomach. "I'd rather not be mingling with the crowd from the Grand."

"You might as well wear the dress your uncle bought—I can only imagine the cost." Father rubbed a thumb over his chin. "Though I suppose he can afford it."

The dress, while gorgeous, was far too ostentatious for anything she'd ever wish to attend—and would draw too much attention to herself. The flutter metamorphosed into a full-fledged beating of wings in her gut.

"It's about time you got a taste of what passes for high society around this island every summer." Father pulled on his shirt collar.

"This isn't a ball. Just the theater." And a small-island theater at that. She would be overdressed in the extreme. Although perhaps not—given what she'd observed some of the women wearing to dinner the night she had parlor duty.

"You know, daughter, you're sounding like an island snob." Father picked up his paper and began to read.

"I am not. . . ." But he was right.

Jack ran up to them, his orange-and-green-striped shirt a blaze of movement. "Sadie's here." Jack bent over and clasped his knees, panting. "Out back."

At two o'clock in the afternoon? "For me?"

"Yup, she ain't here for Bea, that's for sure, 'cause she told her to fetch you, and I said I would."

"Can you bring her around?"

"Nah, Sadie said it's private stuff." He wiped his nose with the back of his hand.

"All right." She rose. "Father, I'll be in my room if you need me."

He raised a hand. "I'll be fine."

Sadie stood between the back entrance and the laundry building. Still dressed in her maid's uniform, her complexion appeared flushed.

"I need to talk with you, Maude."

"Let's go to my bedroom." Inside, Maude allowed a moment for her eyes to adjust to the dim interior. "Why aren't you at work?"

They passed a group of guests who were headed toward the parlor. Maude smiled at them.

Sadie kept her head bowed until they were alone again. "I'm not fired, if that's what you mean. But it's not because of Stillman's want of trying."

"Old battle-ax."

The two mounted the stairs to the second floor and headed to Maude's bedroom.

As soon as the door closed, Sadie huffed a sigh. "Mrs. Fox intervened for me. But that isn't my reason for stopping."

"What, then?"

Her friend sat on the cushioned wicker seat she'd occupied on a great many afternoons over the years. "Maude, I'm concerned about your Mr. König."

"He's not *my* Mr. anything." Maude pressed a hand to her chest. She'd like him to be her Mr. König, though.

"His name isn't even König," her friend whispered.

"What?" Maude's throat grew dry, and she poured them each a glass of water from the crystal carafe on her bedside table. "What's this about Mr. König?"

"I suspect his name is Steffan. Ben Steffan."

Ben, just like Anna had said. Maude's chest squeezed tight.

"And he isn't an industrialist, either."

Breathing shallowly, Maude sipped her water and swallowed hard. "Who is he, then?"

Sadie motioned to her hat and hair. "Do you mind if I take it down?"

"No, go ahead." They'd brushed and dressed each other's hair so many times over the years. Had giggled over all the places Sadie wished to go when she left the island. Yet here they both were.

Her old friend began to unpin her long golden hair, dropping the pins into her lap slowly, one at a time, her lower teeth working at her upper lip like they did when she was nervous and didn't want to say something. "Did you know what your family members have been telling him about Greyson?"

"About Greyson?" Maude frowned. Anna's words rang through her mind.

"I think he's a reporter for the *Detroit Post*."

"You think so?" Was that the real reason he'd shown interest in her?

Sadie slid forward to the end of the cushion. "He's writing a story about Greyson and Anna."

"What for? And why are my family members speaking to him about Greyson?"

A dry laugh accompanied a handful of pins that plopped into Sadie's lap. "They're giving their version of the truth to him."

Maude stopped plucking at the embroidered flower on the bedspread, unaware she'd been tormenting the silk-thread daisy. "Which is?"

Her old friend's huff spoke volumes.

Tossing her head, Sadie's curls fell free about her shoulders. She rubbed her head. "Oh, my aching head. I wish Mrs. Luce could hire me back. I thought it was because of Anna, but I wonder now if it was because your father's payments stopped."

Cold dread settled itself at her feet. Maude kicked off her shoes and pulled her feet up beneath her on the bed. "You have to admit it was no longer Father's responsibility to send Mrs. Luce money."

Sadie's pretty lips parted and held there for a moment before pressing firmly closed. She stood, and the scent of ammonia and vinegar announced the amount of cleaning she'd done that day. "So, you did know?"

"Yes, I knew Mother had paid your wages. And Father took over after…" She blinked back the moisture in her eyes.

"And about the other?" Sadie chewed her lower lip.

"Which was?"

"Greyson's college."

"About what?"

"The payments, silly goose."

"Yes, I heard." Maude clamped her teeth tightly together. If Father hadn't given that money to Greyson's college for tuition, room, and board, he'd still be here on the island. And they'd be married. Rather than regret, relief flowed through her. She drew in a deep breath.

"Well, that's not right that he'd accept all that money and then not marry you. He should pay it back." Sadie lifted her chin.

"That's between him and God." Or had Father asked him to do so and Greyson refused? Maude frowned.

Sadie rubbed her red hands together. "I've never had such raw hands, not even the time Pa insisted I scrub the entire house for his drinking buddies to come and play cards."

Maude pointed to her vanity. "Use some of the Malvina cream—that always helped you."

Bowing her head slightly, Sadie laughed. "You always know what to do."

"If only I knew how to help myself." Maude hopped from the bed and moved to the vanity table. She loosened the jeweled top of the cream jar and offered it to Sadie.

She scooped out a dollop and applied it to her chapped hands. "Thanks."

"You're welcome."

Sadie cocked her head at her. "See how you're trying to take care of me and you're not thinking about what needs to be addressed?"

Sadie clasped Maude's hands. "We both love Mrs. Luce—she's one of the sweetest ladies on the island, and she was no chore to work for. I was grateful your father continued to pay my wages, making it possible for me to take care of her this winter—after you refused Greyson."

"I didn't refuse him." Maude pulled her hands free. "We had a disagreement."

Turning, Sadie grasped the rococo wicker chair and pulled it beside the bed. "Listen to me—you were never in love with Greyson."

"What?" Maude's face flushed. "I loved Greyson."

"As a friend." Sadie tipped her head to the side, her smile knowing.

"As a dear friend." Which wasn't enough.

"Not enough for a marriage. And maybe he knew that, too, for him to turn to Anna. But would you want either of them hurt now?"

Regardless of what Greyson had done, he had been Maude's and Sadie's friend. "Of course not. Why?"

Sadie untied the strings on her cloth purse and pulled out a rumpled piece of paper. "I tucked this in my apron and ran from Mr. König when he demanded I give it back."

"You jest."

"It's the honest truth." Sadie made a crossing motion over her chest. "I imagine there could be a scandal."

"What would be a scandal?"

Her friend stood and took a step toward Maude, passing her the wrinkled typewritten page. "Anna's expecting a baby in a few months, for one reason."

Maude set the page in her lap. "She's not!" But she recollected seeing the Luces looking at baby items at the mercantile.

"But that's not the worst of it." Sadie squeezed her lips together. "Take a look at what he typed."

Maude raised the sheet and scanned it. Greyson and Anna weren't described in derogatory terms, but the writer unflinchingly laid out the facts about each. She cringed.

"That's not all." Sadie wrung her hands. "I saw all kinds of notes that he wrote up about your family, Maude. And I think he wants to paint you as some tragic islander whose hopes were ruined by Greyson and Anna."

Maude sighed loudly. "Do I look tragic?"

"No, of course not." Sadie blinked. "In fact, you've taken this whole thing with Greyson better than I could have imagined."

Because she'd never really been in love with Greyson. But Anna Forham—did she not love him, either? Anna thought Greyson was a Cadotte heir. Had he really tricked her into marrying him?

"And Maude, I hate to think this, but is it also possible that Mr. König is Mr. Steffan and is after your inheritance? I saw a business card for Benjamin Steffan, with the *Detroit Post* and telegrams from the editor there—a Mr. Banyan. I remember that man's name because my father was incensed by Mr. Banyan's columns. He wrote nasty editorials about workingmen taking advantage during the economic downturn last year."

Maude held up a hand, cutting off her friend. "What inheritance?" Her bedside mechanical clock seemed to slow its ticking.

Sadie moistened her lips. "Robert mentioned something—since your father cannot inherit."

Maude was too dumbfounded to speak. Roses floating in the bowl on the side table gently stirred as Maude shifted positions.

"Make sure you understand who this man is and why he is here," Sadie added.

A journalist from the Detroit newspapers. Maude had been fooled again. But she'd rise to the occasion. "He's accompanying me to the theater tonight."

"Send word to cancel." Sadie ran her fingers through her long blond tresses.

"Oh, no. I'm going." Maude gave a curt laugh. "But thank you for your warning."

A good thing Father was doing better. Tomorrow she'd finally heed Uncle Al's advice and head to the attorney in St. Ignace.

By herself.

For now, though, she'd need to get ready.

Throughout the two hours of primping, beautifying, hair curling, and singeing, Maude berated herself for even bothering to continue this charade with Friedrich. Or Ben. What was his true name, anyway? Although she was furious—devastated even—she'd felt the strangest calm settle over her. Shock might be what she was experiencing, for this detached sensation reminded her greatly of her emotions after Mother had died.

Sucking in a breath, she waited as Bea tightened her corset strings.

"Enough!" she called out when she thought her breath might fail.

Bea giggled as she finished off. Then she removed the Worth gown from the armoire. "How could a dress be more beautiful?"

"Uncle Robert has an eye for beauty."

Hoisting it high, the girl held it up to the light that filtered through the lace curtains. She gasped. "If I had a gown like this, I'd get married in it."

Maude wouldn't be marrying. She'd not be fooled again. Greyson. Now Friedrich. Or Ben. Or whoever he was. She stretched her shoulders, trying to relieve the cramp between them.

"You goose, it's aqua and bright blue—like a peacock. I believe Reverend McWithey would frown upon such attire for a wedding." Still, it was so gorgeous, Maude couldn't stop picturing herself floating toward the front of the church, Father holding her arm, and handsome Friedrich—no, Ben— waiting with the preacher.

"Wouldn't care. If this were mine, I'd wear it anyway, no matter what anyone said."

If it weren't for Father's agreement to bring the girl on and house and feed her, where would Bea find herself now? On the streets of the mainland? How could her fellow islanders have snubbed her so? Hurt throbbed in Maude's heart.

"Come on, slowpoke. I've got other work to do." Bea's impudent words dispersed Maude's kind thoughts.

With the girl's help, she stepped into the chiffon silk that practically glimmered as the fabric moved around her. The contours skimmed her hips, cinched in at the waist, and then gently swathed around her bodice in a series of tucks and flounces. This must be what a princess felt like. Except this princess had learned her prince was a pauper—as she may be soon, depending upon Uncle Robert's whims. She had to find out what her inheritance was.

"Bea, will you make sure my day suit gets pressed—I'll need it for tomorrow."

"The ugly gray one?"

"It's not ugly, it's practical and the new style."

"Call it what you want. It's still hideous. But I'll take it down to the laundry."

Bea fastened the back of the gown, each increment up the dress pulling it tighter, constricting her movement more, until Maude feared she might need to wriggle and tear free from the garment and run.

Maude ran her finger around the low décolleté. "I don't want this."

"The neckline's not indecent, if that is what you mean." Bea cocked her head to the side and examined Maude. "Sadie has worn something similar and gotten all kinds of notice."

Feeling her cheeks heat, Maude shook her head. She wasn't about to criticize her friend's choices. "I mean—this gown is too fancy for us island folk. I feel absurd."

"Pooh! What do you mean us island folk? You're beautiful and rich and might as well look like you are. I would if I were you."

"You wouldn't." Islanders were modest. And they weren't rich—not like the Vanderbilts or Rockefellers.

"I would." Bea grinned. "Mr. König will keel over when he gets a glimpse of you."

Mr. Steffan. "He won't—he'll think I'm putting on airs." Just as he'd been doing.

Chapter Twenty-Three

$\mathcal{S}$tone-cold fury accompanied Maude as she mounted the steps to the theater, "Friedrich" at her side. Would he reveal the truth about himself tonight or would he continue to deceive her? Pulling the gown's thin material a little too vigorously, her ankles and calves were on view to all those around them. She tried lowering the hem of the gown but feared she'd trip, and she didn't wish to take the hand offered to her by that deceiver.

"I think you're having trouble. Should I carry you up?" The masquerader's wicked grin taunted that he might.

"No, you shall not." Perhaps he was determined to cause his own scandal.

Maude wadded the material in her hand and by keeping it close to her knees she was able to complete the rise. At the top of the stairs, she released the silk and cringed when a ring of wrinkles remained.

"Here." He grasped the peacock feather in her left hand and transferred it to her right. "Hold it in front. . ."

Cocking his hip, he demonstrated for her—placing the feather at the edge of his tuxedo coat. This jocular stance drew a laugh from a blond woman standing nearby in a rose satin gown. Simple and elegant, the woman looked like a swan. And Maude like a robin overdressed in a peacock's feathers.

What did it matter, though? This man, this liar, intended to make a mockery of her friend. Greyson may have made bad choices, but he was still an islander and he'd been her pal all of her life.

"This is a mistake. I should go."

Laughing, Friedrich handed her the feather and Maude used it to cover the mess she'd made of her gown. With the twin doors to the theater open, sound from within burbled out. A great many summer vacationers attended. All those people from the Grand. Some whose rooms she had cleaned. She'd pretended to be something she wasn't, too. The anger she felt toward her escort dissipated some. But who was this man, then, if he wasn't a wealthy industrialist from Detroit? Was he truly Ben Steffan, the reporter?

The voices from within lacked the uniformity of the Mackinac accent. While they had a Scotsman, Frenchwoman, or Finlander here and there, most of the inhabitants possessed a similar pattern of speech. How in such a short time had a German-accented voice so charmed her? And why, even as she knew she'd break things off and never see him again, did she want to cling to him? Heaven help her, for her heart still yearned for his.

❤

Maude's responses to Ben were, so far this night, curt, and she wouldn't keep his gaze. He led her forward, toward the entrance to the theater where mocking laughter echoed from the box office.

"See here, you'll not keep me out." The deep voice continued berating the ticket manager.

Maude squeezed Ben's arm. "Mr. Thompson works so hard to bring lovely entertainment to the island. He doesn't need to put up with this."

A large man in a too-tight coat wagged his finger in the proprietor's face. "Do you know who I am?"

"Come on." Ben clasped her elbow.

He guided her through the clusters of couples who awaited the performance. The men in attendance, however, surveyed Maude from beneath half-closed eyes. He wanted to tell them to put their eyes back in their sockets.

With a gentle turn, placing Maude behind him at an angle, Ben tapped the red-faced man on the arm.

"What do you want?" The screaming man was Mr. Searles, an iron-ore magnate.

One night in the men's social room, Searles had divulged that he'd brought in a half-dozen bottles of bourbon in his trunks because the previous year the Grand had limited replenishment of the stock in his room.

"Oh, it's you, König." The inebriated man threw his hands up. "Can you believe they've not held my tickets for me?"

Ben tapped his fingers to the brim of his hat. "You were supposed to pick them up from the concierge, sir, not here."

"I'll be d——." Searles sputtered out a slew of cuss words.

"No profanity!" Mr. Thompson pointed to the sign on the wall, beneath which was another indicating there was to be no spitting on the premises.

Searles swayed slightly as he turned toward Maude. "Say, don't I know this little filly?"

"No. Miss Welling is an island resident."

"An island girl?"

The crowd began to press forward into the playhouse, the attendant taking their tickets.

"Why don't you take a cab back to the Grand, get your tickets, and then return for intermission?"

Hopefully the sot wouldn't return.

"Maude Welling?" Mr. Thompson called from the ticket booth. "Is that you?"

She moved forward to speak with the proprietor, her words inaudible.

"Well, I was gonna ask if you knew that drunkard, eh? It seems your gentleman friend does." Thompson puffed out a breath. "Can you verify who he is so I can admit him?"

Maude nodded gently. Curls that trailed her bare shoulders and back undulated like a waterfall. "I'm afraid I do."

Thompson's eyes widened. "Well, call him over then, eh? But stay away from him."

"Yes, sir." She returned to Ben's side and whispered, "The beauty of island life—being told by every adult older than one's self what one should do. And islanders protect their own."

Accusation lit her eyes. Did she know about the article? Had Sadie read his notes and told her?

Mr. Thompson called out, "Mr. Searles, please return to the window." He waved the big man forward.

The ticket salesman tucked a piece of tobacco into his lean cheek. "Listen up, you'll get in—because Miss Welling says so. But if I hear of one more cuss word coming out of your big mouth, you'll be gone."

"Why, I—you. . ." Mr. Searles's jowls shook in outrage. "How dare you?" Ben stepped alongside him. "I suggest you accept this man's generosity and go inside to your seat. And stop making a scene." His low voice, audible only to Thompson, Searles, and Maude had the desired effect. The bully reached out his hand and grabbed the ticket offered to him before he harrumphed off inside, jerking on his cravat.

♥

As the crowd surged forward into the theater, the women's scents of jasmine, geranium, and gardenia swirled into an overpowering aroma. Trying to avoid the admiring gazes of the men, Maude glanced at the women— shocked by the open hostility in their eyes. A shudder began at the base of her neck and traveled down to her strapped pumps. She didn't belong here. Not with these people. And they knew it, too. Those women must recognize Maude as one of the maids from the hotel. That had to be the reason for their behavior.

Friedrich bent down to whisper in her ear, the scent of bayberry and pine enticing her, despite her determination to hold herself distant from him. "You're the most beautiful woman here."

Turning her head toward him, his lips brushed against her cheek. Then he pressed a deliberate kiss where the accidental touch had occurred, sending a thrill of victory through her. But for what? That he thought her the most desirable woman in this place? That he'd been willing to announce his affection in public in front of all these people? Greyson had done the same. He'd wrapped his arms around her at the top of these very steps last summer and had kissed her full on the mouth in front of everyone, some laughing aloud, while she'd frozen there like a ninny. He'd laughed afterward. He had another fish on the line while he dangled her in the Straits. Greyson's cool lips hadn't provoked the response Ben's had. Yet another man deceived her. What was wrong with her?

Tucking her arm into the crook of his elbow, Friedrich guided her toward the door. Nearby, the beautiful young woman Evelyn Stanton, whispered something into her friend Gladys's ear.

Evelyn sidled closer, her pink muslin dress accentuating her curves. "Mr. König, so good to see you. Aren't you going to introduce us to your friend?"

"This is Maude Welling." Her escort held his arm farther away from his body and stepped back, as though displaying her.

Maude blinked at him. What was he doing? *Relax, he is simply being polite.*

Gladys's pretty face showed no recognition. "Are you staying at the Grand, Miss Welling?"

"No, I live on the island."

"You live here?" Miss Stanton laughed, as though the idea were absurd. "I didn't know anyone actually lived year-round on the island."

Tiny lines formed around Friedrich's eyes as he narrowed his gaze. "You think people only come for the summer and then the entire place is empty?"

Reaching into her reticule, Maude retrieved her handkerchief and dabbed at her face, feigning perspiration but inhaling the delicate rosewater it had been soaked in before she'd hung it on the line. Hopefully the scent would calm her nerves.

"Miss Welling is the daughter of the most prominent businessman on Mackinac Island."

Maude had to protest. "I wouldn't say that. . . ." Especially since Father wouldn't inherit. She couldn't believe Friedrich would make such a claim.

The interior doors opened. Now she could make her escape before either of these young women, whose rooms she had tidied, took notice of her as their former maid.

Gladys tapped Friedrich's arm. "Is Mr. Williams here tonight, Mr. König?"

"I don't know."

"We've been reading all of his columns from last month." Gladys tugged at her lace-edged cuffs.

"Daniel is such a wonderful journalist." Evelyn Stanton sighed.

Gladys nodded. "And he recommended we read Benjamin Steffan's articles, in the *Detroit Post*, too."

"Made us both want to visit Detroit and attend some of the wonderful social events he had covered."

"I wonder if someone from the island newspaper will be covering this theatrical presentation." Gladys scanned the stream of theater patrons.

"I'd love to be mentioned, wouldn't you, Gladys?"

"Yes. How about you, Mr. König?"

"Nein." His curt retort caused the two young ladies' eyebrows to rise. But he didn't care. This conversation didn't need to take place right now. "Come along, Maude."

♥

Friedrich guided Maude into the slightly musty building—his hand firm on her back as they separated from the two young women. The familiar give of the wood floor beneath the burgundy-patterned carpet reassured her. This was the same theater she'd always attended, despite a glance around the room suggesting otherwise. The men's fancy hats, which they now removed, weren't worn by islanders. Neither were the women's elaborate jewels, which glittered beneath the gas lamp fixtures. While the Grand Hotel had electric lights, most establishments in town didn't.

An usher led them to their row. Marcus Edmunds, a notorious flirt, stood and shook Friedrich's hand. He gestured to a young woman whose ample cleavage almost spilled from her ruby-toned gown.

"You know Gracie Malone."

"Mr. König, so good to see you out. We've not had the pleasure of your company at this quaint establishment before." Gracie giggled.

Quaint? Maude ran her finger over her feather, wondering where she'd set the silly pretentious thing.

"No." Friedrich grinned down at Maude before turning back toward Miss Malone. "I've been busy with other pursuits."

Marcus leered at Maude, and she wanted to gag. "Like this beauty?"

"Miss Welling, this is Mr. Edmunds."

"Call me Marcus—everybody does."

Certainly all the wealthy young women he pursued called him by his given name. Not that she ever would.

Her companion gestured for them to sit. Thankfully, he sat next to Mr. Edmunds so she was spared rubbing elbows with him.

Maude tried to burrow down into the overstuffed velvet-cushioned chair. What should have brought comfort, as it normally did, suddenly seemed lumpy and stiff. She angled the peacock feather across her lap.

Finally, the lights were dimmed and the production commenced. As angry as Maude was with Friedrich for his duplicity, she was still painfully aware of his presence next to her and what could have been. How could she still yearn for his kiss when he'd spent his entire time on the island deceiving her?

When her companion took her hand in his, her heart picked up a beat.

He leaned in and whispered, "Are you all right?"

Nodding, she felt his side-whiskers brush her cheek before he straightened. The warm evening made the room hot, and the scent of men's heavy Macassar hair oil practically suffocated her. Onstage, the actors continued on with the scene. The crowd remained transfixed. All Maude could do was force herself to breathe slowly, shallowly. *I will not have a spell.*

She prayed as the show continued, but her anger, disappointment, and fear brewed like a toxic gas that filled her being.

They shouldn't have come here. This theater had been an escape for her since she'd been a child—a place where she could magically travel to places far away without leaving the island. Now, though, the painted frescoed walls closed in around her.

The crowd erupted in applause as the scene ended and the curtains closed.

Her breath stuck in her throat. *Stay calm, this will pass.* Maude took short breaths in and out, becoming dizzier by the moment. Frantically, she pulled her hand free from her escort's and pressed a hand to her chest as those dreaded sounds began—the wheezing.

"Maude?" Friedrich leaned in toward her.

"Does she have lung problems?" Edmunds leaned forward and looked at Maude.

People around them rose and moved toward the aisles, their scents of perfume, wool, and leather accompanying them. Maude wrapped her arms around her middle and rocked, willing calm into her spirit. *Lord, please, help me.*

"Yes, I believe she does." Friedrich took her hand. "Edmunds, please go find a doctor!"

Maude closed her eyes.

"Let's get her outside."

"Might this stuffy little playhouse have brought it on?" harrumphed Gracie.

The Island Theater was a fine establishment. Maude gasped and drew in an outraged breath, accompanied by a definite wheeze.

"Can you walk, sweetheart?" Friedrich pulled her up.

He'd called her sweetheart. But he was betraying her friends and possibly her family. She leaned into his arms, pressing her face against his chest. *Lord, let me breathe. Don't let me die. Not here in front of all these strangers. People who don't care about me. Who don't know us.*

Us. Tears overflowed down her face. There would be no us. This man planned to ruin her friend.

Two strong arms wrapped beneath her as Friedrich skillfully guided her through the crowd cluttering the aisle. "Make way. Let us through."

As she struggled to breathe, Maude overheard snippets of conversation. "It's that girl with König."

"The maid?" The sneer on the person's voice squeezed Maude's chest further.

"What's he doing with her?"

Outside, Friedrich found a bench and sat. He sat her next to him, an arm wrapped around her. Cringing, Maude closed her eyes. How could she both despise this man and yet desire his presence?

Edmunds jogged up to them. "The doctor at the Grand is off tonight."

Gracie eyed her with suspicion. "One way to get a man's attention."

"*Sind Sie witzlos?*"

"What did he say?" Gracie clutched Marcus's arm.

No one informed her that she'd been asked if she was witless.

"Dreadful play so far, compared to the number we saw last year in Detroit." Marcus coughed into his hand.

"But not so bad as to bring a fit on," Gracie simpered.

Edmund's laugh was echoed by Gracie's higher-pitched one.

Annoying as Friedrich's friends were, out in the fresh air, a steel band seemed to uncinch from around her lungs. Maude sucked in a deep breath. "Please, just take me home."

Stan rode by, his carriage unoccupied.

Edmunds winked at Friedrich. "Maybe you should skip the rest of the play and get a cab to take you up to Lover's Lookout."

Maude fisted her hands. "It's called Arch Rock, not Lover's Lookout."

"I think she's had that planned all along." Edmunds laughed.

Danke Gott Edmunds had returned to the theater. Ben was tempted to punch the man.

Ben listened as Maude's wheezing quieted. "What do you think brought this on?"

"All those overpowering scents in the room." She looked up, her eyes wet. "And I had an upsetting event today."

"Oh?" Had Sadie told her?

"I think I'm all right now."

He pointed across the green. "There's the coffee stand. Caffeine can stimulate the bronchial tubes."

"I can walk."

She stood, and he followed suit, taking her hand in his.

They crossed the lawn to the tiny whitewashed building.

"Coffee?"

"Thank you. Black for mine and for my. . ." He wanted to call Maude his sweetheart. "She likes lots of cream and sugar in it." He longed to be the one who fixed this beautiful woman her morning coffee every day. First, though, he'd have to share with her about who and what he was and see if she could accept his request to court her as his true self. Taking their coffee, they moved to a bench.

"I need to tell you something," Ben said. "I am a society reporter, from the *Detroit Post*, and my name is actually Ben Steffan."

"So I've heard."

When had she learned? Chills gathered at his cummerbund and raced up his back beneath the borrowed tuxedo.

"Sadie?"

"Yes. Why are you really here on the island?"

He exhaled loudly. "I want to be an editor. This was my chance for a big story. My boss has all but promised me a huge promotion. . . ." With more money, he could bring Maude with him to Detroit.

Rubbing his thumb across her knuckles, he suddenly felt ridiculous. What was he thinking? He'd never be able to provide for her like her parents had.

And who was he to trust in Banyon—hadn't everyone else in his life let Ben down? He'd likely turn in the piece and return to find O'Halloran sitting at Ben's desk and himself demoted to junior. Sick dread filled Ben's gut. Banyon would tell him, "Try a little harder next time, son."

"You'll return to Detroit?" Maude sipped her coffee.

"That's where my job is. If I moved to another paper, I'd have to start all over again." And after this piece he'd have zero chance of ever moving to the *Detroit Free Press*. Unless he didn't send it. He tasted his coffee. Just as bitter as that brewed at the *Post*.

"What's so special about this story?"

"Nothing really." Except that he'd have to keep her name out of it. Which meant doing an additional article of some importance to placate Banyon. "Just a man who did a woman wrong—two women actually." It was a lie—this story wasn't nothing—it could be everything to Greyson Luce. And Banyon must be seeking vengeance on Forham for something.

She exhaled a puff of air, sending the curls on her forehead bobbing like the nearby waves on Lake Michigan.

"I tire of people taking advantage of one another," Ben said. "Of life's injustices." Was he really angry with God, for what had happened to his own family?

"I agree."

"You do?"

"Yes," Maude stated. "I think you've taken enough advantage of my family."

Chapter Twenty-Four

The ride from the island to the Upper Peninsula and the attorney's office was everything Maude hoped it would *not* be. Rain pelted the deck at an alarming rate, whitecaps slammed against the boat, and passengers crowded within the cabin of the ferry. Finally, she disembarked at the dock with the rest of the travelers and followed the queue down to the main street in St. Ignace. Light but steady rain continued, and she aimed her umbrella to keep gusts of wind from blowing straight at her.

The delightful scent of cinnamon buns wafted from a bakery with deep pink awnings. She'd have to swing back and make a purchase on her return. For now, though, she wanted to see Mr. Hollingshead. She continued down the boardwalk until she spied his shingle. She shook out her umbrella before she went inside. Although she expected to be met by a secretary, a pretty young woman, her bun askew atop her head, sat on the floor playing blocks with a toddler.

Maude set her umbrella inside the stand by the door.

The woman rose and wiped her hands on her dusky gray skirt. "May I help you?"

The dark-stained mahogany door to the left likely led to the attorney's office. Maude didn't have an appointment. She moistened her lips.

"I've come to see Mr. Hollingshead."

"Your name?"

"I'm afraid I don't have an appointment. My name is Maude Welling. . . ."

Her eyebrows rose in alarm. "Miss Welling?"

Why would this young woman fear her? "Yes, my family is represented by Mr. Hollingshead."

Face flushed, the young woman turned and picked up the child. "Yes, my husband should be out shortly. Have a seat while I run upstairs for a moment."

Like a chicken running from a fox, mother and child fled the room, heading to the back of the building, presumably to the stairs. After she was gone, Maude crossed to the coatrack and hung her dripping raincoat.

After she returned to the seating area, Maude sat and gathered her skirts around her then crossed her ankles. A large wall clock indicated it was already half past the hour. Because of the storm, the ferry had taken longer than she'd expected.

The office door swung open, and a tall young man emerged, speaking in a solemn voice to an elderly woman who leaned heavily on her brass-headed cane. He walked past Maude, cocking his head ever so slightly as though questioning her appearance in his office.

The silver-haired woman retrieved a large black umbrella from the stand. Then Mr. Hollingshead opened the front door for the frail lady.

In a moment, he turned to Maude, his eyes scanning the area around her, as though looking for his wife and child.

Maude pointed to the back. "They've gone upstairs for a moment."

"Ah." He nodded and clasped his hands together. "I'm Steven Hollingshead, how can I help you?"

"I hoped to speak with you about some family matters of a legal nature."

"Come on into my office." He gestured toward the open door and Maude rose.

Once inside, he pointed to an overstuffed leather armchair, and she sat as he rounded the desk and took his seat. He pulled out a notepad.

"I'm here about my mother's estate—actually my grandmother's—I'm not sure which or if they are somehow bound together."

"I see." He held his fountain pen over the pad, head bent. "I apologize, please tell me your full name."

"Maude Jacqueline Welling."

"Miss Welling?" His chin jerked up, his eyes wide. "You've finally come."

She shifted in her chair. "I. . ."

"I summoned you months ago."

He'd sent for her? "I received no word."

The attorney's Adam's apple bobbed. "I'm afraid I require some identification from you before we can proceed."

"Identification?" She clutched at her reticule.

"Of course—I must ensure my clients' privacy, and I must be sure you are who you claim to be."

Claim to be? "What proof are you seeking, sir?"

His cheeks grew florid. "Something that shows, for instance, that you are Maude Welling of Mackinac Island."

"Oh." She opened her purse. "I have my library card with me. Will that suffice?"

"I must have the exact address of your home, as well."

"Address? Everyone knows where the Winds of Mackinac is located and you, sir, should know we use the post office for our mail on the island."

"Yes, quite right."

She passed him her library card and he inspected it before returning it to her. Then he began tapping his fingers on his desk. "Are you worried about something, Mr. Hollingshead?"

"No, no, all seems to be in order. Do you mind telling me who your parents and grandparents are?"

She drew in a slow breath. "My mother, Eugenia Swaine Welling, and father Peter Welling. Maternal grandparents Jacqueline Cadotte Swaine and Carter Swaine."

"Good, very good." He pulled a thick file from his drawer and set it atop his desk. "Miss Welling, might I also ask if you retain an attorney from the island?" His well-formed lips pulled in tight.

"No. Why do you ask?"

His features pulled in several directions as though he was working out a puzzle and didn't possess all the pieces. "No reason. Well, here, let's review."

Maude pulled her chair closer to the desk. For the next half hour, she listened to him rattle off the specifications of her grandmother's will. Some she had him repeat.

She drew in a deep breath. "So it's true that my father owns none of the holdings he and my mother managed?"

"Correct. As stipulated in your grandmother's will, her heir's spouses wouldn't inherit upon their deaths but their children would, when they came of age."

Which meant she and Jack inherited their mother's property. "At twenty-one?"

"Yes."

Which meant she inherited on her upcoming birthday. "I don't understand. Why would she do that?"

"It seems that your grandmother had been very disturbed about your grandfather Swaine making a muck of things, excuse my language, of the Cadotte holdings that she'd inherited."

Maude recalled the stories of the extreme distress her grandmother had suffered when he'd died and she'd discovered her estate was almost ruined. She'd been left with a small child, Robert, and Maude's mother to raise alone and had become a focused businesswoman, restoring the businesses.

"Miss Welling, you also must remain on the island, to live there, in order to profit from your holdings."

"Robert isn't married and he's not lived on the island in almost a year." *Until now.*

The lawyer leaned forward and rubbed his chin. "I'm afraid I can't discuss your uncle's situation with you. I can say that it's not clear, from the will's terminology, as to whether your grandmother only stipulated for her grandchildren or also for the children. If you'd like, I can suggest another attorney who could advise you, if you wish to take any action."

"Action?"

"Such as contesting the will or certain provisions."

Her mouth was so dry. She needed a drink. Something sweet that would chase this bitter taste from her mouth.

"But what does this mean for us for now? For Winds of Mackinac?"

"You and your brother live on the island, correct?"

"Yes."

"So you fulfill that stipulation. I understand your brother is twelve."

"Yes."

"So his assets would need to be protected by the current sole heir, as would yours until your birthday."

"So my uncle is legally responsible and must remain on the island?"

The lawyer cleared his throat. "As I said, it's not entirely clear if the stipulations apply to Robert Swaine or not. At present, we should assume that at the minimum he must reside at least a portion of the year on the island. If you or he wishes, action could be taken to have a judge determine his status."

Maude's head began to ache. She held up a hand. "No, I don't think that's necessary." *Not now anyway.*

"I'm at liberty to share that he has kept all profits from your businesses in a separate account for you or your brother to draw from as needed."

"Yet none for my father?"

"I'm afraid we fear he cannot, at present, given the codicil in the will. Nothing other than the direct expenses of the businesses he manages."

Poor Father. No wonder he was so out of sorts. "So he's been relying on Robert, since our mother's death, to okay withdrawals?"

"I'm not sure that Robert is requiring that of your father." Mr. Hollingshead rotated his wedding band in a slow revolution. "He's not happy with his mother's stipulations."

"Is that why he's been staying in St. Ignace?"

"Pretty much." The attorney glanced toward his tall oak filing cabinet on the far wall.

"So my father truly has nothing from the estate?"

"I imagine he had the good sense to pay himself a salary over the years. I would hope so."

"But he owned none of the assets."

"Correct."

And Maude, and eventually Jack, owned not only the inn but all the other businesses. Would this entire situation cause Father's heart to finally give way?

"There are some more legal requirements in the codicil, but as your family's attorney I'm not sure we need to concern ourselves at this time."

"Such as?"

"In the future—should there be another heir who came forward."

"My other two uncles died in the war."

"Can you be certain they had no children?"

Maude blinked.

He raised a hand. "Not to worry about these things now. I'll meet with you later to spell out a few other contingencies."

"Thank you for your time."

"You know where your accounts are held, Miss Welling, don't you?"

"I believe so."

"You can't change the accounts without your uncle's permission, nor can you transfer amounts out of the accounts in excess of a set amount."

"Which is?"

"You'd need to ask your uncle."

"I'll do that. Good day."

He made to rise, but Maude dipped her chin at him as she stood. "I'll let myself out, thank you."

She put on her coat and grabbed her umbrella then exited onto the street. For a moment, the sun peeked out from behind gray rain clouds. Maybe a hot drink and pastry would settle her nerves. She dodged small children tossing a ball to one another on the sidewalk. Finally, she paused by Jo's Bakery, its glass windows smelling of a fresh vinegar cleaning. Maude opened the door and went inside, the scents of cinnamon, bread, and sugar enveloping her.

"Help you, miss?" The auburn-haired woman behind the display case smiled at her and pulled a small plate from atop a stack.

"I'd love to have one of those cinnamon rolls."

"Here's a good fat one for you." She slid a spatula beneath a large roll covered with cinnamon, white frosting, and butter. "Tea or coffee to go with that, dear?"

"Coffee, please, with lots of cream and sugar."

The woman laughed. "That's the way I like it, too."

Maude paid and carried her snack tray to a small circular metal table that faced a wall of various antique-framed mirrors. She took a seat but was startled by the reflection in the mirror. A wan-faced, red-eyed, frizzy-haired, and rumpled-looking young woman stared back at her, looking as though she'd lost her best friend. Pitiful. Maude looked pitiful.

The bell to the bakery tinkled as the door was opened. In the mirror, Maude spied a dark-suited man standing behind her. Attorney Hollingshead. He headed toward her table.

"Miss Welling?"

"Yes?"

He shifted from foot to foot like a small boy who'd done wrong. "I need to ask you something."

"Please join me." She sucked in a deep breath and waved toward the empty seat. "But I'm not sharing my roll." Maude gave a short laugh.

"Yes, well, that's fine." He sat, his legs spread wide as he leaned forward. "I need to know if your father ever sent someone over to speak with me on his behalf."

"Not that I know of." Greyson? Had he come to find out what Maude would inherit? Anger heated her face, and she hastily took a bite of her cinnamon bun, bending her head low over the plate.

"I know this may sound crazy, but a gentleman made inquiries here a few weeks back but didn't leave me his card."

Maude savored the tangy roll then swallowed and looked up. "Perhaps Father did, but I don't know who that would have been." She'd give Greyson a piece of her mind if he had come over.

"Well, here's the strange thing. He introduced himself as Friederich something. Cooney?"

Friedrich König had been here. "Oh?" She kept her fork lifted over her treat.

"The gentleman greatly resembled a reporter who I'd met at a lawyers' conference in Detroit."

"What?" The utensil fell from her fingers and clattered onto the plate. "Who?"

"Ben Steffan. But what connection does he have with your family?"

"None." *None at all.* Her stomach threatened to heave up its contents. Ben had confirmed last night that he was not Friedrich König and instead a reporter working undercover on an article, but now she was to understand that he was also investigating their legal affairs?

"Well, then, I may have been mistaken." He laughed.

Hollingshead adjusted his bow tie. "I'm relieved. Do please let me know who your father sent so that I can get a good night's rest, again, will you, Miss Welling?"

"Certainly." What about her? Would she ever rest well again knowing that Ben Steffan had weaseled his way into her family for a story and apparently may also be seeking to learn whether she possessed any fortune? Why would God allow this to happen?

But something inside her begged her to trust Ben. She'd seen too many glimpses into the kind man he was. She had to trust God, too.

Hours later, Maude arrived home with clothes still damp, although the weather had cleared up. The breeze on the boat had only intensified her chill. Now she stripped off her clothes and planned to don a simple-but-warm dress for dinner, after which she intended to speak with her father.

Three sharp raps preceded Bea's entrance. Maude hastily turned away from the door.

"Let me help you, miss."

Bea freed her of the clinging garments. Maude dried off and whisked into her dry undergarments and a soft, light wool dress.

"Mrs. Fox will be arriving about seven."

Maude groaned.

"Don't you like her?" Bea adjusted the dress's collar. "She's the best thing for your father."

"I like her just fine. But can you please stall her if she arrives early? I need to speak with Father, right after dinner."

An hour later, as she ate her last spear of lemon-glazed asparagus, Maude took assessment of her father's mood. He seemed cheerful, joking during dinner, and he'd even allowed her brother to depart a few minutes earlier without eating all of his vegetables.

"Father, I went to see Attorney Hollingshead today."

Jaw slacking, her father pinned her with his gaze. "And?"

She blew out a puff of air. "He told me."

He harrumphed, but his cheeks didn't grow red, as she thought they might. "Quite a pickle, isn't it?"

"It's most distressing, Father. And I hope you know that I believe what Grandmother did was wrong."

"My dear, I lost my own mother at a somewhat young age, not much older than you." Her father looked at her as though only just realizing she wasn't a child anymore. "I was only in my twenties then. And to now have lost my wife, your mother, I can only say that *nothing* Jacqueline Cadotte Swaine did to me could have hurt more than losing them. Nothing."

Maude swallowed. "But it isn't fair."

"No, it isn't. But Jacqueline was a bitter woman." He sliced his asparagus into minuscule portions. "Not that I blame her. I can't imagine how shocked she must have been by your grandfather's foibles."

Both sat in silence, the scent of the boiled ham dinner lingering in the air. What could she do? Father began eating one tiny morsel of asparagus at a time.

Maude drew in a deep breath, wishing she could exhale the sudden sadness that had permeated the air. "I was wondering. Since you knew about the codicil, why did you not wish for me to run the inn?"

"I didn't want you running yourself into the ground like your mother did, managing this place."

"But—" Mother's death wasn't brought on by overexertion, and they both knew it.

"My own mother worked so very hard on the farm. I sometimes wonder if that is what killed her, too. I don't want you to have to have such a big responsibility."

"Father—"

He held out a hand, silencing her. "And there's more. Things you know nothing of, that have influenced my decision."

Someone cleared her throat. Ada Fox stood in the doorway. "Please excuse my interruption. There was no one up front, and I thought I heard your voices."

"Ada!" He rose and went to her, kissing each offered cheek. "Come in. You're just in time for coffee and dessert."

Jack popped his head in. "Did I hear dessert?"

"No vegetables, no dessert, young man." Father wagged a finger at her brother.

"Aw, Dad." He ducked his shaggy head.

Ada smoothed back a lock of Jack's hair from his forehead. "Peter, why don't you allow him, just this once? As a favor to an old friend. I remember the delicious pastries your mother used to make. And I don't remember you ever being denied partaking of them."

He laughed. "You're right."

Jack zipped around Ada and sat in his place, despite Maude's warning glance that he should still be standing until Mrs. Fox was seated. "So you knew my other grandma? Grandma Welling?"

"Indeed I did." Ada turned her direction from Jack to Maude as their father pulled out her chair for her. "I understand you suffer the same affliction that killed your grandmother, Maude. I'm so sorry to hear about your asthma attack."

Father's shoulders stiffened and he remained standing. "When did this happen, Maude?"

Ada's mouth slackened, but then she pressed her lips tightly together.

Maude pushed her plate away. "I should have told you, Father, but I'm fine now."

"Children." Father clucked his tongue. "What can you do with them, Ada?"

"Love them, I imagine. That's what I would do. Had I any." A sheen of moisture glowed on the woman's eyes.

Father sat and shrugged his shoulders inside his coat as though uncomfortable. "Ada, what do you mean about my mother dying from asthma?"

Jane entered the room pushing the coffee cart. She poured coffee and began adding sugar and cream. Maude startled at the realization that their maid already knew what Ada took in hers.

"I received a letter from our old Sunday school teacher back home, informing me that your mother had succumbed to her asthma." Ada leaned back as the servant slid coffee in front of her. "Thank you, Jane."

"Ye're welcome, ma'am."

Father reached for his handkerchief and dabbed at the perspiration that dotted his brow. "I thought her heart had failed her and she'd worked too hard."

"Oh, your mother did work hard—but the doctor said it was the hay that caused her final attack."

"Really?" Father rubbed his chin.

"I'm sorry, Peter. I thought you knew."

"My father only said that she'd worked herself into the grave. I thought he meant her heart had given out."

So there *was* a reason Maude experienced these spells, despite François's amateur psychiatrist attempts at diagnosing her as mentally unsound. The breathing issues seemed to run in the family. "Thank you for sharing that, Mrs. Fox. I'll be sure to tell the specialist when I see him next month." She'd finally made another appointment, and this time she'd keep it.

Father sipped his coffee and tilted his head at her. "Might want to wait until haying season is over, dear."

"Good idea." Ada accepted a piece of cherry pie from Jane. "If you can wait until they've brought it all in, you'll likely have less difficulty. And I'd be glad to accompany you."

"What about me?" Jack eyed the pie as Jane slid a slice in front of him. "Can I go?"

Ada and Father exchanged a pointed glance.

"You'll be traveling a great deal in the near future, son."

"I will?" He forked a huge chunk of pie into his mouth.

"Yes."

Ada patted his arm. "I've heard all about your athletic abilities, Jack. I'm hoping that very soon you'll be able to enter some competitions downstate."

Maude leaned back in her chair. "While I run the inn?"

"Yes." Father set his dessert fork down. "I'm not much on women working so hard, but if you, like your mother and Ada, insist. . ."

"Oh, I never insisted." Ada pressed her napkin to her mouth. "That was your mother who believed I needed training in a vocation."

"My mother?" He frowned.

"She paid for it. I thought you. . ."

From the looks being exchanged between Ada and her father, this looked like a conversation she didn't need to hear.

"Jack, if you're done, let's go play Parcheesi."

"Tiddlywinks first! And I want to finish my pie."

"We'll bring your pie over to the parlor with us."

"Sure, then. But I'll whip you and whoever else joins us."

"I know."

Ada's eyes sent a silent thank-you as Maude led Jack from the room.

Seemed there was more than one grandmother who manipulated and controlled people.

Chapter Twenty-Five

$\mathscr{A}$fter breakfast spent at his typewriter, Ben strolled to the end of the Grand Hotel's long porch, ignoring the young ladies clustered on either side. He gritted his teeth as he reached the far banister. End of the line. For both the porch and for him as Friedrich König. He'd blown his chances with Maude. He'd have to submit his story and be gone or lie low. Somehow. But how? He removed his hat and tapped it against his thigh.

The concierge approached him, carrying several placards. Mark Twain's visage and the date and time of his arrival were inked on the front. Ben had all but forgotten, so besotted was he with Maude Welling. Where Twain went, journalists were sure to follow.

How many papers would send reporters up so far north and pay for hotel and food?

"Mr. König, do you have a moment?"

"Yes?"

"Robert Swaine, the ship captain who is one of our shareholders, requested that you introduce Mr. Clemens, that is, Mr. Twain."

"Me?" Did Swaine want to expose him in front of everyone? Was that his plan? "I don't think so." But Clemens had been good to Ben over the years—sending him encouraging notes.

"Also, when Mr. Twain arrived, he specifically stated that if you were here, he wanted you onstage to introduce him."

"I see." Ben scratched his chin. Clemens hadn't seen him without his beard since he was a young, wet-behind-the-ears reporter.

"Quite an honor, sir."

And a potential nightmare. "Are there many journalists coming for Twain's event?"

He pulled a small notepad from his vest pocket. "Only a few are staying here. A couple of owners' sons who do columns as a hobby."

Oh no, that might include Anna's brother. Ben's stomach clenched. "I. . . will be leaving soon."

"You don't say? A shame."

"I've enjoyed my stay." *And regretted it in many ways.*

"I heard a quote attributed to Twain that's become one of my favorites."

"What's that?"

" 'Twenty years from now you will be more disappointed by the things that you didn't do than by the ones you did do. So throw off the bowlines. Sail away from the safe harbor. Catch the trade winds in your sails. Explore. Dream. Discover.' " The concierge laughed. "Don't know for sure that it's Twain's, but I think whoever said it was right."

The things Ben hadn't done. There had been many. But right now one musical instrument after another played so loudly in his mind that he couldn't think straight. He began to sweat and tugged at his collar. He went to his room and remained there until after lunch—hiding from what was to come.

Ben went downstairs to the ballroom's entryway, where Twain would be giving his speech.

A maid cocked her head at him. "You're fine to go in, if you want, but we're directing all those who aren't guests to go to the public areas."

He nodded in acknowledgement and stuck his head inside the room before returning to the foyer.

Noise carried down the halls. He recognized a flock of journalists who'd descended upon the hotel like seagulls looking for a tasty morsel. Ben ducked into an alcove near the hotel's tea shop, when he heard his name being called.

The desk clerk, Mr. Morris, caught Ben's eye and motioned for him to come over. "We have a message for you from a Mrs. Luce."

Ben rubbed his chin, suddenly wishing he had his beard back. It was time to really be Ben Steffan again. "Mrs. Luce?"

The man leaned over the shiny varnished counter. "Mrs. Greyson Luce." The man's pursed lips left no doubt that he believed Ben to be involved in some illicit activity.

"Thank you."

The slim man pressed a rose-scented lavender linen weave envelope into Ben's hand. He stiffened. The note looked like a love letter, which of course he knew it wouldn't be. He pointed to the letter opener in the man's supply tray. "May I borrow this?"

"Certainly."

Ben sliced into the envelope and read the single sheet within:

> *Dear Mr. Steffan,*
> *G. T. Harris, Father's best journalist, will be arriving*
> *today. He has a lead on a story about an impoverished*
> *journalist posing as a wealthy German industrialist*
> *seeking to wed a wealthy island heiress. Isn't that*
> *scandalous?*
>
> > *Cordially,*
> > *Anna*
>
> *P.S. I feel certain we could help squash this story with some*
> *reciprocity on your part.*

Chasing an heiress? But he hadn't. Ben swallowed hard. Anna's veiled threat was crystal clear. If Ben didn't submit his story, then Harris's wouldn't be published, either.

"I have another for you, sir." Mr. Morris held a cream-colored envelope aloft.

His landlady's name was neatly printed above the imprinted return address for a hotel near the boardinghouse. They had an agreement that no messages would be sent to the hotel unless there was an emergency. He swallowed.

"Thank you." He tucked the missive inside his jacket pocket and headed toward the stairs to go up to his room. As he turned the corner, he spied a group of musicians gathered inside the ballroom, the doors open wide. How did they feel about an author displacing them this afternoon?

Ben entered his room, removed his jacket and patted the pocket for the letter. Then he sat down in the corner chair by the desk, reached into the drawer for an ivory letter opener, and slit it open:

Dear Benjamin,
I have terrible news. The boardinghouse burned, and
everything in it. . . .

Ben's mouth fell open—all his belongings—his books, his instruments—destroyed. He closed his eyes. *Why, God, why me, why now?* He had nothing, was nothing. Nothing but an imposter. And he had no story.

Get ahold of yourself. He shook his shoulders and took a deep breath, the pastor's words from Sunday's sermon echoing in his ears: "Everything you have comes from God, by His will, and for His glory only. Don't ever fool yourself into thinking that anything here on earth truly belongs to you. We took this church for granted, and we failed to care for it. But by His prompting and the obedience of people on this island, we are rebuilding this church, to His glory and for His will."

He'd need to add a job as a pianist and even take on pupils just to make a dent in what he'd lost.

Thy will, not mine.

He continued reading the missive. The poor woman lost everything, but all of the boarders had gotten out alive. Had he been there, on the top floor, would he have been so fortunate? Something dripped down onto the paper, leaving a wet blotch.

After setting the letter down atop the desk, Ben rose and went to the window. *I don't even know myself anymore.* Character traits he'd taken for granted, that defined who he was had been yanked away. He was no actor. And the longer this charade persisted, the less he liked of who he was becoming.

"You're a kind young man, Benjamin—the type of man I'd wish my Anna would marry." Both he and the Prussian-born woman knew that would never be. She knew from whence he hailed and how his uncle had run them off. He recalled how she'd thanked him profusely when he'd lifted her, a dying woman, into her carriage after her footmen couldn't seem to manage. What would she think of him now, were she yet alive? Had Anna made a terrible mistake with Greyson? Or was she simply like Ben—someone who had followed her own path and now dealt with the consequences?

Had Mrs. Forham loved her daughter so much that she'd overlooked Anna's propensity to flirt, tease, and dangle another young man in front of a rival? But he'd been no rival—he'd simply been a newspaperman there to report on her father and her family and whatever events they attended where something newsworthy happened.

Standing here in a room he'd soon vacate, going to who knew where with nothing and no one to greet him, Ben suddenly felt ten years old again. Großmutter, when she was dying, spoke directly and succinctly to each of them in her last few months. Her words had gotten him through many a difficult night when he'd worked hard so that he could study, improve his English, and write. Without her encouragement he'd never have landed the job at the *Detroit Post*. And now—to be so close to being offered assistant editor. . . He pushed a hand through his hair.

He'd taken Mrs. Forham's utterances in the same vein as his grandmother's. But they weren't. Mrs. Forham may have been expressing her wishes to combat the fear she had at leaving her eldest daughter behind in the world—that she'd find a kind man, not the rakes she'd been chasing about town with. Ben stretched his shoulders.

"What about my wishes for you?"

Ben looked around the room, so real was the voice he'd heard calling to him. Like a sweet voice accompanied by a brief snippet of a brilliant piano concerto.

He opened his Bible and went to Ecclesiastes. Was he chasing after the wind? What was God's will for him?

Hours later, Ray arrived and readied Ben. "You sure look fine, sir. And don't that beat all that you gonna introduce Mr. Mark Twain?"

"Thank you."

"There's a steady flow of decked-out guests, business owners from town, and a bunch of newspapermen downstairs."

"Is that right?"

"Yes, sir. And some rustic-looking people from the mainland, too."

"Lumberjacks even?"

"Might be a few, but no checked flannel shirts that I saw!"

"I better get downstairs." Ben brushed a stray speck of lint from his sleeve.

"You'll do fine. The good Lord'll be right beside you, sir."

"Thanks, Ray."

A sharp rap on the door startled both men. Ray went to the door.

"I need to speak with Mr. König." Ada's tight voice wavered.

"Yes, ma'am, he's about to head down for Mr. Twain's presentation."

"Tell them he'll be down shortly, Blevins."

"Yes, ma'am."

Ada closed the door behind the departing servant, a newspaper tucked under her arm. She swiveled to face Ben and offered him the *Times*. "Go to the 'International' section. And you might want to sit down." She pointed to the bed.

"What is it?" He turned to a page marked by the corners being folded in.

"I thought you should read this."

Ben scanned the top headline. "GRAND DUKE FRIEDRICH KÖNIG OF BAVARIA DIES AT AFRICAN PLANTATION." He sank onto his bed and continued reading. "My uncle."

Her countenance softened. "I wondered. Because of your use of the name."

Ben nodded then resumed scanning the article. "Malaria killed him. He'd just turned fifty." His mother had died before reaching forty, heartbroken after Magdalena had died. Mother and Father both became chronically ill from the conditions where they lived in Chicago.

"The paper just came, but guests from the mainland likely already know." Ada's voice was soft and maternal. "And they may have questions."

"Right."

Ada clasped her hands at her waist. "Would you like a few minutes to compose yourself before you go down?"

Ben breathed a sigh and stood. "I'm angry still, at what that wicked man wrought."

"He's met his Maker now." Ada dipped her chin.

"Yes." Ben ran a hand over his jaw. "I pray he didn't poison his son with his beliefs."

"That young man will have some difficult days ahead of him. I see from the article that he's quite young."

"I never met my cousin." He'd read the rest of the article later. "I better go downstairs before I'm late."

"Just wanted to make sure you saw that, just in case people ask you about it."

"Danke." He followed her out the door, locking it behind him, then hurried down the back stairs. He'd never imagined his uncle would die so early. He'd expected him to outlive Ben, even, as he had the rest of his family.

Mark Twain paced outside the rear door that led to the ballroom's dais, as a burly blond man looked on. When he saw Ben, he strode toward him, clasped both his hands between his and shook them. "My boy, look at you now."

"So good to see you, sir." A tremor coursed through Ben. Maybe Ada was right; maybe he should have taken a few minutes to compose himself.

"I'm sorry about your namesake." The author's bushy eyebrows worked together.

"I just learned of his death." Sweat broke out on Ben's brow.

Behind the wall, the noise of happy patrons carried through—women's high-pitched voices and laughter, and deep men's voices initiating jokes that had brought on the women's glee. All were apparently in high spirits and weren't the decorous sort Ben had found attending literary events in Detroit. Their happiness loomed incongruous against his railing emotions.

"Quite a crowd, I was told." Twain tugged at his vest. "And it sounds like it."

Drawing in a long breath, Ben cracked the door open and looked through. There in the front row sat the wealthiest of the Grand's extensive guest list.

A proud-looking beauty with coils of cinnamon curls trailing her shoulders entered on Robert Swaine's arm. Maude. She'd come. Ben hung his head. He didn't deserve her.

He turned to Twain. "I don't merit the honor of presenting you, sir."

Smiling, he clapped Ben's arm. "The honor is mine."

What did he mean?

The hall clock chimed the hour. "I better get in there."

The servant crossed his arms and stood, feet planted wide apart. "I'll be right here if either of you need anything. And we have a man on the other side, too."

Mark Twain often spoke his mind and had offended a great many people. But did they really think someone would come all the way to Mackinac Island to harass the celebrated author?

Taking his place on the dais, Ben waited momentarily until they quieted. "Ladies and gentlemen, it is my great honor to introduce Mark Twain, undeniably one of the most beloved authors of our time."

"Here! Here!" Some of the rowdy journalists called out.

I can do this. Glancing at his notecards, Ben drew in a fortifying breath as he proceeded to name Twain's many accomplishments. Heads bobbed in agreement and applause punctuated the announcement of some of his books. "And it is without further ado, I give you the renowned Mark Twain."

Applause and foot-stomping shook the room. Some of the reporters whistled.

Twain moved forward and Ben gathered his notes, preparing to depart the stage, but the author drew alongside him. "Wait."

Then Twain gestured for the crowd to calm. He smiled benevolently at those assembled. "I do love to tell a story, you know."

Laughter erupted.

He raised his palm. "I want to tell you a story about a young man who inspired a character in my book *The Prince and the Pauper*."

Ben leaned back, sensing the strain in the fine wool of his tailored suit coat. He now possessed only one set of clothing to his name.

"This young man alongside me, sold me a paper one windy day about fifteen years ago."

Several fellow journalists, standing on the side, scribbled on their notepads.

"There was something about that little German boy that bothered me. His aristocratic voice, his bearing, his way of looking down his little nose at me as he offered me my paper as though it were a treasure." The author chuckled.

The room hushed. Ben's eyes moistened. He wanted nothing more than to run. But where would he go?

"When I asked his name, he proclaimed himself as Benjamin Friedrich König Steffan." Twain paused and scanned the room. "I told him that was quite a mouthful for a little chap."

The crowd tittered, a few present exchanging puzzled looks.

He turned and looked up at Ben. "He's certainly grown into that big name, hasn't he?"

Polite laughter ensued.

"I couldn't leave it at that. I have one of those noses"—Twain tapped the side of his nose then turned to the side, displaying his profile so that the crowd laughed—"that can't resist sniffing out a story. So I followed that boy to a tenement building in Chicago, where he lived with his parents. And I started doing my own little journalistic snooping around."

Ben leaned in. "Please, sir, Mr. Twain, say no more."

Twain's shaggy eyebrows bunched together. "That newsboy was the nephew of the archduke of Bavaria. He'd begun his life at a grand estate. But life brought changes."

In the front row, Gladys leaned in to say something to Evelyn. The electric lights illuminated the bronze highlights of Maude's hair, and her eyes widened.

"He was like my little prince who'd become a pauper. Like the story in my head, I had right before me a living and breathing example. And I couldn't get that proud little boy out of my mind. I've followed his career over the years, as he has blossomed in Detroit."

"For those of you who haven't heard, the archduke died this past week." He half-swiveled toward Ben. "I think that might leave you second in line to his title."

Ben's head began to swim. All he wanted to do was run and hide.

Twain waggled his eyebrows. "I'm guessing I could get another story out of my friend now. Maybe one about a restored aristocrat searching for his future duchess from among all the fine young ladies at the Grand Hotel!"

Mortified, Ben bowed slightly as the audience applauded. He turned to leave. He'd go search out a rock cave and hide in it until Twain and all the entourage left the island.

Chapter Twenty-Six

The next day, having been summoned to the Winds of Mackinac by Maude's father, Ben wasn't sure what to expect. He arrived in his own clothing. Stan gave Ben a salute as he dropped him off at the inn. At least no one at the hotel had asked when Ben was returning to Bavaria. *Never.*

Beatrice opened the front door and bobbed a curtsy to him before he entered to find Peter Welling pacing in the hallway. The floral arrangement Ben had ordered was perched on a plant stand, as though it were simply one purchased to decorate the inn.

Welling jerked his thumb over his shoulder, pointing toward his office. "We need to talk."

What did the man know? He followed the man as he stomped down the hall to the office. The door clicked closed as Ben waited to be directed to sit.

Welling stood, his thumbs tucked into his suspenders. "Are you considering returning to Europe?"

So someone finally asked. Ben gave a curt laugh. "I'm an American journalist."

Maude's father tapped a newspaper on his desk. "And reporters say you may be second in line to a title."

"I'm sure my cousin, who'll receive the hereditary title, will marry and produce many little König heirs."

"Do you love my girl?"

Prickles of irritation scurried around Ben's neck collar. "I do."

The man pinioned him with his icy gaze. "Do you understand about her...peculiarities?"

"An attack of the lungs is an illness—not an oddity."

"Ah, so you don't fully understand." Peter Welling's sardonic smile irked Ben. "Have a seat."

He didn't want to sit—would rather remain standing so he could bolt out the door, if needed. But Ben lowered himself onto the closest chair. Perhaps Welling was referring to his daughter's stint as a maid. "Sir, I don't think Maude's service as a maid was due to some emotional instability— rather she was trying to prove herself to you."

"Unnecessary—I know my daughter is capable of running this or any other business on the island, including the Grand Hotel, by herself."

"But..."

Welling raised his hand. "And I do know what you've been up to— putting together a story about Greyson Luce and that poor girl he married." He shook his head.

"Poor girl? She's a wealthy young woman who pursued him." And half the eligible young men in Detroit. How could Welling be so naive?

The man's openmouthed stare accused Ben of idiocy. "Shame his mother will be crushed when she reads your column—you're one of her favorite writers, you know?"

"No, I didn't." He gave a short laugh. "I suspect I shall be her least favorite from hence forth."

"Hard to say—Mrs. Luce values honesty."

"As do I." But was it cruel for him to expose the truth?

"But please leave my daughter's name out of the article." He brought his hand down with a smack on his desktop, causing loose papers to rise and then fall back again in disarray.

Swallowing, Ben was tempted to rise, to leave the room. "I hope to do so."

"But you love her, don't you? Want to marry her, even?"

He did. Ben nodded slowly. Suddenly he felt ten years old, sitting outside his uncle's office as he ordered his mother and father from the estate in Bavaria. And that day he'd rearranged every plan he had in his head for his life. No longer did he aspire to become a musician like his parents, to play in the orchestra and travel across Europe, to return to their ancestral home for respite. No, he'd be his own man, earn his own way, and rely upon no one but himself and his own hard work.

With this story, he might have a crack at providing a life for Maude and himself. "It's my wish to obtain a small house for us in Detroit and to take her there."

"I see." Salt-and-pepper eyebrows rose and fell. "Maude will be heart-broken, you know."

Why? "I know she loves this property, the island, but. . ."

Her father's lips bunched up. "She'll never leave here. And you threaten her situation if she does."

Ben rose, the odor of stale tobacco in the room suddenly annoying. "How?"

"Thought you were an investigative reporter—aren't you? You go and find out." Welling waved a dismissive hand at him.

Heels clicked down the outer hall and stopped at the door. "Father?" Maude stepped in.

"My dear, you'll be pleased to hear I have granted Mr. König permission to marry you."

He'd not said so, nor had Ben asked. Ben stared, his chest tightening. He couldn't blurt out that they'd known each other only a few short weeks. He felt like he'd known her all his life and had finally returned home.

Maude's eyes widened, and she raised a hand to her mouth. She took several steps toward Ben, the scent of geraniums accompanying her.

"I don't believe I'll be marrying Mr. König." She emphasized his phony last name. "And I believe you've misconstrued Mr. Steffan's interest in me as being personal." She moved beside her father and planted a kiss on his cheek.

Peter Welling pushed his daughter gently away and held her at arm's length.

Ben cleared his throat. "Well, I can't say I blame you, Miss Welling. But I assure you, my interest in you is of a very personal nature." His voice rose with each successive sentence. "Although I do believe a marriage would be premature. Perhaps you'd reconsider, in time?"

"Perhaps."

"Well, that's all settled then, daughter." Welling gave a curt laugh. "And do you know where you'd live with Mr. König if you reconsidered?"

Maude's face went blank. "Where?"

"In Detroit," Mr. Welling supplied, his voice low, well modulated. "How would you like that, my dear?"

"I don't see that as a likelihood." Maude clutched her hands at her waist.

Ben shrugged his shoulders. "Detroit is where I work."

Perspiration dotted her fair brow. "I feel confident that I'll never be living as Mrs. König or Mrs. Steffan in Detroit."

Welling pulled a cigar from a nearby box.

Maude tried to grasp the cigar from her father, but he pulled it out of reach. "The doctor said you need to stop smoking. It's bad for your heart."

Her father laughed. "Ah, but another doctor has suggested my problems are all in my head."

"In your mind?" Maude stomped one delicate foot on the wool rug.

"Yes, Ada is accompanying me to a specialist in Mackinaw City, who has seen cases like mine caused by stress."

"Stress?"

"Yes, such as having an obstinate daughter who insists on becoming a businesswoman. Just like my beloved Ada did, leaving me while she pursued her career."

Had Ben misheard? Adelaide and Peter had been in love? Maude blinked rapidly, as though she, too, was trying to comprehend what her father was saying.

Too angry and frustrated to exchange even the most basic of niceties, Ben took his leave. He didn't need any more of this humiliation. He'd turn in his story, obtain his promotion, and be gone.

As Ben steamed out of the room, he almost ran headlong into Maude's little brother, who stood just outside the office door. "Where ya goin', Friedrich?"

He blew out an exasperated breath of anger. "I don't know."

Jack cocked his head. "I heard someone say your name is really Ben Steffan."

"That's right. Ben Steffan. I'm a reporter for the *Detroit Post*."

"Are ya sorry?"

Ben waited for further explanation.

"For lyin' to sis."

And to Jack, too. "I am sorry."

"Me, too, Mr. Steffan." Tears ran down the boy's cheeks, and he turned on his heel and ran.

Ben hung his head as he left.

He'd hesitated in sending in the story. Anna had threatened him, but with there being no further romance between himself and Maude, Harris wouldn't have a story to write. Ben could get his article in tonight.

He crossed the street, passed the bike rental stand, and stopped beside the lake. If he were thinking of this situation like an objective reporter, he'd think. . .what?

Spying several smooth stones, he retrieved them and tossed them across the water. The pebbles skipped over the cerulean pool before finally plunking into the water.

This story he was writing about Greyson Luce could save someone from future heartbreak. He'd leave Maude a copy of the story before he left the island, something showing he'd not used her name. And while he hated to portray Anna in such a negative light, at least someone should learn from her choices. Her poor mother. . .

Jack zipped by on his bicycle, darting in and out of the carriage and pedestrian traffic as if he didn't care what happened to him.

Didn't he?

Chapter Twenty-Seven

Maude knocked on Jack's door. He'd not come down for breakfast. Father told her to let him sleep in, but she had a niggling feeling Jack was up to something. He'd had a conniption when told that she wouldn't be seeing Ben again. Of course her crying episode had upset him, too, but what could she do? She couldn't protect her brother from life's difficulties and their effects on his loved ones.

She waited and knocked again.

"Are you sick, Jack?" When he failed to respond, she opened the door. Gauzy curtains waved in the rose-scented breeze.

His oak captain's bed lay empty, one of the drawers beneath it slightly ajar.

Birdsong carried through the open window. Distant laughter drew Maude closer. After raising the blinds fully open, she peered out. The new guest's bike was gone from its spot, yet she'd just seen the gentleman in the parlor. Had Jack taken the bicycle?

She left the room and hurried downstairs to find her brother.

The bell above the front door jingled loudly as she reached the bottom of the stairs and entered the lobby. The door opened. Ben had the audacity to return!

He removed his hat and stepped inside. Dressed in a shabby suit, although quite dashing by islander standards, he stood in the hallway, his expression flustered.

She turned and went to him.

He took her hands in his. "Maude, is something wrong with your brother?"

"I don't know. Why?"

"He was crying, and he was riding like a verrückt, like a crazy boy, all over the street yesterday and again when I just saw him." The rings under Ben's eyes suggested he'd not slept well. "He wouldn't even respond when I called to him. Not that I blame him."

"Where was he?"

"About fifteen minutes ago, I saw him riding down Garrison Road, into the interior of the island."

"That's not too far from the arch." Maude moistened her lips. "Jack's favorite spot when he's upset is to sit near that limestone formation."

"What's the quickest way to get there?" Ben glanced out into the street, where Stan was pulling away from the curb.

"Ada just purchased a light carriage, a new red gig, and is showing it to Father, out back."

"Come on."

♥

Thank God the horses easily responded to his direction as they'd sped toward the rock. Ben kept tight control over their movements. And this light gig was quick.

As they neared the cemetery, Maude pulled on his arm and pointed. "My mother is buried here—it was Grandmother's wish—in the Cadotte family area."

Ben directed the horses to a walk. From the road, he spied a bright yellow-and-red floral heart-shaped form propped against a headstone situated near the front, adjacent to an imposing statue of an angel with outstretched wings.

"Look—that's the homemade wreath Jack and I made last night for Mother's grave. I should have come out with him when he placed it here."

Maude's brother had experienced so many losses this past year. "Jack was concerned that your father might die."

"I should have talked with him and reassured him more. But frankly, Ben, I'm worried, too."

He wrapped an arm around her. She didn't resist when he pulled her near and kissed the top of her head. "I should have seen the signs of deep sadness, this grief, in your brother—I've experienced them all myself."

She peered up at him from beneath her long lashes. "When you were forced from your family home?"

"Yes. And when my sister, Magdalena, died."

"How did you react?"

"I think Jack is a daredevil on his bike, like I was, taking papers into some of the worst slums of Chicago." Like the boy trying to reach extreme speed when he ran—Ben had always pushed himself harder, longer.

"Look. That's Robert's carriage." Maude pointed toward a landau, waiting at the base of the arch.

Ahead, Swaine waved to them and scrambled from his carriage toward the popular tourist site. Thankfully, with the overcast skies portending rain, no one was about. High above, Jack sat on the top of the arch, his feet dangling over the other side. Gawkers might frighten the boy on his precarious perch. "With this light drizzle, that limestone could be slippery."

A crease marred Maude's brow. "Jack has been up there dozens of times, but he knows better than to be up there alone. Or in the rain." She held out her palm as raindrops began.

Ben slowed the gig and pulled in behind Swaine's landau. Swaine stared up at the top of the curved, but jagged, rock formation.

With the rain the previous night and the dewy morning, the slick rock could easily cause Jack to fall. Ben had to get to the boy.

"I'm going to go up." Maude began pulling at her shoes.

"No, let me talk to him." Ben squeezed Maude's hand and leaned in to press a kiss to her forehead.

Swaine tried calling up to Jack, but the boy shook his head violently, sending pebbles scattering down below and pinging off the rocks. Holding a twist of rope, Swaine slowly backed down as Ben ran to him.

"Can you help me, Steffan?" Sweat dotted the captain's brow. "I've been up there hundreds of times, but it's not a safe place when wet."

"Ja, I understand. Give me some of the rope."

"Let me cut it. If you take half and I have the other half, then maybe we can get it around him and steady him. We'll need to tie something for ourselves, too."

"You have enough for four good-sized sections?"

"Yes, I had some in my carriage, thank God."

God, keep the boy safe.

"I don't know what's eating him. Jack rode up on that bike so erratically that I thought he'd gotten into Peter's medicinal bourbon." Swaine tied rope around his midsection and Ben secured it to a nearby tree.

"I think he's afraid. And sad. And confused." Like Ben had been at the same age. Ben crossed to the opposite side, rope tied and secured as well. If they fell, they'd bang into the nearby rocks, but they'd not fall all the way down, which could be fatal.

Ben checked the cord around his torso and then stripped off his jacket. "I'm coming up there, Jack."

"Go away!"

He carefully climbed up the side opposite the boy, wanting Jack to see him as he approached. On the other side, behind the boy, Swaine did likewise, edging in onto the top of the rock platform.

"Leave me alone!"

"You invited me up here, don't you remember? Last week." Ben tried to keep his tone light. "After we left the Chippewa settlement."

Jack squinted in Ben's direction and nodded. "That was before you got Sis all mad."

"Well, I'm sorry, but she and I are here now."

When he swiveled to look back toward his sister, more rock chips fell. Ben closed his eyes and prayed.

"So you two lovebirds made up?"

"Ja."

The boy turned his head straight ahead and stared out at the water. Ben inched forward, on his hands and knees.

"My friend, what are you doing up here?" A raindrop plopped down on Ben's nose and began to itch, but he daren't lift his hands.

"I'm practicing to be an explorer." Jack tossed a stone down into the deep ravine, covered with trees and bushes.

"Ja? Let me tell you about a boy I know who took a very long journey."

"Was he an explorer?"

"Not really, but maybe. . ." He'd not thought of it that way.

"I don't want to hear it—I'm up here because I'm angry." Jack kicked his foot out and Ben watched as the boy's shoe cascaded down to the bottom of the ravine, bouncing off the rocks and tree branches as it fell.

From below, Maude called out, "Be careful, Jack!"

Her brother turned his head slightly and shrugged.

Ben sucked in a breath as he moved closer, the old pain from his rib beginning to throb. "This boy I knew—he was angry, too."

On the other side, Robert made eye contact and nodded, encouraging Ben forward. He wasn't afraid of heights, but this precipitous position made him dizzy out of a very real fear of falling.

"Why was he mad?"

Ben crept closer to Jack, slippery rock tearing at his skin. "He was very angry because his uncle had been unkind to his family."

"Yeah, I'm mad at my uncle, too."

Swaine momentarily closed his eyes and appeared to be praying.

Jack cocked his head. "What was the kid's name?"

Ben looked down at the water far below him and the child. "His name was Benjamin Friedrich König Steffan."

"That's a long name." Jack swung his feet and the other shoe fell. Down it fell, as did Ben's spirits. *Dear God, help me and this boy.*

"Ja. But he didn't use all those names."

"Does he have a nickname?"

"Ja." He licked his lips. "Ben—but his sister called him *pest*."

"My sister never calls me names."

"Ja, well his did—but he didn't mind because he liked bothering her, too."

His eyes misted. In water similar to this beyond them, his sister's body had been laid to rest, her spirit fleeing to the place where one day he'd join her.

Jack sniffed, and Ben realized the boy was crying, too.

"I miss my mom."

"I know. It must be hard."

"And my dad is sick. Real bad, I think."

Behind him, Ben heard the sounds of carriage wheels crunching over the drive leading to the scenic lookout. Not so scenic today.

"I'm sorry. But he looked well yesterday. I know how it must feel—"

"You don't know what it's like. Nobody does."

On the opposite side, Robert had moved within several feet of the boy. Ben had to keep Jack talking. And glancing in his direction.

"I am Ben, that boy, and my uncle threw me and all my family out of my grandparents' estate in Germany."

Sniffing loudly, Maude's brother's shoulders stiffened. "Who would do that?"

"My uncle inherited a noble title. . . ."

"Like a duke or somethin'?"

"Ja. Like that. When my grandparents were gone, my uncle sent my parents, me, and my sister packing."

"That's mean."

Ben tried not to look down as he brutalized his pants' knees by crawling forward, unsure how long he could balance in this position.

"And so we came to America."

"We're gonna have the best Olympics team from this country." The boy's eyes seemed to focus and brighten, as though seeing Ben for the first time. "Good thing you came to America."

"But, you see, my sister died on that trip here."

Knees shaking, Ben was within reach of Jack, as was Robert, who was poised to throw a circle of rope over the boy, lasso-style. But if he startled him, he could fall.

"She died?"

"Ja, my older sister." Tremors coursed through his shoulders.

"You better sit, Mr. König; you could slip and fall." Jack patted the damp spot beside him.

"If I sit, I'm not sure I can get back up again."

"Oh boy, we better get you offa here, then." Jack looked in the other direction, and Robert offered him the rope.

Perspiration beaded on Swaine's forehead. "Take it, Jack."

"Yeah, I think I need it for Mr. König." The boy took the rope and handed it to Ben.

The boy stood, balancing like a monkey, holding the line. He passed the end to Ben and held on to the taut rope himself.

"Tell me about your family, Mr. König, and hold the rope and scoot back a little at a time, okay? I don't want ya to get scared and fall—so be careful."

Ben swallowed. "My mother was rebellious, like me, and she wanted to be a violinist in an orchestra."

"That ain't so bad." Jack took a half step forward and Ben moved slowly backward. *Mein Gott, this is up high.*

"Aristocrats don't play in symphonies." Ben scooted back again and watched as Jack took a pace forward.

"Why not?"

"It wasn't the thing the royal families in Europe permitted their members to do, even though the rulers loved music and the arts." Nor would they be crawling around on their knees like this. A piece of rock gouged against his left hand, and he bit back a groan. Jack appeared as relaxed and in control as though he'd walked on wet, slippery limestone all his life. Maybe the boy had, and his sister hadn't known.

"Did they let you climb rocks like this?"

"No." Ben's head swam. As long as the boy thought he was rescuing him, they'd be okay. They had to be.

♥

Maude couldn't lose her brother, nor could she stand the thought of Ben pitching over the side of what had been her favorite spot on the island.

She pulled up her skirts and got to the top edge of the arch then waited as Ben moved backward, and Jack forward, toward her. She'd grab him if need be, although she didn't know what she'd do if she did have to get ahold of Ben. Jack, she knew exactly what to do with.

The impudent boy winked at her. If he'd ever deserved a paddling, it was today.

"Tell me about your sister, Ben." Jack used the tone of voice he reserved for the youngest guests at the inn.

"She was pretty, like yours. Magdalena was a great writer—oh, the stories she could tell."

Jack laughed. "My aunt Virgie is like that—she'd talk your ears off with stories if you let her."

Ben ceased his retreat. Maude could see his clothing moving, not from the wind for there was none now, but from trembling. "I. . .I think I realize something up here, Jack."

"What's that?"

"My sister had a gift."

"A present?"

"No, like your ability to run. A gift from God, a talent."

Rain began to fall in light bursts. They needed to get down. Maude bit her lip.

"You think God made me fast?"

"Ja. And he made my sister a gifted writer, and when Magdalena died. . ."

"Yes?" Jack moved closer to Ben and used his bare toes to nudge him.

Ben continued his reverse crawl toward Maude, and she exhaled in relief. "I missed her stories."

"I don't miss Virgie's stories." Jack looked just like a banty rooster up there, strutting toward the end of the arch.

"You will when she's gone." Ben looked up at her brother.

Tears welled in Maude's eyes.

"Maybe. Ya know, Dad says your gift is music."

From behind her, Maude heard Father's and Ada's voices. When Ben's back foot descended onto the platform and Jack hopped down beside him, Maude hugged both of them close to her. She couldn't lose either one. Whatever Ben had done, couldn't she find it in her heart to forgive this man she'd grown to love?

Father rushed up the stairs and pulled Jack into a bear hug and then gestured for him to go to the carriage.

Maude kissed his cheek. "Ben, do what you need to do. Search your own conscience. Then let me know. But realize this—I forgive you no matter what." She'd have to pray about these words that were put in her mouth from something, Someone, besides herself.

He pulled her into his arms, and as the rain pelted down, Ben covered her mouth with his, his masculine scent and the warmth of him, the solidness, lulling her into a sense of protection that she never wanted to end.

Chapter Twenty-Eight

*B*en smacked the return on the typewriter in resounding satisfaction. Completed. Finished. Likely to net him a huge bonus, an advancement, and perhaps a bit of respect.

Someone rapped at the door. "Message for you, sir."

He rose and neared the door. "Slide it under, please, Ray."

A rose-tinted envelope passed beneath and onto the carpet. Ben plucked it up from the floor and opened it.

Maude's perfume wafted from the missive as he opened it. *"I'm waiting downstairs. Come for a ride with me."*

Another faint knock sounded. "Sir?"

"Yes, Ray?"

"Miss Welling wants to know if you'll be coming down or not. What should I tell her?"

Ben opened the door. "Tell her five minutes."

"Sure thing."

When Ben arrived in the hotel lobby, he found Maude waiting, dressed in a brown boxy day suit, her hair upswept beneath a boater hat banded with a matching cocoa-colored ribbon, eyes serious.

"Come along, we're keeping my cousin waiting." A faint smile curved her beautiful lips.

Maude circled her arm through Ben's and commandeered him out the door to a waiting cab, her cousin Stanley the driver.

Soon, they'd entered the carriage and rounded the Grand and then continued down the hill. Other drivers allowed Stan's cab out into traffic, busy this warm sunny day as they headed toward the main street. Only a faint breeze stirred the air. The sapphire waters of the straits lay calm. Waiting.

"How's Jack today?" To have Maude so close, so warm and comfortable beside him, unnerved Ben.

"He's fine, now, thank God." When he pressed his hand over hers, she slid it away, clutching both her hands together in her lap and avoiding eye contact.

"Where are we going?"

"It's a surprise." She arched an eyebrow at him. "I thought you might want to see this before you leave the island."

On they traveled through town and past the harbor, seagulls diving to feast on bread crumbs tossed by tourists at the park.

The cab soon turned down a side street nearby. Slowly they climbed the hill, and then Stan parked the cab beside a simple square-framed house, standing three stories tall.

The whitewashed building's peeling paint made the house an eyesore. Scaffolding surrounded the building, up to the second story. The silver-gray wood on the top level revealed a complete absence of paint. A young man spread paint on the side corner, his back to them, while two other men worked below.

"Greyson! Be careful up there, do you hear me?" A woman's voice carried to them and up to the man, for he paused in his brushstrokes.

"Yes, Mother."

The lady sat on a porch quite a ways from where the man painted.

"Why doesn't she move to where he might hear her better?" Ben whispered to Maude as she lifted her skirts to disembark the carriage.

She turned and cast him a withering look. "You'll see."

The young man removed his hat and wiped his forehead, blond hair glistening.

The door to the home opened, and Anna emerged, her apron barely covering the babe that surely was growing within her. Mrs. Forham's words ran through his mind, *"Please watch out for my daughter—I love her so."* He drew in a slow breath and followed Maude into the overgrown yard.

"Good morning, Mrs. Luce. Anna. . ." Maude's breezy voice held no scorn, no anger, only peace and grace and acceptance.

The older woman remained seated. Anna moved toward Mrs. Luce.

As Ben stepped toward the porch, he heard Greyson descending the scaffolding.

Mrs. Luce sat upright in a wheelchair.

"Mother?" Greyson pushed past Ben, sidestepping Maude, to join his wife and mother on the porch.

The three of them looked at Maude, then Ben.

"Welcome, Maude—we've not seen you in some time."

Maude turned toward Ben, her soft features begging him to understand.

"We mean to remedy that, Mrs. Luce. You see, there is no reason for you to miss church just because Greyson has come home for the summer and Anna is. . ."

Greyson's eyes widened.

Maude continued, ". . .unwell at present. And congratulations, by the way."

What an amazing woman Maude was, to extend such Christian charity. Ben took a step closer and cupped her elbow, watching as the two other men ascended the stairs to paint.

"Come sit in the chairs, Maude. This must be your Mr. Steffan—I've heard so much about him from Anna."

Anna's cheeks reddened, and Greyson cast his wife a look of surprise.

"Mr. Steffan? I think you mean Mr. König."

Ben cleared his throat. "No, Steffan would be the correct name. Ben Steffan." *The journalist who'd planned to write an article documenting all your sins for public consumption.* His face heated.

A furrow formed between Greyson's eyebrows. "Anna's mother thought a reporter named Ben Steffan hung the moon."

"A kind and gracious lady." Kind and gracious—unlike himself.

"So that's you?" Greyson frowned at Ben and then directed his gaze to his wife, who appeared nonplussed.

Mrs. Luce clapped her hands together and rotated her wheelchair slightly. "Now, come sit beside me, tell me all about yourself, and I'll decide if Mrs. Forham should have thought of you like I do of my Greyson."

A smile jerked at Ben's lips. "No man can accomplish that, save with his own mother, Mrs. Luce." He bent over her hand and pressed a kiss to the dry skin.

She giggled like a girl. "Oh, Mr. Steffan, I think I see why Mrs. Forham cared for you so."

Later, as the sun hit full high noon over the house, and Ben's story had slipped away like the magnificent sunsets did every night on the island,

Anna brought out a tray of sandwiches and a pitcher of lemonade. "Mother Luce, would you like to eat inside or out?"

"Inside of course. I must see if this whippersnapper really can carry me as easily as he claims."

Heat climbed up Ben's neck. "Madam, I assure you my boast is good." His article, however, was shot. He rose, dusted off his hands, and stood in front of the woman. She appeared about Maude's size. He bent.

"Do you give me permission to place my hand and arm beneath your knees?"

"Do what you need to do, young man, but I'd be ever so happy to sit in a regular chair at the dining-room table, if you please."

Maude held the screen door open. Inside, Greyson pulled a heavy mahogany chair from a long oval table, covered in an expensive linen table-cloth. Silver had already been set as though for dinner, and china and crystal sat at seven places.

"Would you call in the men for lunch, please, Anna? Give them the soap and those towels, and they can wash up at the pump outside first."

"Yes, ma'am."

Anna Forham Luce—essentially the servant of her mother-in-law. Remarkable. Or was it an act?

Regardless, not only did Ben no longer have any belongings, but he couldn't in good conscience turn in his story. No story—no work. No work—no money. No money. . . Then what?

Back at the Grand, Ben pulled his watch from his vest pocket. He grabbed his valise with a change of clothes. If he caught a cab right now, he could hightail it to Mackinaw City while the sun still shone. The note he'd received back from the music hall said he could stay over the night he auditioned.

The boat from the island seemed to have just departed when Ben already found himself at the dock in Mackinaw City. On the way over, he'd sat there contemplating his two marketable skills: his writing and his music. If the boss fired him, he might even cancel his steamship fare back to Detroit. Knots turned to rock-hard stollen loaves in his stomach. If he turned in his story, which he knew he couldn't, he'd have an assured future.

He could imagine the telegram he'd receive back from his boss:

GREAT ARTICLE *Stop* PROMOTION TO ASSISTANT
EDITOR *Stop* IMMEDIATE RAISE IN PAY *Stop*

New desk, new title on the door, new assignments, a nice little house near the paper. All of that up in smoke, like the boardinghouse that had held his meager belongings. This trip to the mainland was out of desperation. If he destroyed his article, then he must have some way to live. All the nightmares of the hunger and degradation in Chicago had flooded his sleep.

Standing at the Mackinaw City dock, he closed his eyes, allowing the misty morning to wash over him, to mourn what could have been his. It could have been theirs. His and Maude's.

Amazing how empty he felt. If he'd had the promotion, all would have been meaningless without someone to share it with. Without Maude there beside him, what point was there? He'd never felt more alone in his life. He headed off in the direction of the music hall that the Grand's songstress, Lily, had spoken about, and from there he'd visit the newspaper office. He'd definitely stop in the tavern that offered the overnight stay. He could play all the popular songs by ear.

Lord, if it is Your will that I abandon my article and face the consequences, then show me. He first sought out the post office and mailed the copy of the Edmunds article to Banyon. The public interest would likely be minimal, but at least his boss couldn't say he'd had no return on his money. This article, was, after all, what he and the editor had originally agreed on. Before Banyon had slipped in his underhanded plan for someone to expose Anna Forham Luce and her new husband. Doubtful that Banyon even realized his rival had spitefully cut off his own daughter—leaving her with no dowry.

The late afternoon passed in a blur of meetings with managers, the editor of the newspaper, and the owner of the music hall. With each affirmation of interest in hiring him, Ben had breathed easier, his tie seemed less tight, and his palms not so damp.

A foghorn tooted as Ben made his way to a nearby coffee shop. With the heavy mist rolling in so thick, so deep, would he be able to make it back to the island that night?

He pulled a note from his pocket—one from the owner of the *Mackinac Express* newspaper with the salary amount notated on it. Not very much. He fingered it. If he taught piano on the island and he wrote for the paper, he could afford a tiny house in the center of the island.

Ben opened the door to the café, inhaling the scent of freshly baked pasties and sugar cookies, and entered the square room, it's pine plank floors squeaking as he moved toward a small round table.

"Sit where you like, dear," a red-haired matronly woman called over her shoulder as she poured coffee into a gentleman's cup.

As the waitress moved aside, Ben realized her body had shielded Adelaide Bishop from his view. He sucked in a breath and almost rose to leave, but Ada's pointed look held him in check. She sat with a slim ebony-haired man—the physician from the Grand.

The waitress moved to his table. "Coffee?"

"Yes, thank you."

"You want the meat loaf special or the pasty?"

"The pasty, please."

"I'll throw you a little taters and gravy on the side. You're a big man, and I 'spect you'll need a big-man's meal." She chuckled as she poured his coffee. "My husband can put away three of them pasties by himself. He's a lumberjack, though."

All Ben could manage was, "Oh." And as quickly as she'd arrived, the woman was off and headed behind the counter to the kitchen, which was shielded from the interior by a pair of checked curtains.

He sipped the bitter coffee then poured some cream from a chipped tinware container into his mug. He dipped his dented teaspoon into the small crockery bowl of sugar cubes, managing to snag two, and plunked them into his coffee, trying not to let his discomfiture show when the physician rose from the table and made to leave.

Ada also rose, but she carried her coffee mug and a plate of what looked like cookies smothered in hot fudge and topped with whipped cream. A lot of sugar for a tiny woman.

The duo made their way toward him.

"Mr. König, how are you?"

Ben made to stand, but Ada and the man gestured for him to remain seated. "My name is actually Steffan, Ben Steffan."

"I see. I've heard of cases such as yours, but I've never met someone with multiple identities." Dr. DuBlanc tapped his index finger against his pants leg.

Ada let out a low, rich laugh. "He means he's used a pseudonym—he's a journalist. Aren't you, Mr. Steffan?"

"Yes, I am."

"Good. I think I've had enough psychiatric cases for the day." He exchanged a glance with Ada. "Well, I'm off to the docks. Hope they'll take me back over."

"I think I'll catch the next ferry, Dr. DuBlanc." Ada extended her hand. "You'll be returning tonight, won't you, Mr. Steffan?"

"Yes, after dinner. Please sit down and join me."

"Thank you. And Doctor, again, thank you for your help and for having your mentor meet with us. I feel a great relief."

"You're very welcome. I've never had anyone be so grateful to have a psychiatric ailment."

"Much better than heart problems." Ada's features bunched together as she lowered herself into the seat across from Ben.

DuBlanc grabbed his hat from the stand and departed.

Ada leaned in. "Did you send it?"

"My story? Yes." He gritted his teeth.

"The one about Greyson and Anna?"

"No."

"Ah. Are you going to?"

"No."

"I see. So then, you have nothing to give your editor."

"Not exactly. I sent him an article about Marcus Edmunds."

"Little toad, he deserves to be exposed." She sniffed and sat taller in her chair.

"He's charming, even if he is a toad."

"Yes, he's that all right. But how would you like to be the parents of the girl who has been charmed out of her inheritance?" She arched an eyebrow at him.

"I wouldn't."

"Exactly. You're doing someone a good deed."

"I hope so. I pray this article will be a warning." He truly did.

"So what do you suppose will happen now?" A crease formed between her eyebrows.

"I'll probably be dismissed."

"Worst-case possibility? What would that look like?"

He chuckled. "This morning I'd have given you a litany of woes, including the fact that my boardinghouse burned down—along with all my belongings."

She gaped.

Ben continued: "But now from where I'm sitting, things are looking manageable."

"Manageable? You've given up your dreams?"

He drew in a long breath. "I don't know. I'm starting to think those dreams were that of a very frightened boy, and I don't want to be him anymore."

"Ah. So Jack's episode brought some good, did it?"

"Not just that. Many things."

The waitress whistled as she crossed the floor, juggling a plate piled high with a pasty, gravy, potatoes, another plate piled with rolls and bread, and a crock of butter. She set them down with startling efficiency then brushed her hands against her apron. "Now, enjoy."

"Thank you."

Ada eyed him, eyes direct and piercing. "While you eat, I'll talk."

Ben nodded, silently prayed a blessing, and then tore into the fantastic-smelling beef, potato, carrot, and turnip pie that he'd ordered.

"I think I have a story that could get you that coveted assistant editorship spot you've wanted."

"I'm listening."

"Fine. Eat and listen. I'm going to give you the scoop of the century." She laughed.

Prickles of apprehension worked their way up his neck.

"There was a little girl named Ada whose parents died from typhus. She lived in Detroit. The social welfare agency matron found her guarding the bodies of her parents and little sister."

Ben stifled a groan, the food in his mouth turning bitter.

"The nice lady took her on a train far out into the countryside, where Ada lived on a farm. There were many people there, all different ages of children, some adults even. It was what you call a poor farm."

The wealthiest woman in America had grown up on a poor farm.

"In Shepherd, Michigan."

He set his fork down.

"One day when she was out hoeing in the fields, a big black snake slithered past her and she began to scream her head off. And at the nearby farm, a boy heard her cries and came running. His name was Peter, and he was the nicest boy she'd ever met."

"Peter Welling, of course."

Mrs. Bishop pointed to his food. "Eat, before it gets cold."

Ben reached for a piece of bread and slathered butter on it.

"Soon Peter and his family, the Wellings, invited the little girl to visit. She began to attend church with them weekly. And the years went by so quickly. Oh, so fast. And she was sure that Peter would ask her to marry him. And that his family would welcome her with open arms."

"But?"

"Ada was just a charity case to them. And when his mother saw what was happening, what was growing between Peter and her, she sent the girl off to secretarial school in Battle Creek."

"What about Peter? What did he think about this?"

The foghorn sounded again, this time longer. Both he and Ada turned to look out the window. From where they sat, the bicyclists and carriages in the street were no longer visible, blanketed by a thick coat of fog.

"Well, I'd say you could get yourself an in-depth, exclusive interview, Mr. Steffan, since we'll need to be staying the night on the mainland."

He hated to use the paper's money for a hotel. He remembered what the music hall owner had offered this afternoon—free room and board if he played for their dinner crowd for an hour or two.

"I own the Mackinaw Breeze Inn." Ada's voice was nonchalant.

"The new one by the water?" Ben took a sip of his coffee.

"One of the many reasons I came up here." She chuckled. "I feel sure they'd give us two rooms. Might even have my suite available if no one has rented it for the evening. If so, I'll invite you to finish this interview in my parlor there."

"Are you sure? Do you really want to do this?" Apprehension still gripped him, as though God was shaking His head at what Adelaide Bishop was about to do.

"I don't want you to make some of the same mistakes I've made. It might be too late for me, but not for you and Maude."

"Do you think she'd forgive me?" Maude had said she would.

Ada leaned in and covered one of his hands with hers. "You really don't know about that debacle with that controlling grandmother of hers, do you? About the will and the codicil and poor Peter."

"I do know Mr. Welling didn't inherit what he believed was his and his wife's life work. And her relations implied that Maude was the wealthiest young woman on the island. But there were some stipulations on her inheritance."

"The Lord giveth and the Lord taketh away. Blessed be the name of the Lord."
Had he not heard it from her lips, Ben would never have thought Adelaide Bishop was speaking. He had to know more about her. What was the truth? What had made her who she was?

She straightened. "I imagine all that Peter worked for will go to you and Maude once you marry. And later half of that to Jack."

He still couldn't believe Maude stood to inherit. "It doesn't seem fair, does it? That Mr. Welling is left with none of the estate."

"Ah, sometimes God has to put us in a place where He can mold us and ready us for something new. And sometimes He puts friends around us to help us, doesn't He?"

"Yes, I suppose He does." Like the Welling family and now this woman.

"I know He does."

"Yes." Ben could see God's hand in this. Yet he didn't know what he'd do with Mrs. Bishop's story. This article could take him to the New York newspapers if he sold it.

"Well, shall we? I've got a lot to tell you, and we'll need to find you a typewriter if you're to work on my story tonight."

"Good thing I've had my coffee, then."

"I'll have room service bring us up more, have no fears."

Ben looked for the waitress and felt in his pocket for his wallet, but Adelaide gently touched his arm. "She's been paid, tipped, and is in the back enjoying her own dinner."

"Ah. Well, thank you."

"No, thank you. Listening to Peter talk with Dr. DuBlanc earlier, I wondered if I'd benefit from unloading my own history by sharing with someone. And God brought you along."

"But don't you fear what will happen if your true story is published?"

"You haven't even heard the half of it yet."

Three husbands, wealthiest woman in America, eccentric extraordinaire. No, all he'd heard was the story of a brokenhearted girl who'd been rejected and lost the one she loved.

Chapter Twenty-Nine

A sharp rap on the door awoke Ben at five o'clock Sunday morning, as he'd asked. He had a promise to keep on the island. "Who's there?"

"Breakfast, sir."

He'd slept in his undershorts, but Adelaide had procured a silk robe for him. He rose from the ornate brass bed and wrapped the garment around himself. He crossed to the door and accepted the tray from the maid. Turning, he sought a place to set the tray so he might clear the typewriter and his article from the small table near the window. The room was spacious, with high ceilings, and furnished with sumptuous brocade bedding and drapes. It seemed out of place in the somewhat backwoods town. But Adelaide had assured him that guests en route to the Grand Hotel who were stranded in town very much appreciated finding the comforts of her inn.

He set the machine on his bed and gently laid the sheets of typed paper beside it.

Oh, Lord. This is wrong.

He couldn't do it. If he sent in this story, Adelaide's privacy, her very life could be threatened. If people knew who exactly she was, she'd be hounded for loans. She'd be targeted by criminals. What on earth was she thinking? What was he thinking by continuing her interview after he'd realized the implications? Why had he bothered typing the story?

Pride. Greed. And a few other sinful motivations. Nothing driven by a fear of God nor a desire to do His will. This story would have given him the scoop of a lifetime. At the expense of a woman whom he'd now come to respect greatly. All the stories about her life—so many falsehoods, she'd laughed them off.

"God knows," she'd said.

No position, no amount of money could replace what she would lose if he submitted this article to Banyon.

Ben removed the cover from the breakfast plate. A stack of pancakes had the image of a smile on them, made from berries.

A tiny note, tucked under the plate, read, "*Do whatever you believe is right, Ben—Affectionately, Adelaide.*"

Her words were almost identical to those Maude had spoken to him. Was this some kind of test from God? If so, would he pass it?

He knew what was right, pleasing, and a good thing in God's sight. Before he went back to the island, he had some letters to drop off. And if he hit the ferry just right, he'd be crossing the street to the church just in time to accept Reverend McWithey's offer—and to play for the morning service.

Maude sat on the front porch swing, her legs tucked up under her, one of her mother's quilts wrapped around her shoulders. The fog had finally lifted, and ferries again crossed the straits. Ben had left. And he'd not even said good-bye. Sadie told her his room was empty and another guest had checked in. Not—even—said—good-bye. How could he? Tears ran down her cheeks.

The door opened and her father stepped through, carrying a coffee tray. He set it down on the wicker table beside the swing.

"Guess what, Maude?" He looked healthier than she'd seen him in a long time.

Maybe he was gloating because he'd run Ben off the island. "What?"

"You'll be happy to learn that your old man's not dying of heart failure."

"No? You saw the specialist?"

"Yes, yesterday, but not the kind you think." He arched a brow at her.

Her spirits sank. "So you didn't see the heart doctor?"

"Don't have to."

"Why not?"

"Because Dr. Cardona, a trained psychiatrist, confirmed what Dr. DuBlanc already suspected—stress has caused these heart palpitations."

"Is he certain?"

"Yes, he's checked me thoroughly and conducted a psychiatric exam.

I'm not crazy, but I am what he called 'a walking bottle of anxiety,' and he's got some treatment plans for me."

"Which includes what, Father?"

"Hopefully, life on the farm very soon."

"Oh." She wasn't ready to live on a farm. And with no marital prospects, she wasn't sure what would become of her.

"Robert wants to talk with you tonight over dinner at the Canary." Father picked at some imaginary lint on his gray trousers.

"Are you going?"

"Perhaps. If Ada gets back from the mainland. I don't know what is keeping her so long."

At least Father would see his friend. Would she ever lay eyes on Ben Steffan again?

After preparing quickly for church and rounding up Jack and Father and getting them into the carriage, Maude directed their driver to carry them on to church. When they arrived, she swiftly departed to her Sunday school class, breathing easier when she realized that none of her students had yet arrived. She organized her materials, set up her flannel storyboard, and set out the cookies that always kept the boys happy during long discussions. But by the end of the hour, she'd learned that even cookies weren't sufficient to keep her students from asking where the "man teacher" was. She'd only missed one Sunday! The little ingrates wanted Ben back. But so did she.

Maude exhaled loudly as the last child departed, leaving her with Jack.

"Ain't your fault that you ain't him, sis." Jack patted her back, and she resisted the urge to swat at him.

Father knocked on the door frame of the square whitewashed room. "Ready, children?"

Jack ran to him and wrapped his arms around their father. "I'm so glad you're just an old worrywart and not got some bad heart problem."

"Me, too, son. Me, too." Father kissed the top of Jack's unruly hair. "You're getting a haircut tomorrow!"

Maude grinned. "You're sounding more like your old self."

♥

The trio entered the narthex. Maude retrieved a bulletin from the side table. The date, June 30, startled her, and she felt her cheeks flush. This was to have been the day after her wedding to her old friend Greyson. A man so desperate to provide for his mother that he'd snared a wealthy girl as insurance. Yet that apparent ploy had failed him. *Dear God, help them—they and their child are going to need it.*

Odd that the one man she most wanted to share her feelings of pain with was Friedrich—no, his name was Ben. The name was solid. Strong. It suited him. But he was gone. And she'd never felt more alone in all her life. Regardless of what he pretended to be, she'd seen the caring, intelligent, kind, and talented man that Ben was. She'd never met anyone like him who made her feel both excited yet grounded at the same time.

"Good morning." Greyson's mother, assisted by both Greyson and Anna and using two canes, wobbled a smile at them.

"Wonderful to see you here, Mrs. Luce." Father nodded to her.

Jack chewed on his lip before averting his gaze. "Hey, do you see?" He tugged on Maude's arm.

She bent. "Shhh, not now, Jack."

Father fixed him with a penetrating gaze. "Say good morning to Mrs. Luce and Greyson and his wife."

"Mornin'." Jack scrunched his nose.

Mrs. Luce smiled. "Same old Jack. Come 'round and see an old lady once in a while, will you? I miss seeing you."

"Sure thing." Jack shifted back and forth in his brown lace-up shoes. "You still got those bowls full of butterscotch candies?"

"Jack Welling." Maude's reprimand was covered by the woman's laugh.

"Mother?" Greyson directed her toward an empty back pew, and Anna followed.

As they entered the sanctuary, Maude spied a tall, slightly shaggy-haired man with the hint of a beard, attired in a rustic brown tweed jacket and tan pants, sitting at the piano.

Jack elbowed her. "Tried to tell ya."

Maude pressed a hand to her chest as unbidden tears sprang to her eyes. Father squeezed her hand.

He leaned in. "Looks like he hasn't left, my dear. In fact, he looks quite at home."

When they arrived at their pew, Robert occupied it. Father sighed but in the end slid next to him.

Maude tried to focus on the hymns and really sing, but she couldn't help watching, as did the rest of the church, as Ben Steffan brought the music to life.

When Pastor McWithey took the podium, he grinned from ear to ear. "I have wonderful news."

A hush came over the parishioners. Was he going to say Ben was staying on permanently? Maude held her breath in anticipation as Jack wriggled beside her.

"We just received word this morning that an organ has been purchased for the parish."

A titter began two rows in back of them. The pastor cleared his throat. "It has been donated by someone who wishes to remain anonymous."

Had Robert done so? He could certainly afford it, even with having lost two ships of his fleet. A few gasps preceded the congregation clapping. The reverend raised his hands. "We're all very grateful, and I'll be composing a letter to our donor, offering our thanks."

Jack began swinging his feet, and Maude placed a gloved hand on his knee. "Stop, please."

He looked up at her with his puppy dog eyes and leaned against her shoulder. From where he sat, Ben winked at her, and she winked back.

Dare she hope things could be mended?

But after the service was over, she couldn't find Ben anywhere.

"Coffee downstairs?" Robert cocked an eyebrow at them, and she, Father, and Jack followed her uncle down to the fellowship hall.

But Ben wasn't there, either.

"What's troubling you, Maude?" Robert brought her coffee, prepared just as she liked it.

"I seem to have lost Ben."

"We'll just have to pray you find him again."

But the afternoon passed with no word. Nothing from Ben as to where he was. And she had a dinner to get ready for.

Chapter Thirty

$\mathcal{G}$retchen assisted Maude with her hair and dinner gown.

When Maude descended the stairway into the lobby, Jack gave her an assessing look. "You doll up real good, sis."

"Thank you, Jack." She pretended to tweak his nose. "You look like a little gentleman in your monkey suit."

"Hey! I ain't no monkey." He swatted her hand away.

Later, as their family carriage rode up the hill and then past the Grand Hotel, Maude pressed a gloved hand over the jewels at her neckline. Inside that building this Sunday evening, servants toiled.

Father nudged her. "Do you miss working there?"

"I miss the friends I made."

He tucked her arm inside his. "I'm proud of you for doing something you believed in."

The straits glistened as the sun began its descent. Ahead, the Canary welcomed them, bedecked with lanterns, lit and beckoning them to cross the manicured lawn to the grand home.

The front door opened as the three of them descended from the carriage. Grandmother's elderly footman stood there, and for a moment, Maude half-expected Grandmother and Mother to appear there, as well.

"Thought he retired." Jack brushed at the front of his jacket, which bore suspicious residue resembling sugar cookie crumbs. As he ran past them, the evidence fell from his pocket onto the grass—a half-eaten sugar cookie whose enormous size marked it as one from Jo's Bakery in St. Ignace.

"Come along." Father tugged at his lapels.

The manservant took their light evening coats and hung them on nearby decorative brass knobs. He bowed slightly toward Father, and Maude, and then directed his bleary gaze toward Jack. "The young Duvall ladies have requested your presence upstairs for a game of hide-and-seek."

Jack was off like a shot. How many times had Maude played the same game with a giggling Sadie and a guffawing Robert, who'd always managed to find them, usually hiding in a closet?

Sadie entered from the parlor, dressed in an apricot dinner ensemble that brought out her peaches-and-cream complexion. White elbow-length gloves covered her work-worn hands. "Welcome to dinner. Robert should be here in a minute."

Maude kissed her friend's cheeks. "You look lovely."

Sadie ushered Maude and her father into the front parlor, where the heavy black Eastlake furniture had been polished to perfection. How odd it seemed to have her old friend waiting on them here instead of Grandmother's maid. But Matilda, even more bent with age, if that was possible, soon entered the room, carrying an engraved silver tray piled high with crudités and small bowls of salad dressing.

High-pitched girls' giggles carried down the stairs, followed by a racket of footfalls. One by one, the Duvall sisters entered the room, each bobbing a curtsy to Maude and her father. Matilda rolled her eyes then departed, huffing as the girls swiped vegetables from the tray as she passed.

"Miss Maude, Mr. Welling, it's so good to be here in the house, working again. With all these folks here, it's like life has returned to this beautiful home."

All the folks? Were Sadie and her sisters living here?

Lighter footsteps trod down the stairs and Robert appeared in the doorway, dapper in his navy pin-striped suit and yellow-and-blue cravat. "Welcome. So glad you could come."

When she saw the look of adoration he gave Sadie, Maude's stomach sank to her pinched toes, which were shoved inside a pair of satin pumps. She wasn't ready for her best friend and her uncle to be sweethearts.

"Come to the music room. We have a special treat for you tonight."

"Girls! Jack!" Sadie yelled up the stairway.

The footman's eyes widened, but he said nothing.

Maude exchanged a glance with her father. From the set of his jaw, he was likely having the same thoughts she was.

The girls giggled as they clattered down the staircase, and Sadie shushed them. Jack followed, as sedate as an undertaker. Had being in the place where their mother had died upset him? When he reached her, Maude wrapped an arm around him and drew him close.

He cupped his hand around his mouth and whispered in her ear. "I think Opal is sleeping in my room!"

Maude whispered back, "Don't make a scene, Jack Welling!"

From the other room, the haunting notes of "Clair de Lune" wafted toward them. The pianist was accomplished. Gifted even, as whoever it was caressed the walnut Kimball piano. This song, one of Mother's favorites, was a tune Maude had rehearsed over and over again, trying to get the song just right. In her head she could hear, in her heart she could feel how the music should sound. But she couldn't accomplish it on her own. Only one person she knew played that well.

Robert moved alongside her, his woodsy fragrance pleasant. "I've procured the services of Mackinaw City's newest pianist at the Northwoods Hall. We're hoping to find him a position at the Grand as well."

Was it possible that Ben would stay? Tears threatened to flow as Robert nestled her arm through his and they made their way across the Aubusson carpets to the music room.

Broad shoulders strained his brown tweed jacket as Ben's head bent over the piano. He had no sheet music but played with his eyes closed, as though he felt the music. As though the notes flowed through him. Shivers of delight flowed through Maude as tears streamed down her face.

"I give you a man of many talents. He's the island's newest correspondent for the *Mackinac Express*, he's the new assistant editor for the *Mackinaw City Courier*, the pianist for the music hall on the mainland and hopefully for the Grand Hotel as well."

Ben rose from the bench and bowed. "I'll be working very hard. And it's all honest work."

Father stared, his lower jaw open. "But. . ."

Matilda entered the room. "Ada Fox has arrived." She curtsied stiffly then left.

Dressed in soft tones of mauve and yellow, Maude's former supervisor, and the wealthiest woman in America, looked perfectly the part of an island matron, albeit decidedly slender without the many layers of clothing she wore at the Grand.

"Ada." Father strode to her side, took her hands in his, and kissed them. "Welcome."

"Thank you." She beamed as one by one the girls approached her and curtsied and introduced themselves.

Robert ushered them away and brought Maude's friend forward.

"And of course, Sadie you already know." Her uncle grinned as he gazed at Sadie, resplendent in her gown that was cinched at her tiny waist.

"Indeed, I do. And you make the very image of a proper lady, Miss Duvall."

Sadie blushed.

"But I'm most interested in hearing from Mr. Steffan."

Ben rose and bowed in her direction.

"Should I call you Assistant Editor Steffan?" A tremulous smile tugged at Ada's lips, and if Maude wasn't mistaken, fear darkened her eyes.

"Ja."

Maude glanced between the two. Ada's shoulders sagged slightly and a muscle jumped in her cheek. She gazed at the floor as though she were memorizing the rug's pattern and its many colors.

"I'm the assistant editor of the *Mackinaw City Courier*, Mrs. Fox."

The woman's coiffed head lifted, and Maude spied tears in Ada's eyes. "God bless you, young man."

"The Lord has, ma'am. I've found enough employment to make a nuisance of myself in these parts for some time to come."

Bea bobbed up and down in her new Mary Janes. "Does that mean we can celebrate?"

"Do we get cordial?" Opal piped up.

"Yes, can I have the cherry cordial?" Bea clasped her hands to her chest.

"Only a little." Sadie wagged a finger.

Ada moved alongside Maude and whispered in her ear. "My dear, I believe you've found a keeper."

She patted Maude's hand. "Go play a tune with him. One of the songs you enjoy. Go on, now."

Cheeks burning, Maude joined Ben on the piano bench. He slid over, allowing her to take the lower register.

"I thought you'd gone." She couldn't look at him.

"I'd never leave without saying a proper good-bye. But now I won't have to." His eyes sparkled.

"No, you won't." She tried to look away but found herself drawn toward him, taking in his every perfect feature. "But what about the story about Greyson?"

"Gone. Kaput." He met her gaze directly and then took her hand in his, a little thrill shooting through her.

She swallowed. "And your job in Detroit is gone, too?"

"I haven't been officially notified, but, yes, that would be a good guess." He arched an eyebrow at her, and she could imagine him as the aristocratic little boy living on his grandparents' estate. But had he never left, Ben wouldn't be with her now.

"Why don't we play some fun music?"

After he and Maude finished playing, Ben hesitated. He'd rather remain here, his shoulder pressed into her soft arm, inhaling her delicate lilac-and-rosewater scent, while admiring her slender neck and pretty face up close. But he reluctantly rose and assisted the woman he loved from the bench. "Can I get you anything?"

He'd noticed Matilda, the only apparent house staff, struggling to keep up with the steady inflow of refreshments before dinner.

"No, thank you. I believe we'll be going into dinner now."

When Matilda slid the pocket doors back, Peter and Ada followed Robert and Sadie, trailed by the girls, as they moved from the music room into the adjacent dining room. The two mahogany-and-cherry-paneled doors disappeared into the wall, revealing a room so like his home on his grandparents' estate that Ben sucked in a breath. The flocked wallpaper had to have been imported from London because it perfectly matched that which hung in the dining room from his youth. The heavy crystal stemware on the table was from the same French manufacturer who'd furnished his parents' wedding collection—confiscated by Ben's uncle.

Ben strode to the front of the table, which could accommodate eighteen guests. He pulled out the heavy, ornately carved chair for Maude.

From behind them, two male servants attired in green-and-gold waistcoats and trousers emerged through another, narrower, pocket door. One hoisted a massive silver soup tureen, decorated with turtles, onto the eight-foot-wide dark cherry sideboard. He set it there as the other servant delivered a tray covered in assorted rolls to either end of the table, accompanied by small bowls of butter.

Mr. Welling cleared his throat. "Robert, would you say the blessing?"

"Yes, sir." He paused. "Lord, bless this meal, this fellowship, and may what is shared here tonight be truly from the heart. In Lord Jesus' mighty name. Amen."

The dinner passed with happy chatter as course after course was served. While Ben relished the meal, beside him, Maude only partook of several bites of each of the sweet peas, beef tenderloin in burgundy sauce, wild rice, and the chocolate ganache cake that had been specially prepared. He patted her hand. "Are you all right?"

She beamed up at him. "Yes, I'm fine."

One of the servants tapped Ben on his shoulder. "There's someone in the garden out back who wishes to speak to you, sir."

"To me?"

"Yes."

The man gently tapped Maude's shoulder. "And you, too, miss."

They followed him out. Apprehension built as the door swung open. Twilight had just begun. The sky still possessed a blaze of pink and blue as the sun set and the moon made its appearance. But with the many tall trees shading the backyard, dusk predominated.

The entire garden was lit with what looked like a million candles, each nestled in a glass jar.

♥

Maude sucked in a breath of wonderment watching the flickering illumination. This was exactly how she'd imagined her prince would propose to her. She sniffed back the tears, reaching out to touch the potted palm tree, which had been moved from the foyer to the backyard. The wrought-iron bench was draped with a crushed velvet throw, and two round pillows were nestled on either end.

"What is it, Maude?" Ben turned toward her and cupped her face in his firm hands.

"Nothing, it's just that. . ." Maude exhaled then drew in a slow breath full of the aroma of roses, carnations, lilies, and the last of the lilacs. "This was my dream. Sadie must have done this!"

The garden was like a fairyland, with the flickering candles, the gentle breeze rustling the trees, and the scent of flowers surrounding her. Exactly how she'd imagined her prince would arrive and ask her to be his own. She'd given up that childhood fantasy long ago, when she'd convinced herself that her friend Greyson would be a "good enough" husband. It had been wrong to think she should settle for anything less than true love as God intended for her.

"Let's sit." He guided her toward the bench, and they nestled together, his cheek pressed against hers.

Then he drew back and ran his thumb over her chin, sending a shiver of delight through her. "Maude, I know I have nothing to give you. But I'm willing to work hard to support us. I'm not even sure what it is that God has called me to do for a living. I do know this, though—I want to marry you someday. When we've both been completely honest with each other and when you have time to forgive me for the ruse I played at the Grand."

"You were just doing your job, Ben." Maude shrugged. "I've heard it's not uncommon for reporters to assume a false identity to investigate. And that was actually part of your name—part of who you are."

"True, but I should have told you. Should have trusted you. And I wish you'd trusted me enough to have shared about your inheritance."

She cringed. "I didn't know about it myself until a few days ago, and I'm still unclear how this all works. I do know, though, that you'd never inherit any of my, of our, holdings—my grandmother had some kind of strange codicil put into her will. Wouldn't that bother you?"

"That's all right. I think with four jobs I should be able to keep myself going."

He pulled her close, and she inhaled his sandalwood scent, felt the heat of him as he pressed his lips to hers and drew her closer yet into his arms. Surely she was in heaven. He deepened the kiss, and she yearned to pull him even closer but didn't know how that was possible.

A twig cracked and Ben pulled away. "Who's there?"

"Aw, it's just me, you two lovebirds." Jack ambled up from behind a bush.

"Jack Welling, what are you doing here?"

"I snuck out here. I gotta tell ya somethin', Muddie."

She cringed. "What?"

He stepped closer. "About you and me. And our money."

"Our money?"

"Yeah, what Uncle Robert was keeping for us and what shoulda been Dad's." He bobbed his chin several times. "But now you got control of it."

Maude exhaled loudly. "Oh, Jack. Please—not now."

Her brother drew up right beside them, patting the back of her hair. "Here's the way I see it, sis. I need a bunch of money soon for my Olympic training."

Ben cleared his throat and leaned forward.

Maude swatted Jack's hand away from her hair, where pins were now coming loose. "Jack, you are annoying."

"Here's the thing." Jack grinned a sappy grin. "You know I'll be good for it—as far as getting it back to ya later."

"Go away!"

Someone rounded the corner of the house, a lantern swaying in her hands. The light revealed Ada's serene countenance. "Jack, leave your sister be."

The woman sounded exactly like Mother used to. She went to Jack and wrapped an arm around his shoulders. "You run on in and get another dessert before the servants put it all up."

Jack hesitated, rocking sideways back and forth like he did when he really wanted to say something badly.

Ada clapped her hands together. "Jack, I forgot to tell you. I've found a sponsor for you, for your training." Her voice held more hope and enthusiasm than Maude had ever heard the woman muster. She reminded her of how Mother would encourage them and get excited over their projects.

"Really?"

"Yes, I'll pop into the house with you and tell you a little about it, but then I've got to catch up with your father."

The two disappeared into the back of the house.

Ben's warm lips covered Maude's, and she didn't resist. Ben's arms, locked below her waist, pulled her up and against him, crushing her to his broad chest.

He pulled away and leaned his head against hers. "I love you."

"I love you, too."

Once again, he moved his mouth over hers, and she responded to him, not caring if he thought her unladylike or not. He was hers. And she was never letting him go again. She tasted the sweet coffee on his mouth and inhaled his scent of sandalwood, wool, and his own unique male scent. He pressed his face against her curls.

Leaning back, he lifted one lock of hair. "Your curls feel like silk."

He pulled her close again, and she rested her head on his shoulder, enjoying the warmth of her neck against his own.

"Ahem!"

They broke apart. Robert slowly moved toward them on the candlelit path. "I have a couple of things I'd like to say to you both."

Ben stood and held out his hand. "Captain Swaine, this isn't the time nor place for any business discussions."

"But. . ."

"Let me say that I expect to court Maude in a, shall we say, more traditional manner than I've managed thus far."

Maude laughed. "Hopefully this time you can simply be Ben Steffan, and I shall be Maude Welling, inn manager and not a maid."

"Exactly." Robert clapped his hands together.

"Is that all?" Ben's voice held a dismissal.

"No. I've arranged for some chaperones."

Another lantern bobbed as someone rounded the corner. "Robert?" Sadie Duvall marched forward, her sisters trailing her in a line.

Ben leaned in and kissed Maude's cheek. "They'd make good bridesmaids, wouldn't they?"

She pulled away. "Is that a proposal, Mr. Steffan?"

"Soon." He kissed her again. "Would you like it to be?"

"Soon. Very Soon."

Author Notes

The *Detroit Post*, my hero Ben's periodical, is a fictional newspaper. Detroit had many newspapers during the time of this story. Although the *Detroit Free Press* is a real newspaper, this story and the characters associated with this renowned newspaper are fictional. The Grand Hotel, a gem of a resort hotel, still dominates the cliff side on Mackinac Island. Maude's inn was inspired by the Windermere Hotel, a beautiful landmark inn on the island, but Winds of Mackinac is fictional. Both the Grand and the Windermere have lovely websites that share their histories.

This story and all the characters were created from fiction. One character was inspired by a real woman—a reclusive hermit who was the wealthiest woman in America but lived like a pauper. While there are real-life Cadottes and a Cadotte Street on Mackinac Island, all of the Cadotte references in this book are complete fiction, as are the Wellings.

Mackinac Island was a site originally populated by the Chippewa and Odawa people. This was an important area for the Native Americans, especially for trading and, according to my research, at a spiritual level. The French and their missionaries came into the area in the 1600s. The British and the Americans followed. Churches mentioned in this story, such as the historic Mission Church, the oldest church building in Michigan, sought to bring Christianity and services to the Native Americans. The Mission Church is now under the control of Michigan State Parks and is open to the public. It one of my favorite places to visit on the island.

In my research, I found Mark Twain a visitor to the island. Of course since my hero is fictional, he had no real influence on Twain's novel *The Prince and the Pauper*, but it was fun imaging it. Ships sinking in the Great Lakes were an all too common problem at this time. The story of ships sinking in the Mackinac Island harbor, however, is fabricated. The Round Island Lighthouse was indeed being built in 1895 because of the problem that Round Island itself presented by its location in the Straits of Mackinac. The light was not functional until the following May.

Grayling fish were abundant in Michigan but ended up being decimated early in the twentieth century. While you can find delicious whitefish in Mackinac, you won't find Michigan grayling fish on any menus.

And pasties, filled with delicious meat, potatoes, and other vegetables, and wrapped in a pie shell, are indeed a regional favorite.

A Michigan attorney I consulted confirmed that codicils can be added to wills. He also indicated that these cumbersome additions can be contested and overturned by the courts.

A little neat fact: you'll find my grandmother's names on the cover of the book! Maude Carrie (Williams) Fancett was born in 1895, one of the reasons I chose that year for this story. I never knew her, as she died when my father was twelve and she was only in her thirties. The name for my heroine almost got changed by Barbour. I'm glad they let her stay Maude, which was a popular name at that time, and that all three of her names are on this beautiful cover.

I had the pleasure of working on the island when I was sixteen and fell in love with the magical place. I've been privileged to visit often. I can truly say, "My Heart Belongs on Mackinac Island" and am blessed to be able to write, and share, this story!

ECPA-bestselling author Carrie Fancett Pagels, Ph.D., is the award-winning author of a dozen Christian historical romances. Twenty-five years as a psychologist didn't "cure" her overactive imagination! A self-professed "history geek," she resides with her family in the Historic Triangle of Virginia. Carrie loves to read, bake, bead, and travel—but not all at the same time! You can connect with her at www.CarrieFancettPagels.com.

If You Liked This Book, Watch for These Other Titles...

My Heart Belongs in the Superstition Mountains (Carmela's Quandary)
by Susan Page Davis

Carmela Wade lives a lie orchestrated by her uncle, but as she matures into adulthood, how long will she accept a life of fraud? Can a chance encounter with US Marshal Freeland McKay on a stagecoach through Arizona's Superstition Mountains lead to her escape? But what about her scars?

Paperback / 978-1-68322-295-8 / $12.99 / March 2017

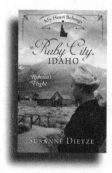

My Heart Belongs in Ruby City, Idaho (Rebecca's Plight)
by Susanne Dietze

It's a mail-order disorder when newlyweds realize they've married the wrong partners with similar names. An annulment seems in order—and fast. But when the legalities take longer than expected, Rebecca Rice wonders if Tad Fordham wasn't the right husband for her all along....

Paperback / 978-1-68322-011-4 / $12.99 / May 2017

JOIN US ONLINE!

Christian Fiction for Women

Christian Fiction for Women is your online home for the latest in Christian fiction.

Check us out online for:

- Giveaways
- Recipes
- Info about Upcoming Releases
- Book Trailers
- News and More!

Find Christian Fiction for Women at Your Favorite Social Media Site:

 Search "Christian Fiction for Women"

 @fictionforwomen